Imminent Danger

A. G. Hayes

Savant Books
Honolulu, HI, USA
2013

Published in the USA by Savant Books and Publications
2630 Kapiolani Blvd. #1601
Honolulu, HI 96826
http://www.savantbooksandpublications.com

Printed in the USA

Edited by Mary Yamin-Garone
Cover Images: Killer with Two Pistols © Igor Kovalchuk |
Dreamstime.com; Pope's Statue © Gian Marco Valente |
Dreamstime.com
Cover Design by Daniel S. Janik

13 digit ISBN: 9780988664036
10-digit ISBN: 0988664038

Dedication

To St. Francis de Sales, patron saint of writers

Imminent Danger

Prologue

With his heart fluttering, the old wino stumbled down a trash-strewn alley, desperately seeking a hiding place. His mind was fuzzy from muscatel and the fact that someone had attempted to kill him at three in the morning in his cardboard box in a shoe store doorway on Hollywood Boulevard.

He leaned against a wall and gasped for air, wondering who wanted to kill him. Not the cops. He could die on the street for all they cared.

Cocking his head, he heard footsteps: slow, measured and deliberate as a pallbearer. A cold wind flicked a crumpled newspaper down the alley and the stink of rotting garbage swirled around him. With an outstretched hand, he staggered forward, bumping along the wall until he contacted the cold iron of a dumpster.

The lid was propped open and with the last of his fading strength, the old man hiked his scrawny body up into the evil-smelling container. He was reaching up to release the bar holding the lid open when a hand grasped his wrist in a powerful grip and a flashlight beam blazed in his face. He screwed his eyes shut, his corneas reacting to a burst of luminous blue light. In the grip of his unknown assailant, he felt the sleeve of his threadbare jacket being pushed up to his elbow. A needle slid into a vein and a sudden reeling in his brain told him a powerful drug was coursing through his bloodstream. Then a voice whispered, "Don't fight it. Just close your eyes."

Chapter 1

Tom Stewart pushed aside a thick report with the name Cerberus stenciled across the cover. The file contained information he knew would elicit an immediate response from the United States Department of Homeland Security (DHS). He reached for his phone and tapped a set of numbers then drummed his fingers impatiently on the desktop waiting for Special Agent Joseph Falk to answer.

Initially Joe Falk had resisted initiation from the FBI into Cerberus but ultimately he acknowledged the need for an organization that covertly supported humankind's highest ideals. Now he and his partner, Susan Koski, belonged to a little-known cadre of specially skilled undercover agents trained to mingle with known dissidents and paramilitary terrorist groups, allowing both agents freedom for clandestine assignments. No questions asked.

Stewart wasted no time when Falk answered the phone.

"Joe, I want you and Agent Koski here in LA at once. There'll be a company plane waiting at Reno-Tahoe at 0800 hours. I'm at the Beverly Wilshire Hotel. Now move. Take off is in thirty minutes." Stewart hung up.

Falk was a thirty-something, wrapped-tight guy with a leathery tan and a brooding, magnetic face sporting a two-week-old beard. He looked at his watch. He flipped on a gray Kangol 504 Cap that had seen better days and sipped the last of his coffee as he dialed his partner. After six rings, Koski answered, panting as she ran the last half-mile of her five-mile morning run.

Imminent Danger

Chapter 2

Greg Grant was a foxy-eyed man in his late thirties. He gazed out the window of his tenth floor Washington, D.C. office and viewed the wide expanse of the National Mall and the reflecting pool in the distance. It was his first week with the DHS. The department, hurriedly created by the Bush administration a few weeks after 9/11, had been beset with problems of organization and acceptance ever since.

Grant had been an investigative reporter for the *Washington Post*. His work caught the eye of the new DHS director who offered him a position after deciding that bringing a media type on board might improve the department's image. Grant had an inquisitive mind and his thinking was always self-centered. He quickly accepted the job. Now, this morning, he was attending a briefing for his first assignment.

He sat relaxed. His slim, six-foot-two frame was arranged with the practiced ease of an actor listening attentively to his boss as he wrapped up Grant's assignment to the Hollywood killings.

"You'll head up the investigation team with two FBI agents. Being DHS, you'll be in charge. Arrangements have been made for you to liaise with LAPD."

Grant sat a little straighter. "Two FBI agents?"

"Yes. They'll act as your photographers—video and still. The Bureau has to learn sometime that now DHS is in charge of national security."

Grant's ego swelled. "I'll be *happy* to bring them up-to-date, sir."

Mikhail Brasinov cruised along Sunset Boulevard, his Slavic features softening as he inhaled the luxurious bouquet of new leather. The eight-cylinder engine of his Ferrari Testerosa purred with the promise of a growl that would occur with a tap of his toe. Glancing in the rearview mirror, he smiled and his large, yellowed teeth reflected back. Tomorrow he'd have his teeth whitened. He planned to fit in—look native when he met with Hollywood's "in-crowd."

Seven blocks north of Sunset a second victim was dead. A scrawny young woman with both arms cankered by needle scars lay propped against a stucco apartment wall on Franklin Avenue. Unlike the man in the dumpster, she hadn't fought the needle and had readily gone along with the offer of a fix. The murderer drove north to Los Feliz Boulevard, made a sharp left onto Fern Dell into Griffith Park. It was an ideal hunting place. A bubbling stream, a winding path between Pine and Cedar trees, masses of leafy ferns, waterfalls, grassy areas and picnic tables; a lovers' lane.

Voices and the bobbing beam of a flashlight alerted the murderer to remove two hypodermic needles from his case on the picnic table. He'd have to be fast to take out two at once; four in one night. His bosses would be pleased. The beam moved from side to side as his victims neared. He heard them now, a man and a woman. Then the murderer remembered his orders were to kill only derelicts and the homeless.

The beam came closer and the man said, "I hope no one broke into the Jag."

A woman laughed. "Don't worry. No one comes up here this late at night. Besides, how often do you get to make love on a picnic table in Griffith Park?"

The murderer remained in the shadows, still and silent as the duo passed.

Chapter 3

"You're late," Stewart growled as Special Agent Susan Koski ambled into the sitting room of his suite at the Beverly Wilshire.

Falk sat next to a thin, scholarly-looking man and squirmed slightly at her tardy entrance. He'd warned her there was no time to stop for coffee when they'd dashed from the cab into the hotel.

"I needed to stop for coffee," the petite blonde said huskily. She lowered a case containing her compact digital video equipment to the floor next to a chair. At the same time, she tried not to spill the tall decaf mocha in her left hand. Stewart eyed his watch. He decided not to directly address Koski's "morning person" comment. She was the second half of Cerberus' most dynamic duo. Falk's exploits were becoming legendary. Koski's were almost mythical. Stewart intended their partnership to continue.

"Agent Koski," Stewart said, "meet Dr. Jack Wolf, Professor of Biology and Director of the Stem Cell Research Program at UCLA. He's also one of us."

Wolf was slumped in a wing-backed chair. He leaned forward, pulled his feet to a standing position, rose an inch from the seat and nodded in way of a greeting.

Stewart continued. "You'll be working with the Department of Homeland Security." Stewart knew the pair had little use for cumbersome bureaus. He held up his hand as Falk leaned forward to complain. "Hear me out, Joe. This assignment is vital to our country's safety. It's possible Mikhail Brasinov could be involved."

"He's a long way from Brno," Falk replied, referring to the Czech

Republic capital where a Bosnian thug wanted for war crimes and on the run from NATO had entered into a working agreement with militant Muslims. He'd made millions. He was a dangerous man; a rich dangerous man.

Stewart nodded. "The CIA is setting up a special team as we speak."

Falk shrugged. "Why are we going to work with DHS?"

Stewart raised an eyebrow. "I don't need to tell you how the President feels about Brasinov's presence within our country's borders. You've both had first-hand experience with his organizational abilities when you were on the *Judas* case in Czechoslovakia and Austria."

Koski and Falk exchanged looks but remained silent.

"You'll both be teamed with an agent from DHS named Greg Grant. Your assignment, as far as anyone is concerned, is to assist him in investigating a rash of serial killings in Hollywood involving street people."

Stewart cleared his throat before continuing. "DHS is fully aware there are Muslim terrorist cells operating in LA and possibly linked to the murders." He paused to allow his words to sink in. "You'll be liaising with the Los Angeles Police Department as part of the ongoing effort by the federal government to mesh local law enforcement with DHS." Stewart sighed. "And we know how that goes.

"You'll go along as photographers. Grant has been briefed that you are FBI. As far as anyone else is concerned you're DHS. Being a videographer will be a breeze for Koski but you'll have to wing it, Joe."

Falk nodded. Stewart lifted a glass of orange juice and pointed to Wolf. "Doctor Wolf had been involved with stem cell biology studies long before public interest was stirred, back when the President finally decided to allocate federal funding for research. He's here to update us on the use of various bioethics and their possible use by terrorists here at home."

Stewart sipped his juice before continuing. "It's imperative *no one* learns you are actively involved in a covert operation to discover what may turn out to be a deadly tool for Islamic terrorists.

"Heightened security and active defensive measures since the end of the Iraqi debacle have done little to slow worldwide carnage by Muslim insurgents. Nonetheless, it's come to our attention that recent murders in and around Hollywood could be the work of terrorists."

"Why kill street people, Tom? What do they expect to gain?" Falk asked.

"I'll let Doctor Wolf explain further. Possibly the victims were chosen at random to test a new means of intravenous injection."

"How much do either of you know about stem cell research?" Wolf whispered.

Koski grimaced. "In the great stem cell debate, I've never given much thought to which side I was on, the stem side or the cell side."

Falk enjoyed her sense of humor as he added, "Me, too. All I know is what I read in the papers."

"Ninety percent of America's population would answer the same way," Wolf replied. "Few really care unless directly affected."

"I had a friend who would have died of diabetes if they didn't have stem cell treatment. I consider it good medicine," Koski exclaimed.

"I'm sure you do, however, as with a large element of medical research and development there are always pros and cons." Wolf paused and contemplated the scuffed toes of his cowboy boots.

"One fact most Americans *are* aware of is the cruelly commercial side of medicine; questions of funding, professional infighting, increasing cost of prescription medicine: publish or perish, corporate scrambling to be the first with the latest. *Not*, I'm afraid, always in the best interests of patients or their problems."

Wolf leaned forward, hands dangling between his bony knees. "It's possible the killer we're seeking has the ability to manipulate stem cells and by so doing change their known behavior. That in itself is nothing new. This treatment is inserted into a person's genes to enable stem cells to survive prolonged chemotherapy treatment. This is a great advantage in cases where a cancer patient benefits from additional chemotherapy after stem cell transplantation."

Koski swirled the remains of her coffee as she listened to his every word.

Wolf slowly rubbed his chin. "Normally, this manipulation would kill newly transplanted stem cells but fortified cells treated by gene therapy can survive. They give researchers another tool in the battle against inherited defects, such as anemia, sickle cell anemia and Wiskott-Aldrich Syndrome."

Koski said, "Our killer must be a medical whiz kid, Doctor."

"Yes. We're beginning to call him the Gene Genie. From what little we've learned, we've come up with a working profile of someone with a background in medical experimentation, especially stem cell transplantation. Whoever it is may have discovered a means not only to clone genes but also to add certain critical qualities to them. Smart genes from say a nuclear scientist intermixed with aggressive genes from a prizefighter or a ruthless business tycoon. Even a serial killer. There's no end to the possible combinations."

Wolf raked his fingers through his sand-colored hair. "There is also the dreadful possibility that our genius could design and create the perfect assassin—a monster that slavishly carries out orders without question."

Koski gasped. "Sounds like a modern Doctor Frankenstein!"

Wolf grimaced. "Worse. Remember the opiate used by the Russian Special Forces in the 2002 hostage situation at the Moscow theater. That reflected a new era in bio-weapons development. Since then, there have been tremendous biotech advances to degrade enemy forces while enhancing one's own troops.

"Our own Defense Department is studying the development of 'calmative' chemicals as well as 'incapaciants' and 'convulsants.' It's possible this is happening with the random killings and they, whoever they are, are experimenting with street people."

Stewart picked up the conversation. "What we have here is the ugly possibility that someone can medically manufacture a killer who can pass through any security check, no explosives and no weapons. He shows up clean on the screen. When the assigned victim is dispatched, they simply kill off the monster and create another assassin when needed."

"Sounds like a plot for a sci-fi movie," Koski muttered.

Wolf nodded. "Performance enhancing drugs are right *NOW,* Koski. Our Air Force pilots use 'no go pills' to induce sleep…what would you think of a microchip smaller than a dime implanted under the skin of a soldier's neck and used to trigger the release of chemicals for 'body regulation' and 'rejuvenating drugs'?" Wolf asked.

Before she could answer, he waved a long forefinger in the air. "They are being studied by U.S. Special Operations Command, the Defense Advanced Research Projects Agency and other Defense Department organizations."

Stewart broke in. "We must find out who this madman is before he decides to try out his method on a wider scale."

"And we've *no* idea who we're looking for?" Koski inquired. "Could this mad genius be a she?"

"Maybe," Wolf responded. "Murder and medicine are equal opportunity employers."

Falk asked. "How do we know this person you're talking about is responsible for the Hollywood killings?"

"The Los Angeles County Coroner's office contacted me when autopsies carried out on two of the victims showed peculiarities. They both were brain dead before they died. One was found in a dumpster and the other in an alley behind Grauman's Chinese Theater. A more complete autopsy is under way. Our intelligence informs me the victims were possibly guinea pigs used to enable the killer to fine-tune the exact amount of evil concoction to inject.

"Being street people, they create less attention to the media. The next victim may well be injected with a corrected dose and become a killer by design."

"There can't be that many people with the ability to do what you say, Doctor. Surely that narrows down the list of suspects," Falk said.

"Yes. We're already checking labs, hospitals and known private industries that have the ability to produce such drugs. We're also keeping in mind that whatever is being used could have been produced offshore."

"If there is anyone with the expertise to know these persons or companies that have the capability to create such a weapon, I imagine you are at the top of the list, Doctor."

Stewart picked up the line of reasoning. "Joe, you're right. Cerberus is working through a list as we speak. Your cover liaising with DHS is just that. You'll be kept up-to-date on the tie-in with a suspected cell here locally, the Brasinov sighting, murders of the homeless. Also, from what little we've learned so far it's possible the ringleader of the cell is a big name in the pharmaceutical business."

No one spoke for a moment as the slow, tick-tock of an antique grandfather clock stretched seconds into minutes.

"What about the police?" Falk asked. "Are they aware there may be a mad scientist out there?"

"Not yet," Stewart shot back. "Let one word get out about the possibility of a mad scientist running around Hollywood injecting people with a psychoactive drug and the police will have a bigger problem on their hands trying to calm a panicked populace."

Chapter 4

Eleven thirty at night and the Hollywood freeway was jammed. Detective Victor Young, LAPD, eyed the red taillights ahead and thought if he had a dollar for each one he'd retire. He still had six years to go.

Young lit another Camel and increased the volume on his police radio. A continuous litany of chanting monotonous voices reporting murder, burglary, robbery, domestic disputes, along with gang shootings and general mayhem; six more years in which his disenchantment with politicians at city hall would grow.

Young drove an unmarked piece of rubbish from police headquarters at Parker Center motor pool on his way out to Hollywood division. His temporary three-month assignment to Undercover Narcotics, Rampart Division, would be over in two days so forty-eight hours filling in for an injured Hollywood Narc would be a piece of cake.

The stream of stop-and-go traffic reached Vermont Avenue when a carload of gang bangers passed him driving in the emergency lane, caps on backwards, loud Rap music thumping from oversized speakers. Young almost switched on the siren then decided not to. He could stop them and be called a Fascist pig and accused of racial profiling. He ground his cigarette into an overflowing ashtray. Whatever legal aggravation he gave those punks, they'd be home tonight before he was.

Inching forward, he thought of his dad, who'd served with LA's finest when they had been just that—the best dammed police force in the nation. Back when cops kept the peace and the citizens respected their dedication to duty.

The traffic started to move a little faster and he eased across the lanes for the off ramp at Cahuenga Boulevard. He took one last look at the scumbags roaring up the emergency lane. He knew damn well his dad *would* have nailed their asses.

The wall clock showed 1:05 a.m. The desk sergeant glanced up as Detective Young entered the front entrance of the Hollywood station. He crossed the well-worn floor tiles, passed a battered wooden bench containing two drunks handcuffed to the cuff-hooks and stopped in front of his desk.

"Welcome to the real world, Victor," the white-haired cop drawled. "I heard you were coming to spend a couple of days with us. How are things at Rampart?"

Young shrugged. "My Spanish is improving."

The sergeant didn't give a damn how anyone was, especially those outside of Hollywood division. Glancing at a note on the desk, he informed Young he'd be working with Detective Bob Gulliver.

"I thought Gully was with Robbery Homicide downtown."

"He was. He got transferred to us a month ago."

Young knew a transfer out of Robbery Homicide wasn't an upward shift. Young grunted. "What happened?"

"Internal affairs. I wouldn't ask if I were you."

"Where can I find him?"

"He's waiting for you in the squad room."

Gully was seated at a wooden table, tapping a keyboard with two fingers and transferring notes to a PC. He glanced up. "Morning, Victor. Long time no see."

Young pulled a heavy wooden chair out from the table and sat facing him. "Where is everybody?"

"The brass ordered everyone on the streets. Another vic found an hour ago in the 6400 block on Fountain. A citizen called in a description, someone in a long black coat running from the scene."

"Great!" Young pushed out of the chair and crossed to the squad room coffeepot. "You want some?"

"No. I want to run our orders for tomorrow past you then go to bed."

Chapter 5

After leaving the meeting, Koski and Falk headed to a small hotel in West LA where Stewart had arranged their accommodations. They spent the rest of the day studying the latest Cerberus files on various terrorist cells and their suspected activities in Southern California.

Several hours later Falk tossed the last file aside. "Let's go eat. We need a break."

It was after eleven when they finished dessert. Koski pushed her dish to one side. "Reading those files, you'd think we'd have a better handle on illegals entering the country."

"Yeah. This country's in deep shit. Homeland Security's going to be hard pressed to *ever* cure that problem."

"So we get attached to this guy, Grant. Is he at the same hotel we're in?" Koski asked.

"No. He's staying with someone in Beverly Hills."

"How do you know?"

"I asked Stewart just before we left. You were powdering your nose."

Koski arched her eyebrows. "A woman?"

"No idea."

"Fine. I'll make it my job to find out."

"I doubt we'll have much free time." The buzz of his cell interrupted and he quickly answered. "Right. Got it. We've a beaurocar. We'll find you." Falk left some bills on the table as he rose. "Dr. Wolf. He's at the morgue."

The smell of formaldehyde at midnight can ruin a perfectly good dinner. Falk and Koski, ID tags hanging from their necks, entered LA County morgue. A stoop-shouldered janitor led them at a snail's pace through dimly lit underground corridors to a set of double doors with a row of gurneys lined up like taxicabs; the difference being that the occupants of these transporters were no longer in a hurry to arrive at their destination. Green sheeted, their big toes labeled, they waited in silence.

The shiny double steel doors whooshed open and Dr. Wolf, dressed in surgical greens, walked out. He beckoned them to follow as he re-entered the room.

Inside, they donned scrubs, gloves and masks. They had both experienced morgues in the past and unless you worked there full time, it was always an uneasy sensation being in such an environment. An icy coldness filled the room; a chill one inhaled along with the odor of chemicals and freshly cut bodies. The sibilant sound of continuous running water sluicing the granite operating slabs added another dynamic to the frigidity.

"Over here." Wolf led them past three unclothed corpses. The first table held a black man with his throat slashed open. A young girl on the second slab had been shot in the temple. The middle-aged man on the third looked as if he'd died in a traffic accident. The top of his head was peeled down over his eyes.

Wolf stopped at the fourth table. "Take a look." Falk's eyes followed the direction of Wolf's finger pointing at a scrawny emaciated old man with the top of his skull neatly removed by Wolf's cordless Stryker cranial saw. The smell of scorched bone still lingered over the table.

Koski and Falk stared at the wrinkled gray matter. The outer edges of the brain had a peculiar discoloration.

"You'll notice the bluish hue beginning to show." Wolf pointed with a thin, steel, pencil-like object at the area. "Here in the cerebrum is an indication that before he died he had lost the ability to speak or to have original thoughts."

"*Before* he *died?*" Falk echoed.

"Yes. I believe this man lived for several hours after he had been injected and programmed to carry out commands."

Wolf's eyes went to abstract speculation. "The toxic drug surged through his brain, flooding the cerebrospinal fluid, destroying the nerve cells of the cerebral cortex, inhibiting those nerve fibers from carrying signals to other cells, other parts of the brain and the rest of the body."

"An hour or two later it's possible the victim could have begun to feel ill," Wolf continued. "A feeling not unlike an unsettled stomach or the start of the flu. I'll show you evidence of other victims that have died under similar conditions and indicate the miniscule entrance wounds they suffered. This will alert you to how difficult it is to locate the puncture wound and how, in some cases, it could be overlooked altogether. God forbid this formula is ever used in spray form, as Serin was in a Tokyo subway a few years ago."

"Amen." Koski muttered.

Driving back from the morgue, Koski mused over their meeting with Dr. Wolf. "It's evident that at the moment Wolf has no idea what type of toxic material was injected into those people."

"Do I detect a tone of dissatisfaction with our latest assignment, Koski?"

"Not really. However, five unsolved murders in less than a week! Shouldn't there be a more aggressive attempt to find the killer?"

Falk felt the same way. "Murder of homeless people doesn't stir up the media enough."

Koski stared out of the car window. "Yeah. It'll have to be significant, something more exciting, an event that'll rouse the Fourth Estate to their usual frenzy to be the 'first with the worst'."

"Especially, if as Stewart said, someone big in the pharmaceutical industry is involved."

Imminent Danger

Chapter 6

Falk's doorbell rang at 6 a.m. He rinsed off shaving soap, grabbed a towel and went to the door. "Who is it?"

"Greg Grant. I'd like to take you both to breakfast. Not too early am I?"

Falk opened the door. "No problem. Come in." He indicated the couch. "Take a seat, I'll be right back." He headed to the bathroom, donned pants and a dress shirt over his tee shirt and boxers and reentered the living room.

Grant stuck out his right hand and flashed his brand new DHS badge in his left, level with his face. "Glad to meet you, Falk. I'm looking forward to working with members of the Bureau." He glanced toward the bedroom. "Agent Koski still asleep?"

"I doubt it. She's most likely halfway through a five mile run." Falk pointed to a connecting door. "We have adjoining rooms."

"Give us time to chew the fat."

Falk relaxed in one of the upholstered chairs and assessed what he saw —someone who made assumptions and was used to running the show. Arching an eyebrow, Falk asked, "How did LAPD react when they discovered DHS was about to become involved, Mr. Grant?"

"Call me Greg. DHS Washington cleared everything with the mayor's office. We'll have full cooperation with LAPD—official feedback, access to murder scenes, investigating officers, medical examiners, etc."

"Mmmm, another agency's presence at crime scenes during an initial investigation is normally against police procedure."

Grant sniggered. "Yeah, but times change. That's why the DHS was created. When you have influence, you have power. Hope we didn't ruffle any FBI feathers."

"The Bureau understands." Falk realized he was talking to someone who was already a legend in his own mind.

"Of course." Grant quickly added, "Rest assured this is not the first time I've worked with covert operators."

"Greg, I'm glad to hear you say that. How about a cup of coffee while we wait for Agent Koski?"

Grant leaned back and laced his fingers behind his head. "Sounds good, Joe."

Susan Koski ran with long easy strides, breathing the fresh morning air before the usual haze blurred the Hollywood Hills. Six-thirty a.m. and the streets began to fill with traffic. She saw their hotel ahead and hoped Falk had put on a pot of coffee.

Normally they would have run together but decided it was wiser to split up until they knew how events would proceed. Nearing the hotel, she noticed a vehicle parked halfway down the block. Her natural powers of observation noted it was a green Toyota Rav4. The man sitting behind the wheel was reading a newspaper and looked out of place. She knew the vehicle hadn't been there when she'd left the building earlier.

The SUV suddenly drove off. Instincts made her memorize the California license plate number—NTV925. She caught a glimpse of his face as he glanced back.

Once in her room, Koski jotted down the number and headed to the shower. Fifteen minutes later, dressed in faded blue jeans, a white cotton turtleneck, navy blue jacket and a pair of Reeboks, she opened the unlocked adjoining door to Falk's room.

"Ah, here she is now." Falk got to his feet.

Grant set his coffee mug on a side table and rose from the couch. "Happy to meet the other half of the duo," he said with a seemingly genuine smile. They both knew he was thoroughly briefed on both of them and fully aware of their background and accomplishments with the Bureau.

Koski took an instant dislike to the man as she said, "Nice to meet you, Mr. Grant."

"Call him Greg, Koski. Mr. Grant doesn't stand on ceremony."

"I'm taking you two to breakfast," Grant announced. "I'm starving. Where would you like to go?"

Koski caught the twinkle in Falk's eye. "They say the Polo Lounge serves a great breakfast."

Grant's smile faded momentarily. They knew he couldn't justify breakfast at "The Lounge" on his government expense account. Then he blurted, "Great idea, Joe."

"I'll grab my purse," Koski purred. "Meet you downstairs." She returned to her room and scooped up the note containing the license plate number and headed for the elevator.

Sunlight already streamed across the crisp pink tablecloth and the waiter adjusted the blinds to lessen the glare. Service at the Beverly Hills Hotel was, as usual, impeccable. Grant nodded to the waiter with the aplomb of the archbishop to an altar boy. He dominated the conversation all through breakfast and it seemed he was not about to stop.

"There was this time in Chicago. I headed up a team investigating city hall politicians suspected of paying off teamster bosses..." He stopped in mid-sentence as his cell phone chimed. "Grant."

Koski absent-mindedly wet the tip of her finger and tapped crumbs of a jelly donut off her plate and into her mouth, enjoying the fact it had cost Grant nine dollars. She looked forward to Falk's suggestion on where to go for lunch.

Grant covered the mouthpiece. "It's the office." He continued talking on his phone. "No problems. Everyone's very cooperative. I've contacted my photographers and scheduled a meeting with LAPD at Hollywood Central this morning. I'll keep in touch."

He flipped the phone shut and beckoned the waiter as he signed his name in mid-air.

Walking to their car Grant said, "When we meet with LAPD I'll do the talking. I know how to handle local yokels."

"We appreciate that, Greg." Koski oozed. "We really do."

Falk hid a smile.

Imminent Danger

Chapter 7

"Pease, that son of a bitch..." Paul Horn stopped in mid-sentence, turned back from the tinted floor-to-ceiling window overlooking the Pacific Ocean and wiped his brow with the back of his huge hand.

Roughly rearranging his six-foot-four, 220-pound frame on a delicate Chippendale chair, he stared across the well-appointed office of Enrico Pegmanti. "I'm sorry, Enrico. After all, Martin is your son-in-law."

"No problem." Despite his eighty-seven years and small stature, Pegmanti was still a giant in charge.

Horn continued. "I believe Martin's department was close to reproducing genes on demand. Maybe we made a mistake letting him go."

"That remains to be seen." Pegmanti leaned back and his swivel chair creaked. "I have information that Martin was lying. He wasn't just close. He *could* reproduce the germinating acceptance genes *now* if he wanted to."

Horn sat upright, the abrupt movement of 220 pounds of suddenly rearranged inertia applying a vicious torque to the chair. His eyes glittered behind rimless glasses. "Why would he lie?"

Pegmanti grasped a solid gold letter opener in his blue-veined hand and tapped the tip on the polished teakwood desk. "Paul, you've been head of our sales division for over twenty years. Perhaps in that rarefied atmosphere you've lost touch with the *inner* workings of Pegmanti Chemical Industries." He spun the letter opener in slow circles.

"Martin is keeping the progress of his embryonic stem cells and blank state cells to himself. After I'm dead, he'll announce a breakthrough. Ergo, the rewards will be all his!" Horn pushed out of the chair, crossed to the window and with his back to Pegmanti, gazed thoughtfully at the Pacific, a strange smile on his face.

Chapter 8

Martin Pease, always a clever student, had been quickly accepted at Cambridge University when he was seventeen. He had chosen to study medicine. During his years there he made tremendous strides and became looked upon as an up-and-comer in the future of medicine and sciences. Then in the summer of 1948 his world, as he had known it, came to a sudden and disastrous end.

At Cambridge he was close to home, having been born in the town of Newmarket. He was the only boy. His two elder sisters were married now. The other person in his life was Fiona, his fiancée of two years. Fiona, already considered part of the family, spent weekends at Pease's home. One weekend toward the end of term, Fiona and Pease's parents drove down to Cambridge to visit him.

After enjoying a pleasant lunch at one of the riverside pubs, Fiona and Pease strolled together, discussing plans for their future wedding. Later they said their farewells and with his father at the wheel of his car, they began their return trip. It was the last time Pease saw them alive.

A few miles outside of Newmarket, a horse transporter skidded out of control and into the family car, killing everyone including the truck driver.

Pease was inconsolable in his grief. Less than two weeks after burying his parents, he sold the family house and took advantage of a scheme offered by the U.S. government at the end of World War II. It encouraged people with certain specialties to immigrate to America.

Now twenty-two and in the first year in his chosen homeland, he knew he wanted to return to the world of medicine. He contacted his mentors at

Cambridge, who gladly arranged access to the right people in California who could assist him in transitioning into research and medical science at UCLA.

Doctor Rita Massy was the first to welcome him when he entered the room of glittering personalities. He smiled wryly at the memory.

"Over here, Martin. There are people who want to meet you. I've told them all about you."

In the early 1950s, Beverly Hills overflowed with charming people; men of power and foresight; women of elegance and cunning; and those who simply bided their time and waited.

Over the next few years, Massy and Pease worked together in the field of cognitive neuroscience at Pegmanti Chemical Industries (PCI). In time, they became good friends, both passionate about their research. Theirs was a platonic relationship.

Goldie Pegmanti, Enrico's only daughter, had fallen in love with Martin and they were married. She reveled in their large house in Beverly Hills, a wedding gift from her father, and she adored throwing parties.

As the years passed, however, Goldie forgot how to love Pease because he was consumed by his work. There was never any discussion of a divorce. They were both too 'Catholic' for that. Besides, old man Pegmanti would have cut them out of his will. Although he was a mean-spirited, hard-nosed businessman, Enrico still believed in the sanctity of marriage. The old Catholic traditions from Italy were firmly locked in his soul.

Goldie and Martin simply lived in separate quarters and went their own ways. Enrico was rarely a visitor to the rambling domicile and knew nothing of this arrangement. Appearances indicated that Doctor and Mrs. Pease were a contented, middle aged couple that had found a comfortable, lasting way of life.

In time, however, Martin Pease and Rita Massy became secret lovers. Their clandestine affair was never discovered.

Six days ago, after years of research and what had become the hard labor of marriage to Goldie, he received an unexpected "Golden Handshake." Enrico Pegmanti soon realized his mistake.

Pease cleaned out his desk, collected his personal effects and downloaded *his* formula from the company computer, replacing it with a fake. He returned home and used his laptop to transfer ten million dollars from the PCI's research account to his secret Swiss bank account. The transfer was cunningly designed to be untraceable. It would be months before anyone at Pegmanti had a clue as to what had happened. Even then there was no way anyone could *prove* he was involved.

He had wrapped his cunning into the intricacies of megabytes, hard drives and a million other details of computer cleverness. A few taps on his keyboard was all it took. Despite his craftiness, Pease was an extremely worried man.

Martin Pease had rented a room in a seedy motel on Pico Boulevard in Santa Monica for a meeting with Rita Massy. He sniffed the stale air as he perched on the edge of a rickety wooden chair. He took stock of his surroundings, realizing how drastically his life had changed.

Rita was offered the position as head of research with Laser Research Laboratories in Pasadena. She left PCI and their lives had drifted apart.

Pease never had the slightest indication that Rita Massy was anyone but a talented and extraordinarily gifted scientist, deeply involved in her chosen discipline. That was the day he received a death threat. He also was informed that Rita was a third generation Saudi Muslim, a sleeper, waiting to respond to the call from those who were in power long before the formation of Al Qaida.

Massy revealed that fact at the end of a romantic dinner for two in a cozy corner of Musso & Frank's Grill in Hollywood. She explained that her father married an English woman and immigrated to the United States in the late 1920s. He anglicized his name from Abu Tala al Masry to Albert Massy. Rita was born in New York City.

Years after the WTC attack, Massy confided her allegiance to the militant faction of Islam to Pease. She threatened that Goldie and her father would be killed without hesitation unless she was given access to the latest stem cell formula he was developing along with his top-secret delivery system.

Pease rued the day he revealed his research to Massy. He had developed a system to replace the needle injection method. He'd discovered that he could distribute medication into the human system without leaving the slightest sign of penetration. He also was able to infuse from a distance that had grown from a few feet to fifty yards with absolute accuracy.

He sighed. He'd been a fool in happier days. Now his ex-wife and Enrico Pegmanti were virtual hostages. Their lives were in jeopardy unless he agreed to work with Massy and allow his work to fall into the hands of the enemy. He begged her to reconsider what she was doing. His stem cell manipulation process, used in conjunction with the delivery system, provided her with supremacy to kill or create. She was totally unmoved when Pease accused her of creating a silent killing machine.

Shocked she would even dream that he would willingly become part of such a diabolical plan, Pease had flatly refused. She scoffed at his naiveté. Was it worth the loss of two lives so dear to him?

He had learned too much too late. Now he stiffened at the sound of a light rap on the door. Quickly he crossed the shabby room. "Who is it?" There was a rustling sound. A sheet of expensive writing paper slid under the door. The paper was a signal.

Chapter 9

Martin Pease opened the door and a smartly dressed woman entered.

"You look pale, Martin. Are you feeling ill?" Rita Massy asked.

"I'm fine."

"You've lost weight. You look like hell, frail, that's the word."

Rita Massy was green-eyed with auburn hair stylized and modern. She moved with surprising agility. Glancing with disdain at the room and furnishings, she plucked a white handkerchief from her Dior jacket pocket, flicked the seat of one of the two wooden chairs beside the window and sat down gingerly. She crossed her shapely legs and with a fingertip, moved the drab yellow drapes a couple of inches and peered down the street.

"There's no one out there," Pease said. "This place is safe."

"No place and no one is safe," she replied.

"I need a drink." Pease went to a kitchenette and returned with a Bombay tonic.

She flicked an imaginary dust mote from her tailored skirt. "We decided to let you complete your research on the delivery system—*now*."

His hand trembled as he took a long drink. Then he shook his head. "No."

"We have another target."

"You said five, not six," Pease said quietly.

"Follow orders, Martin, and you'll be able to go to Switzerland and spend your money."

Pease nervously rattled the melting ice cubes. "Why a sixth?"

"My people want a *clean* kill, one that doesn't leave needle marks."

"Meaning?"

"Doctor Wolf from UCLA was called in for consultation at the morgue. I believe you know him?"

"Of course. But why was he consulted?"

"Someone became interested in unusual findings during a routine autopsy of one of the early victims."

"What kind of unusual findings?"

"Needle marks."

Pease stared at her incredulously. "Needle marks would raise no questions on a derelict. Besides, those low-lifes are tagged and put on ice for weeks before anyone looks at them."

"Not this time." Massy got to her feet. "Your next formula delivery must be forensically clean. If it is, the arrangements for you to leave for Switzerland will be completed." She smiled, "Otherwise the seventh victim will be very well known and the method of death obvious."

Massy crossed to the door and paused. "You won't be able to spend all that money with your throat cut."

After she left, Pease refilled his glass and sat quietly in the dingy room, thinking back over the years. He had made a stupid and deadly bargain. Pease knew he must comply. Three lives depended on it.

Chapter 10

Half a block south of Hollywood Boulevard, on Vine Street, is a bar called *The Grape*. You go in through a side entrance off the bus station parking lot.

Twelve noon and the place was jammed; producers and writers rubbing shoulders with electricians and craft workers amid loud conversations and clashing dishes.

Rita Massy found it to be the perfect place to meet her contacts. Sitting at a small table against the wall, she slapped the bottom of a ketchup bottle, applying liberal amounts to her cheeseburger.

A husky man in his mid-thirties, blond crew cut and a ready smile, pulled his plate closer. "Careful. You're going to get that stuff all over my lunch."

"Don't worry. I'm an expert." The next moment a gush of ketchup erupted from the bottle.

"Yeah, right, but not on ketchup removal."

No one would have suspected either was there to finalize a killing.

Never mentioning names or locations, Massy laid out her plan. "I want him to die on camera." She pushed a rolled copy of the *Hollywood Reporter* secured with a thick rubber band across the table.

"Everything you need is in there."

Crew Cut chomped a bite out of his BLT and chewed, thoughtfully eyeing the magazine then slid it off the table into his jacket pocket.

Massy left five minutes before him and sat in her car at the end of the parking lot. She watched Crew Cut leave. No one followed. Massy waited another few minutes then vacated the lot, drove south on Vine and hung a right onto Sunset before she realized a car behind might be following her.

She tightened her grip on the steering wheel and glanced in the rearview mirror. Maybe it was her imagination. Suddenly she slammed on the brakes. She had almost hit the car in front of her. Damn! She was actually ruffled. She'd never had a problem before.

The car she was certain was following her went past. The driver was staring straight ahead, beating her through the green light by three seconds.

Massy sat at the stoplight and watched the car vanish among the traffic. Was she getting too old for this? The light changed and she moved forward.

Chapter 11

Chief of Police Warren Bradbury sat behind his desk in Parker Center tapping his leather-bound blotter with the tip of his large forefinger, emphasizing each slowly enunciated word. "*I...want...every...available... man...assigned...to...these...Hollywood...killings. Two mayors and the DHS are on our ass. Understand?*" Bradbury glared at the top LAPD brass assembled in his office. "Forty-eight hours. I want that bastard, whoever it is, in custody within forty-eight hours. *Get to it.*"

Captain Howard Garvey hesitated before pushing out from his chair. He wanted to tell the Chief that wasn't enough time but he knew this wasn't the time or place. He was among the last to head for the door when Bradbury called his name.

"Stay here, Howard. We need to talk. Shut the door and sit down."

Together the two men represented over fifty years of dedicated service to the City of Angels. "Go ahead, Howard. Tell me there's no way we can nab this guy in the next forty-eight hours."

Garvey noted the edge in his friend's voice. "Okay, Warren. There's no way." Quickly he raised a calming hand before the Chief could reply. "No way unless you tell me something I don't already know."

Years ago they had been partners riding a black and white when to "Protect and to Serve" was the new motto of the LAPD.

"Department of Homeland Security," said Bradbury. "We're going out as they come in. Police departments across America will end up reporting to the DHS in the near future." Bradbury leaned back in his chair until it creaked. "Cities, towns, sheriffs, State Police, even the Feds are going to feel the ripple effect. America's War on Terror is going to change law enforcement as we once knew it—forever."

Garvey knew it was true. The invisible barrier of little fiefdoms that had long hog-tied inter-agency investigations nationwide over the last hundred years had been swept away by the stroke of the President's pen when he created the Department of Homeland Security.

"Short of martial law, DHS will become the primary law enforcement agency in America." Bradbury's voice carried a note of sadness. "Howard, tomorrow three members of the DHS will be working with your people at Hollywood division. Give them all the courtesy at your command."

Koski awakened before Falk. She lay motionless, watching him sleep beside her. It was not yet dawn and the new day still un-warmed. She pulled the covers up around her ears, undecided if she would go on her run. The license plate she had written down proved to be nothing other than a driver making an early delivery to the hotel. At least that was the feedback. Nonetheless, she wasn't satisfied. There was *something* about that car.

"You running today?" Falk mumbled.

"How'd you know I was thinking about running?"

Falk turned on his side and grinned. "You'd be having a guilt trip if you didn't."

Koski was a petite bundle of energy, half asleep or not. She rolled on to her side and placed her feet on Falk's bare ass. She catapulted him from the bed. "*Your* turn to run. I'll make the coffee."

Falk twisted from the bed onto his feet and faced her, hands resting lightly on his hips. Koski pushed aside her short-fringed hair, allowing the covers to slip down and reveal her small, well-shaped breasts. "Of course you don't have to run. There *is* another means of morning exercise."

Falk felt himself stirring and his erection grew larger. Moving to the bed, he pulled back the sheets, reached down and scooped her naked body into his arms. She quickly slid her arms around his neck.

Slowly he lowered himself to a sitting position on the edge of the bed with her in his lap and whispered, "You're right. We'll work out together. You can make the coffee later."

Koski straddled him and they slowly sank back into bed.

Falk had made the coffee while Koski showered. She walked into the kitchen swathed in a yellow terry robe. "*I* was going to make breakfast."

"Decided I'd better get started in case Grant showed up."

"We agreed we'd meet him at the Hollywood station," Koski said.

"I know." He flipped a partially burnt flapjack in the air and it landed half in and half out of the pan. "Damn electric stoves. You can't control the heat like you can with gas."

"Yeah, right. Let me finish that."

"No. You get dressed. I'll fix us some eggs."

Koski headed for her room and hesitated, looking back over her shoulder at the big tough agent fumbling around the kitchen and smiled, knowing she loved that man a little more each day.

Imminent Danger

Chapter 12

Falk, Koski and Grant arrived at morning roll call in the Hollywood station and were begrudgingly accepted. DHS or not, they were still a federal team on LAPD's turf.

Captain Garvey introduced the trio, instructing the assembly to work closely with the investigators and give them every courtesy in a combined effort to apprehend the killer. Garvey then announced that Grant wanted to say a few words.

"Good morning. My name is Agent Greg Grant." He turned slightly. "Agents Joe Falk and Susan Koski, my photography team. We're looking forward to collectively investigating a possible terrorist action." He paused. "As far as the media is concerned we're seeking a serial killer; nothing else. If there are any leaks we'll know where to look. I hope I make myself clear. Any questions?"

Victor Young sat in the back of the room. He raised his hand. Grant nodded and pointed. "Yes. The officer seated in the back."

"Can you explain why the murders of these street people have a tie in with terrorists?"

"Not at this time. Any other questions?"

Again Young raised his hand. "Yes. If the DHS is watching over us doesn't that indicate the government has little trust in our ability to do our job?"

"Not at all. The government needs your expertise and your ability to work the problem at a local level. We are here to learn and to liaise with local government in a manner that will minimize any bureaucratic bottlenecks."

Another hand went up. It was Gully, Victor's new partner. "Does the DHS have any intelligence that it can share with the LAPD?"

"No, although you can rest assured anything DHS gathers will be sent immediately to Parker Center and transferred through regular channels to the field. Let me say again. We're here to assist, not hinder, your regular procedural policies."

Captain Garvey stepped forward and thanked Grant for his input. "Take over, Sergeant. Let's get on the street."

Moments later Grant, Koski and Falk sat in Captain Garvey's office. Grant leaned forward eagerly. "Okay, Captain. How's this going to work? Do we get our own black and white or what?"

Garvey shook his head. "Parker Center has deemed it wiser to assign you three one of our communication vehicles. It'll give you room for yourselves and your equipment."

"We need flexibility, Captain," Grant said. "To check out the crime scenes, question people in the area. Basic police work."

"I understand. It's been arranged for you to be taken to each crime scene. Nonetheless, we can't issue you a police car."

Grant bristled. "Why not?"

"We have no standard procedure for a federal task force being in place with us at a moment's notice, Agent Grant. We're doing the best we can to cooperate with the government."

Grant grimaced. "Very well, Captain but I assure you it won't be long before every law enforcement agency in the nation is given standard procedures on how to cooperate with the DHS." Grant checked his watch. "How soon can we get this vehicle loaded?"

Falk decided Grant had about as much tact as a Sherman Tank when it came to forging a link with LAPD.

Koski and Falk rode in the back of a police SUV. Grant was up front with the driver as they headed north on Beachwood Drive. It branched into Ledgewood, a winding road with the big Hollywood sign looming on their right.

Koski craned forward as the driver took a sharp turn and the sign went out of view. "Joe, I never dreamed I'd ever get this close to that sign."

"It used to spell out HOLLYWOODLAND at one time," the driver explained. "Originally, it was an advertisement to sell real estate up here, way back."

Grant butted in. "And possibly where one of the killings took place."

"The fourth murder in the series we're investigating, yeah, but not the first murder in the area," the driver said. "A number of homicides have occurred up here over the years; a couple of suicides, too. Young women unhappy about their careers climbed to the top of the letters and jumped."

No one spoke for a while. They continued up the hill and finally pulled to a stop.

"They found the body over there." The driver pointed toward a thicket of oleander thrusting up from the hillside onto the sidewalk. The houses on the street consisted of small to medium-sized stucco homes in white, pink, even blue.

Built back in the 1920s and 1930s, they sold for around eight to ten thousand dollars. Now they commanded prices in the hundreds of thousands.

Grant got out and pointed. "I'll take the two houses on the left. You and Koski check out those three on the right."

Imminent Danger

Chapter 13

Koski and Falk drew a blank at the first two houses. Elderly people occupied both and had no wish to answer any more questions.

The third house, the blue one, gave Koski a glimmer of hope. A curly-haired young Latino woman dressed in well-worn jeans and a t-shirt emblazoned with the letters IBM (*Italian by Marriage*) opened the door.

"Hi. What can I do for you?"

"Mind if we ask you some questions?" Koski inquired.

"Are you with the police?"

"No. We're working with the DHS doing a follow-up."

Koski and Falk flashed their DHS ID's. "Sometimes people remember little things they might have forgotten when they were interviewed the first time."

"Right. Come on in." The young woman opened the door wide and stepped aside. Falk and Koski crossed the threshold and were immediately in a small, neat living room decorated with furniture that must have been in vogue when the house was new. "I was just brewing coffee. Take a seat." She indicated the choice of three well-worn easy chairs or a long, overstuffed couch. They opted for the couch. "How'd you like your coffee?"

"Two blacks will be fine. Thanks," Koski replied.

Falk whispered. "Is Grant still in the house across the street?"

Koski got up and peeked out the window. "Must be. I can't see him. Why?"

"I don't want him around while we're interviewing this gal. I want an exclusive here." The young woman returned and placed two mugs on a side table. "Couldn't help overhearing. Am I an important part of the investigation?"

Falk picked up one of the mugs and sipped the brew. "Good coffee. We didn't get your name."

"Nell Fynn. That's with a Y."

"Important? I don't know. Tell me. What do you know?"

"Hold on." Nell went back to the kitchen, got her coffee, returned, then folded her shapely form into one of the easy chairs, resting the mug on her right knee. She glanced from one to the other as if deciding whom to address. She chose Koski.

"I'm a writer. That's one of the reasons I live up here." She took a sip. "That and the fact I'm broke most of the time. Lucky for me this place was bequeathed to me by an aunt. She was a great lady and I bless her memory every day."

Koski leaned forward. "Nell, did you give this preamble to the cops when they were up here asking questions?"

Nell studied Koski over the rim of her mug. "No."

Koski nodded. "Then why us?"

"I want to communicate with you two."

"Why?"

"I need background on the DHS for a book I'm writing."

Koski glanced at Falk and they both grinned. "Fine, Nell, but first *we* have questions. You say you live up here and don't go out much, right?"

"I do get out but not much. My VW is almost twenty years old and I'm trying to conserve its strength. That and I'm busy with the book."

"I suppose the police asked plenty of questions so bear with us," Falk said.

Nell shrugged. "No problem. Take your time."

"On the day the body was found out there," Koski nodded toward the window, "did you hear or see anything out of the ordinary?"

"The cops asked the same question."

Falk raised an eyebrow. "And?"

"I said no. I couldn't recall anything. Then a few days later I remembered something. I was going to call them but changed my mind. I decided it was nothing."

Falk leaned forward. "Tell us, Nell."

"It was the night before they found the body. I was working late, must have been after two in the morning, and I was getting ready to turn in when I heard a car coming up the hill. We don't get too much traffic up here late at night. It was moving slowly. I could tell by the sound of the engine. Anyway, I looked out the window, you know, curious.

"At first, I didn't see the vehicle because it was driving without lights. There was a full moon and I saw it as it came past the house. Couldn't tell you what color it was but I recognized the make."

"A Rav4, maybe?" Koski asked.

"Hey! How'd you know that? Yeah. It was a Rav4. I love that little car. Soon as I get enough ahead I'm going in debt for one."

"Did it stop?"

"Don't know. I went to bed after it passed. I was bushed. How'd you know it was a Rav4?"

"Woman's intuition," said Koski gently. "Too dark to see the license plate number, right?" Nell nodded.

"You should have called the cops back."

"I suppose. I thought it might be a couple of young kids coming up here to make out."

Falk broke in. "In a Rav4?"

"Yeah. You're right." Her laugh was bubbly.

"Thanks anyway," Falk said. "You've been a big help. If you think of anything else or notice something out of the ordinary give us a call. Here's our number."

Nell took the card and studied it. "Any chance of giving you guys an interview sometime, you know, DHS and what it means to the civil rights of the average citizen?"

"Can't promise anything. We'll have to see how things go." Falk stuck out his hand and she shook it vigorously.

"I'll keep my fingers crossed, Agent Falk."

"Just one more question, Nell," Koski said. "Your t-shirt says IBM. Are you married?"

"No. It was my aunt's. It came with the house."

As the police communications vehicle headed back down into Hollywood, Koski drummed her fingers on her knees, a habit she had when deep in thought. It irritated the hell out of Falk. He reached out and held his hand over hers. She saw the look in his eyes as he tipped his head toward the front passenger seat. They clearly indicated, "Don't say anything."

Koski went silent but restarted her drumbeat and watched the trees and bushes flash past as the driver headed to the next scene.

Chapter 14

Three minutes into reading the early evening news, the anchor died; slumped forward across the news desk. Camera One quickly cut to the weather map.

Crew Cut stood near an exit then quietly walked off the set amid the sudden confusion.

Rita Massy watched the drama on TV. She smiled and pressed the off button on her remote. This time there would be no telltale discoloration of the brain that caused medical examiners reason to suspect foul play. Her mobile rang. Massy had prearranged for the call to be brief. "Go to your place. I'll be there within the hour."

Massy parked in the street outside an apartment in Burbank, a few blocks from Warner Brothers' Studio, a white two-story stucco in need of paint. How could anyone live in such a place? She alone had paid this man enough in the last few months to enable him to live in far better circumstances.

Massy passed through the front entrance into a courtyard of withered plants and two drooping palm trees. A small swimming pool filled with murky green water and surrounded by a chain link fence completed the picture of neglect that hung over the entire complex.

Pausing at the bottom of a set of stairs leading up to a balcony encircling the second floor, she scanned the upper units. All the apartment doors faced out onto the pool area. Number 223 was in the middle of the row.

She climbed the stairs, hearing sounds of various television shows as she passed the apartments. A child cried in the distance and a door slammed.

Imminent Danger

Then she was at number 223. She kicked on the door with the side of her shoe, noting closed Venetian blinds covered the windows. Massy kicked harder. Then, taking a handkerchief from her pocket, she grasped the doorknob, turned and pushed the door open. Once inside it was apparent the place had been tossed. She closed the door with her shoulder. Whoever had searched the apartment had done a thorough job. The shabby living room was trashed with broken items. Drawers were pulled out and contents scattered. Even the cushions on the worn-out couch had been ripped open.

In the filthy kitchen she viewed a pile of dirty dishes stacked in the sink under a slowly dripping tap. She headed down the hall to a bedroom. The door was open. Crew Cut lay stretched across an unmade bed with his throat slashed and surrounded by the wreckage of another savage search.

After the initial shock of finding the man dead, Massy's brow beaded with a sweat of fear. The prototype delivery system she had passed to Crew Cut at lunch! She'd told the dead man to guard the weapon with his life. Had his killer found the device?

Massy, light-headed, heart racing, cursed the fact she should have arranged with Crew Cut where to hide the damn thing in case of an emergency. Checking the time, she realized the killing must have taken place shortly after the phone call, just over an hour ago. It was now 7:15 p.m. She had no time to waste. Someone might return.

Moving swiftly and using her handkerchief, she carefully opened the front door a crack to be sure no one was on the balcony. Satisfied, she slipped out, closing the door softly.

Two minutes later she sped up Barham Boulevard, heading back to Hollywood. *She should have taken her time, checked the body, searched for any clues that might tie him to the dead newscaster.* Damn. For a moment she almost turned back then decided it was too late. She couldn't risk someone in the building seeing her. Tightlipped, Massy shuddered at the thought of having to face the cleric and update him about the murder and losing the weapon.

Chapter 15

It was nine p.m. when the police communications vehicle pulled into the Hollywood precinct parking lot on Ivar Street. Greg Grant glanced over his shoulder. "I have an engagement tonight otherwise I'd invite you both to dinner."

The team had spent a long day scrutinizing each murder location, including the latest death at the television studio.

"Thanks. We'll get something on the way back to the hotel." Falk rubbed his hand across his chin. "Interesting day."

Grant nodded. "Yeah. We have some good footage. We'll meet here in the morning at eight. I have a couple of ideas that could move us ahead."

"What's the chance of getting an official car of our own?" Koski asked.

"I'm working on it." He swung the passenger door open. "You guys get plenty of rest. See you in the a.m."

Koski watched him cross the parking lot and climb into the passenger side of a black Mercedes parked beside the building. "Dinner dates with a woman driving a Mercedes," Koski muttered. "No wonder we're working for him."

"Temporarily," Falk replied. He pushed open the car door. "C'mon. Let's go." Falk slapped the driver on the shoulder. "Thanks for being the chauffeur in this charade today. We appreciate it."

The driver looked surprised. Grateful someone had voiced thanks. He gave a tired smile. "You're welcome. Say, if you guys like seafood try the Shack over on Cole. It's the best."

"Thanks. We'll do that." Walking to their car Koski linked arms with

Falk. "That young writer up in the hills. What do you think?"

Falk shot her a questioning glance. "Meaning?"

"She said she doesn't get out much and wanted to interview us..."

Falk unlocked the car door. "I saw you jot her phone number down when we were drinking coffee. Get in, call on your cell and tell her we'll pick her up in fifteen minutes." Falk climbed behind the wheel, switched on the ignition and the car's interior filled with Mozart's Symphony No. 14 "Jupiter" as he eased the vehicle forward.

The halibut was superb. The trio finished their meal and sat in a comfortable booth at the Shack.

"The driver was right. We'll have to come here again," Koski murmured as she finished the last bite.

"My dad used to say truck drivers and cops knew the best places to eat." Nell reached for the breadbasket, pulled apart the last sourdough roll and wiped her plate clean. "And starving writers always accept a meal no matter who recommends the place."

"And investigators want the truth when they buy a meal," Falk said. "That Rav4 you saw the other night, you'd seen it in the area before, right?"

Nell stopped chewing as a surprised look flitted across her face. "How'd' you mean?"

"One of your neighbors said they'd seen a green Rav4 driving around a couple of times during the day. They remembered because it drove past slowly as if the driver was lost or looking for an address. Whoever it was also could've been scoping the area for a place to dump a body."

Falk watched as she finished eating the last of the bread then took a sip of water.

"Okay. I saw the car a couple of times."

"Why'd you hide the fact?" Falk questioned softly.

"I didn't want to get involved."

"In what?" Koski asked.

"The driver stopped outside the house several days before the body showed up on the hillside. I was out in the yard and he called to me. He said he was looking for a place to rent. Cool looking guy—said he was a musician, slept days and needed some place quiet."

Falk cut in. "Would you remember the guy if you saw him again?"

"Sure. I told him I loved his vehicle and wanted to get one like it when I had the money. He laughed. Said he'd come and see me if he ever decided to sell. He gave me his phone number."

"Notice anything about him?"

"Like what?"

"You're a writer. Describe him."

Nell looked skyward. "In his mid-thirties, dark hair and brown eyes. Couldn't tell his height since he was in the car but I'd guess five nine or so. Most Hispanics are about that height."

"You're sure he was Hispanic?"

"He looked Spanish although he didn't *sound* Spanish."

"Then why did you say Hispanic?"

"Guess it's because there are so many of us in Southern California. He could've been Italian. I don't know."

Falk pressed. "Middle Eastern perhaps?"

Nell shrugged. "That, too, I suppose. How'd you know I'd seen the car before?"

"When Agent Koski asked if you recognized the car in the darkness you came up with a Rav4 without hesitation. It's not a car most people mention as a first guess so we decided to ask you again."

"What are you going to do now?"

"Take the phone number he gave you."

"It's at home. I stuck it in my phone book. I didn't memorize it."

"Fine. You can give it to me when we get back to your place. I want you to call and ask if he'll sell the car if you raise the cash. If he says yes, find out when you can have a test ride."

Back at the house, Nell made the phone call, letting it ring several times. She glanced over at Koski and Falk shaking her head. "No answer. Like I said, he's a musician, most likely still out on a gig. You want me to keep trying?"

Falk looked at his watch. It was already past midnight. "No. Call him tomorrow. If you get him, give me a call on my cell. The number's on the card I gave you."

Falk drove back down the winding hill. "Turn the heater up, Joe." Koski nodded sleepily as the CD played softly and the warm air swirled around them. Falk concentrated on tight curves and a narrow road without streetlights when suddenly he felt something cold press firmly on the nape of his neck.

"Pull over and no heroics." Koski resisted an automatic reaction to reach for her Glock Nine and remained motionless. Falk parked the car.

"Kill the engine and lights, hands on top of your heads," a male voice commanded.

Blackness and silence filled the car. The voice continued. "Now listen up. I know who you are and why you're in town and I've something to sell."

"What?" Falk asked staring ahead.

"Information the DHS needs to know."

"How did you find us?"

"You want to buy?"

"I'll answer that when I know what you're selling."

"Fine. Drive back to your place and we'll talk."

Chapter 16

They had not attempted to overpower the young man who now sat on a straight-backed chair in Falk's living room, covering them with an automatic. Koski and Falk sat side by side on the couch. The man was olive skinned, slight of build with chocolate colored eyes reflecting that he'd learned about life the hard way; on the streets.

"I'm a gangbanger from East LA and me and a few of the gang became mixed up with a group of Middle Easterners. They said they could show us how to make big bucks, fast. It sounded easy. We thought they were drug dealers looking for local talent. The money they offered was wild. Later, when they had our trust, they told us what they really wanted."

He rubbed the back of his left hand across his mouth. "I need something cold to drink."

"Pepsi?" Koski asked.

"Yeah. It'll do."

He lapsed into silence until she returned with a bottle and a glass. He waved the glass aside and gulped from the bottle before continuing. "Turns out they wanted to use us." He took another long swig. "Mexicans can go anywhere in California and not worry about racial profiling. That profiling is a pile of shit anyway and a waste of time. Hell... Arabs can buy whoever they want to do a job. All they have to do is go where cops are hated. Easy as that."

"What made *you* change your mind?" Falk questioned, sensing the gunman was nervous despite his bravado.

"I haven't yet. I want to see what you guys have to offer."

Falk smiled. "A true patriot, I see."

The young man finished his soda. "If we make a deal it'll have to include putting me into a witness protection program in a new location far from LA with new ID and my own house."

"Ambitious plans, young man."

"I intend to improve my lifestyle."

"How did you find us?" Falk inquired.

"I'm a *thinking* gangbanger. I have my ways."

Falk nodded. "But you were fooled by a group of Arabs."

Lowering the empty bottle to the floor, the man nodded. "You're right. But I learn fast, man, and after we've made our deal I'll be living better than you."

Falk swapped a glance with Koski. "I'll have to arrange a meeting with my boss. It'll take a few days."

"I'm staying here until he comes and makes the deal." He nodded to Koski. "She'll stay with me as my guardian angel."

"You could have been followed," Koski said softly.

"Let me bring you up-to-date, lady. Nell phoned and told me you were going to pick her up and take her back to her place. I hitched up there and waited until you returned. You know the rest."

"Not quite. Tell us about Nell."

"What's to tell?"

"She's *not* a gang member?"

"No way. She's a freelance writer. She plays music to eat otherwise she'd starve to death. We met at a club in LA six months ago. I liked her music. She plays a wild clarinet. I got her a few gigs around town.

"Nell phoned me earlier and said a couple of DHS agents were taking her to dinner and then bringing her home. She was stoked, man. Said she was going to try to get an interview. I decided it would be a good time to introduce myself."

"You'd been driving around her neighborhood. You told her you were a musician looking for a place to live."

"Yeah. I told you. I met her a couple months ago at a club on Crenshaw.

We got talking and she told me she lived in the hills overlooking Hollywood. Anyway, a few days ago I was ordered to look for a lonely place to dump a body and thought of the area up near her place."

"Did you tell her you were a musician *and* a gang member?"

"No."

"Who told you to look around?"

"One of the Arabs."

"Why?"

"Man, they don't tell you why. Anyway, I drove up, Nell was out in the yard and we gabbed awhile. She admired my car. We made small talk and I said I'd sell her mine when I was ready. Then I mentioned I was looking around for a place to rent."

"Did you leave your phone number?"

"Sure. Nell said she'd keep an eye open for a place."

Falk leaned forward. "You're going to have to return our weapons if you want me to call my boss."

"You said it would take a couple of days."

"I lied. What's your name?"

"Call me Marco."

"Okay, Marco. What's it to be?"

"I give you my gun. You call the cops and I'm whacked, right?"

"Not if what you have to tell us is worthwhile."

Marco lowered his voice. "It'll be worth plenty."

"Then you don't have a problem. Give it to me."

Marco handed him the automatic. "Call him. Now."

Imminent Danger

Chapter 17

Tom Stewart arrived within the hour, walked in, tossed his raincoat across the back of the couch and asked, "Where is he?"

Falk pointed. "In the kitchen. Koski's making him a sandwich." Koski and Marco entered. Marco carried a plate. He slumped into an easy chair, eyed Stewart and took a bite of his sandwich. Falk brought Stewart up-to-date while Marco chewed.

Stewart's voice was husky and his disposition edgy from having to get out of bed and drive to the hotel. He joined his fingers behind his head and leaned back. "Okay, Marco. Tell us your story."

The young Hispanic related his experiences with the Arabs, as he called them. "They needed us to act as spies, hit men, any assignment that might trigger a security check." He paused. "As long as the government continues to use its present methods of racial profiling those guys will find others to do their work."

"You don't seem to have much patriotism, Marco."

"You're wrong, man. That's why I'm here. I was born in East LA. I'm an American. You know how many people are living in LA who *aren't* citizens —illegals working low-end jobs *if* they're lucky to find work?"

Marco's face tightened. "Some dude offers them big bucks to do something, they do it. No questions asked." Marco got up and paced the room. "I'll be straight with you, man. I knew this country was in big trouble when people like these Arabs could buy anyone as easy as buying a loaf of bread."

"What made you change your mind and come to us, Marco?" Stewart asked.

"They killed my best friend. They said he was going to go to the police."

"Was he?"

"No. It was their excuse. He refused to carry out an assignment."

"What was the assignment?"

"Place a bomb in a trash container near the snack bar at Dodger Stadium just before the end of the game. He told them he wouldn't do it, man. Didn't want to hurt no women and kids. Two days after he refused, I found him sitting in his car, dead. His throat cut."

Stewart asked. "You want to tell us who they are and seek protection, right?"

"I want to make a *deal*." He pointed at Falk. "Like I told him. I want a guarantee of the witness protection plan. A house fully paid for and a new location."

"Is that it?" Stewart questioned.

"No. I also want one million dollars. Cash."

"You're out of your mind, Marco. The government doesn't pay out that kind of money."

"I'm not finished. I'll stay with the gang for another six months and feed you information that'll be worth more than a million bucks. Hell, every time the government dropped *one* of those smart bombs on Iraq at the start of the war, they cost that much. All the taxpayers got for their money if the missile went off track was crushed rock and some dead goats."

"What makes you think you can give us information worth a million dollars?"

Marco flicked off a few crumbs and smoothed his shirtfront. He cut his eyes to Stewart and gave a sly smile. "I don't want to be rude, but your two agents," Marco nodded toward Koski and Falk, "are working with the cops trying to find who the Hollywood serial killer is, right?"

"Go on."

"I can tell you more than the cops know right now. The killings are experimental tests to discover the best means to deliver a mind-altering drug that can turn a person into an assassin or a suicide bomber on command."

Stewart glanced at Falk and back to Marco. "How do you know that?"

"It's what I do. I keep my ears and eyes open. And these guys trust me."

"Why?"

"Good help is hard to find, man."

Imminent Danger

Chapter 18

Stewart had agreed that Marco contact him through Falk within forty-eight hours, at which time he'd be advised whether he would become a paid informer. Marco phoned Falk the next morning at 6 a.m. They arranged to meet at a Mexican restaurant, José's, on Alvera Street, a tourist attraction near Union Station in downtown LA.

Falk hung up and looked into Koski's room moments before she was about to leave for her morning run. "Why call you so soon, Joe? He only left a few hours ago. Maybe we should go together."

"No. Contact Grant. Tell him I was called into the bureau and I'll check with him later. Stick with Grant until I join you. Gotta go."

Alvera Street is a short, quaint street of shops and small stalls selling Mexican goods, everything from jumping beans to piñatas. Falk found the restaurant—and Marco—sitting in a red leather booth facing the door.

"Coffee?" Marco asked. Falk nodded.

"Let's eat." Marco slid a plastic covered menu across the table. "I think better on a full stomach. Try the eggs and salsa. Gets the brain working."

"Coffee's fine." Falk eased into the booth. A server appeared, filled a thick mug with steaming coffee and pushed it toward him. "I thought we were going to wait a couple of days, Marco?"

"I decided to show goodwill and give you a tip."

"Why?"

"Goodwill. Understand what I'm saying?"

"No."

The server returned and placed a large plate of refried beans and eggs and a deep bowl of salsa in front of Marco, along with a covered dish. Marco tapped the dish. "Warm tortillas. You like one?"

"I'm fine."

Marco shrugged, scooped a forkful of beans into his mouth, snagged a tortilla, folded it in half and stuck one end into an egg, breaking the yolk. "You should eat, man. Breakfast's the most important meal of the day."

Falk nodded and sipped his coffee. It was strong, not bitter.

"I'll be straight with you, man," Marco continued, eating and talking at the same time. "You heard of *Jamul* right?"

Falk nodded. "The pop singer?"

"He's more than that, Agent Falk. He's a show business legend." Marco plucked another tortilla from the dish, rolled it into a tube and jabbed it into the salsa.

"He's also big with the Arabs and I don't just mean music and entertainment wise. He has homes all over the world. Right now he's at his pad in the marina. You guys at the DHS should check him out."

"What does he do for the Arabs?"

"Hey! I don't know yet. All I know is Jamul became a born again Islamic, and whatever it is he does for their cause, he does for free. It's up to your boss. If he agrees to my demands, I'll find out."

"You could have saved this information for Stewart and made brownie points."

Marco took the last tortilla, shrugged and wiped his plate clean.

Chapter 19

Crew Cut's murder received little notice from the news media. The Hollywood serial killer was still the lead story. The most concerned person was Rita Massy. She'd been called to meet with her boss and report what had happened. She parked in the subterranean garage, entered the express elevator and punched in the penthouse's security code.

Her boss was a tall, handsome man. He was on his cell, pacing impatiently back and forth across a white wall-to-wall carpet three inches thick. "She's here now. I'll call you back." He flipped his phone shut and slipped its compactness into his shirt pocket.

White slacks, a long-sleeved red silk shirt, a pair of red tennis shoes, his hair pulled into a black shiny ponytail and the man thought he looked cool. Rita Massy thought he personified a pimp. Massy's boss opened his arms like a preacher greeting his flock. "Doctor Massy, come in, take a seat. Would you like something to drink: coffee, tea?"

Both knew the dance had started. Smooth courtesy thinly covered the distrust in both their hearts. "Nothing, thanks. I'm fine."

"I see our last subject went out in grand style. No problems I take it?" He indicated a chair.

"No problem with the execution. And there'll be no questions at the autopsy." Massy leaned back in the soft comfort of the deep leather chair.

"Were you satisfied with the delivery device, Doctor?"

"Absolutely."

"This person who carried out the execution was one of your people, I believe."

Massy stiffened slightly. "Yes. I've used him on several occasions."

"Trust him then, do you, Doctor?"

"Of course," she replied.

The tall man turned toward the floor to ceiling window and stared at the view. "I had him eliminated. He's been around too long."

A wave of fear shivered into her gut and she fought to hide her reaction. She needed to move. Pushing out of the easy chair, she joined him at the window and gazed out at the panoramic view. She was the first to speak. "You did the right thing."

"You surprise me, Doctor." He turned quickly, fastened a viselike grip on her arm and led her away from the window. "You also allowed him to take the weapon back to his apartment." His eyes were slits as he moved his face close to Massy. "A foolish move, doctor. Luckily my man discovered the weapon. I have it in safe keeping."

Massy felt the grip loosen slightly then a long slender finger tapped her shoulder. "You look pale, Doctor. Sit down, relax. I won't be a moment." Massy took a deep, shuddering breath and slumped into the chair. The bastard was playing cat and mouse.

Within seconds he returned with the prototype wrapped in a towel. Placing the bundle on a side table next to her chair, he slowly unwrapped the towel and stood back to admire the killing tool.

"A wonderful device indeed," Massy's superior said softly, any sign of his anger now gone. Both stared at the black plastic object that was the shape and size of a small flashlight. He reached down and with the solemnity of a priest raising a chalice, held the weapon cupped reverently between his large powerful hands. "So light. It feels like a toy."

Massy watched mesmerized as he turned it from side to side then took it in his right hand and aimed directly at her. "You say the new model is even more advanced, longer range, truer accuracy, even smaller! Amazing. And to think it doesn't make a sound when fired."

He lowered the weapon. "Is that the correct term, fired?"

Massy swallowed hard before attempting a reply. "Perhaps a new word will have to be coined." She felt perspiration trickling down her back. Had her boss continued with his previous fit of anger she would be dead by now.

"You will need a new assassin, Doctor."

"Yes. I have an expert in long-range work. He's already skilled with the new weapon."

He smiled and aimed the device toward the window. He held the position for a count of five then suddenly spun and stared at her. He moved in closer and placed the tip of the weapon on her nose. "I'm certain you'll see that this expert does an excellent job, Doctor."

Imminent Danger

Chapter 20

After Doctor Massy left, the tall man returned to the window and gazed out across what had been rice paddies years ago. It was now a yacht harbor surrounded by upscale apartments and known as Marina Del Rey.

Located between Venice and the Los Angeles Airport, the Marina is a place of recreation, habitation and fornication. Apartments full of swinging singles, slips full of powerboats, yachts and sailboats, all tied down in neat rows, making a city of wealth and power; floating assets.

Jamul lived in the penthouse of one of the twin cylindrical apartments that soared over the display of nautical richness. It was 9:05 a.m. Even though it was April, the sun ignored the fact and beamed kindly on the Marina. The ocean twinkled in response.

Jamul walked onto his balcony and stood facing the Pacific, focusing a large pair of binoculars on a white-hulled Grand Banks trawler as it rounded the breakwater sailing into the main channel of the Marina.

"Home is the sailor, home from the sea," Jamul whispered as the trawler cruised proudly the length of the almost deserted waterway. Jamul owned the craft along with two more identical Grand Banks. Each boat was registered under a different name. Jamul's name didn't show on any of the manifests. His name did appear, however, on one of the largest yachts in the Marina. Purchased through a broker in Gibraltar and outside EU and American waters, the vessel remained unaffected by tax considerations. The brokerage house was an establishment guaranteeing confidentiality at all times.

Elvis Presley, at the height of his success, had once owned FDR's yacht, the *Potomac*.

Sadly, it was no longer for sale and was now part of a maritime museum in Oakland, California.

Jamul had searched every major ship brokerage in the world. He finally located his dream, the sister ship of FDR's beloved *Potomac*. Jamul knew the original yacht was 196 feet long so he added another twenty-five feet. In addition, a bright blue Bell 206B-111 Jet-ranger helicopter perched on the ship's helipad.

No way was Elvis ever going to upstage Jamul. He named the craft *Caviare*. It was rarely put to sea. A full time crew whose duties were to maintain the bright work always kept the yacht in perfect condition, ready for business meetings or dinner parties at a moment's notice, whatever Jamul decided.

Jamul's position in life called for such amenities. Being adored as a demigod by those between eighteen and thirty-five from all around the world had placed him in a position of absolute power in the music industry.

His story of rising from the ranks of poverty in New York's Spanish Harlem to singer/entertainer of choice to the younger generation had been extolled ad nauseam by the world's entertainment media. With superb management, Jamul possessed a magnetic personality and a singing voice with the range of Caruso, the charm of Sinatra plus a magic of his own that no one could explain. He was a star with one name and beloved by millions.

Jamul lowered his binoculars, walked across the balcony and back inside the penthouse. He owned homes in many countries and traveled constantly, using his own private jets. Jamul had secretly embraced Islam ten years earlier. To the public he was a man with the voice of an angel. In truth, he was a man with the soul of a serpent.

The Grand Banks sailed to its mooring, tied up and no one looked twice. Within less than a half hour of docking, Jamul was entertaining three passengers from the trawler in his penthouse. His manservant served Arabic coffee. Jamul served the three with up-to-date Bosnian passports, showing they had arrived into the country legally with visas valid for three months. United States Customs or airport security hadn't troubled the travelers. They were to join Mikhail Brasinov at his Beverly Hills apartment within hours.

Deception is an arrangement of light and dark... The people trained to see white where there is black.

Jamul was black and he could easily make Rita Massy see white.

Imminent Danger

Chapter 21

Falk's cell phone buzzed as he drove back to Hollywood from breakfast with Marco.

"Where the hell are you? You were supposed to meet me at eight." It was Grant.

"Didn't Koski phone and tell you I'd been called into the bureau?"

"No one called. I've been phoning your hotel and just located your damn cell number."

Falk's mind raced. What happened to Koski? "Look, Greg, you know the way it is sometimes. You'll have to excuse us for today. Okay?"

"DHS will take a dim view of this, Falk. We don't operate this way."

"Greg, I'm driving. You're breaking up. Can you hear me? Hello, Greg?" He switched off and headed for the hotel.

Falk checked both suites. No sign of a struggle. Koski would have called if her plans suddenly changed and she decided not to meet with Grant. Where was she? Falk returned to his suite, thinking of the sudden request to meet Marco for breakfast; an arrangement to get him out of the way while someone snatched her?

Mikhail Brasinov studied the passports and handed them back to the two men who had arrived at the Marina. "Very good. We're working with super pros now, better than the old days, eh?" Both men nodded. "Good. Your first assignment will be to kidnap an FBI agent, a young woman. Do not harm her. She has information we need."

The burlier of the two scowled. "You want us to kidnap an FBI agent?!"

"Yes, and take her to a boat in the Marina. You'll be briefed in detail. I

Imminent Danger

want *nothing* to go wrong, understand?"

Chapter 22

Koski was flat on her back in total darkness. She had regained consciousness with a splitting headache and attempted to push into a sitting position but the pain was excruciating. She flopped back onto what felt like a cot or bunk. She didn't attempt any moves other than slow deep breathing. Dampness—salt air—the smell of stale coffee and diesel oil and the sound of lapping water seeped into her consciousness.

She was on a boat. Pushing up onto one elbow, she forced herself to overcome the nausea. Still dressed in her running clothes she quickly pulled up the right leg of her sweatsuit and reached for her ankle holster. Her fingers fumbled for the .22 automatic she always carried when out alone in the early morning. It was gone.

The creaking sound of a hatch opening startled her, then a shaft of daylight stabbed into the darkness and a woman's voice called down. "Has the headache diminished yet?"

Koski shifted on the bunk, shaded her eyes and blinked up at a dark shape in the hatch entrance as the woman spoke again.

"You're not tied or handcuffed, and as long as you obey orders you won't be harmed. If you don't, you'll be killed."

Koski had experience in situations where she had learned firsthand to be silent. Say nothing. Listen. Answer questions and if they didn't already know the answers, lie.

The woman continued. "No doubt you could use a cup of coffee. Black or white?"

"Black," Koski mumbled.

Rita Massy stared through the eye slits of her ski mask at the woman curled on the bunk. Doctor Wolf, in a casual conversation with Massy, had unknowingly disclosed the interest the DHS had shown concerning the mysterious deaths and the resultant findings of brain discolorations during the autopsies.

Locating the address of two of the investigating agents hadn't been a problem. The hatch closed. Blackness returned and Koski cursed softly. One minute she had been running her morning miles and the next woke in a whorl of pain.

In the City of Angels, in an area known as Silverlake, Detective Victor Young entered his small rented house. The once bright yellow stucco had faded to a dingy white and was surrounded by overgrown flowers and weeds.

Jacaranda trees in blue bloom next to a bright red bottlebrush were the only two living things in the garden that Victor could name. Red and green had been Jenny's colors. Green eyes, red hair. She'd known the name of every flower and plant in the garden.

Young missed her with an ache he knew would last as long as he lived. He closed the door softly.

Three years had passed since she went to the store to buy groceries on a warm summer afternoon. She never returned, having been killed in a robbery that went wrong. Young discovered later that his wife had gone to the store to get fresh garlic for her spaghetti sauce. She'd asked him what he wanted for dinner just before he'd left for work. Now he stood on the exact spot he'd been when he called back. "Spaghetti, and don't forget to put garlic in the sauce this time." They'd laughed and he kissed her goodbye.

"I won't," she said. "I'll pick some up this afternoon. Take care of yourself, Vic."

Take care of yourself, Vic. She never failed to send him off to work with a kiss and those words. Over the last three years Victor Young became an embittered man.

The winking green light of the answering machine in the living room caught his eye. He tapped the play button and heard Captain Garvey's voice.

"You have a new assignment, Detective Young." Victor noted the sound of urgency in the Captain's voice. "One of the hotshot investigators from the DHS has gone missing. Call Falk on his cell phone soon as you get this message." The Captain gave the number then the line went dead.

Young stared at the machine. Captains didn't usually call detectives at home and give them an assignment. He made the call.

Joe Falk was still at the hotel and was rechecking Koski's room for the slightest sign she might have left as a clue to her whereabouts when Young called.

"Falk."

"This is Detective Victor Young, LAPD. I've been assigned to work with you." He paused, uncertain how to phrase his next sentence. "It's regarding your missing partner."

"Where can we meet?" Falk barked.

"Your hotel, twenty minutes. I'll leave now."

"I'll be in the lobby."

Imminent Danger

Chapter 23

Falk recognized Young coming through the front entrance. "You're the guy with the questions. I remember you from the briefing. Let's get a cup of coffee and I'll bring you up to speed."

Stewart had given Falk the okay to tell detective that he and Koski were undercover FBI, not DHS photographers. He said it made for better working conditions. Stewart was right.

Young set his cup down. "I thought I was stuck with a news photographer who didn't know his ass from a hole in the ground about police procedure and I was to play nursemaid."

Falk smiled thinly. "There are a few news photographers who do, Victor."

Victor leaned forward, eager to gather facts and get started on their search. "Yeah, right. *Very* few. So the last you saw of her she was in her room getting ready to go on her morning run. You know the route she takes?"

"No. She changed it daily, for safety's sake."

"She could've been followed from the start. Let's make a few inquires," Young said.

Their first stop was a 24-hour convenience store several blocks from the hotel. The clerk remembered seeing a young woman jogging past the window shortly after he went on duty at 6 a.m. Nothing unusual. He often saw joggers from the hotel running in the early morning. When questioned further by Falk, he remembered a car drove past a couple of minutes later, driving slowly—a Rav4.

"Can you recall the color?"

"I think it was green. I'm not certain."

"Thanks." He turned to Victor. "Koski told me she saw a green Rav4 outside the hotel the other morning. She took the plate number and ran it through the DMV. Turned out it belonged to a guy making a delivery."

"You still have the number?"

"Yeah. I jotted it down." He removed a small notebook from a pocket and thumbed a few pages. "Here it is—'NTV925'."

"We'll run it again," Victor said. "Get an address and see what we can find."

Less than an hour later they had an address on June Street, a section in Hollywood consisting mainly of homes and small apartments built in the 1930s. The street number proved to be a house in the rear.

They parked out front and walked up the buckled concrete driveway. Young knocked on the door of a house with peeling brown paint on the window frames. No answer. Falk tried the bell. "No one home," the LAPD detective muttered, peering through a grimy window.

"Can I help you?" a woman's voice called.

Turning, Falk saw a heavyset woman standing on the back step of the front house. She held a yard broom across her ample chest as if it were an AK47.

"Police." Young removed his wallet and flipped it open.

The woman relaxed a little, came forward and scrutinized Victor's picture. "What about him?" She pointed the broom at Falk. Victor raised his eyebrows. Falk showed his ID. The woman looked surprised. "A cop *and* a DHS man!"

"This isn't TV, ma'am," the detective replied. "We're looking to ask the occupant a few questions." He jerked his thumb toward the peeling paint.

"He's not in."

"Know when he'll be back?"

"Never. He's dead. Killed in his car early this morning." She lowered her broom, "A wreck on the 405."

"How do you know?" Falk asked.

"Cops came by to see if he had any next of kin. Must've gotten his address from his driver's license," she said softly.

"Did he?" Falk said.

She shook her head. "None. He lived alone."

"Did he drive a Rav4?"

"All I know is it was a small green SUV."

Falk thanked the woman then they walked back to their car. His new partner turned on the ignition "We can get a search warrant."

Falk nodded. He was thinking of Koski and hoping she was still alive.

They headed north on Highland Avenue. "It'll take a couple of hours to get the warrant," Young explained.

Falk grunted, staring straight ahead.

Captain Garvey pulled the necessary strings. In less than an hour Falk and Young were on their way back to June Street with a warrant. Victor hung a left off Highland and they saw the red lights and heard the sirens of two fire trucks winding down as they turned onto June. Black smoke billowed skyward.

"That's the house!" Falk shouted. Young drove onto the curb. They leapt out and ran toward the equipment as firefighters unraveled hoses up the driveway. Two-way radios crackled as people gathered in the street. Orange flames licked through the roof of the rear house. A black and white screeched to a stop and two cops bailed out, ordering rubbernecking neighbors back.

Falk and Young flashed their IDs to the fire captain. The broom woman stood on the curb near her house as firefighters poured streams of water on the roof to lessen the chance of sparks igniting her place.

The captain wasn't impressed. "I've no time to talk. You'll have to wait until we have this under control." He turned away, rasping orders into a handheld radio.

"Whoever torched the place got matches faster than we got the warrant," Falk growled. They moved to one side, shielding their faces as the roof of the rear house collapsed sending up a shower of sparks and a shuddering wave of heat.

"We're back to square one," Young groaned.

Falk shook his head. "Not yet... Come on. I want a few more words with the broom lady over there."

She was waving her arms and yelling to keep pouring water on her roof. Catching sight of the two who'd interviewed her earlier, she scowled. "Can't you see I'm busy?"

"I think you can leave everything to the LAFD, ma'am. There's nothing you can do. We have some more questions. Let's go over there out of the way." Falk indicated a spot under a singed palm tree. "Did you see anything suspicious since we were last here?"

She glared at Falk. "Damn right I did."

"Tell us."

"You weren't gone five minutes when a green car drives up the driveway. At first I thought it was him."

"Same color?" Young asked. "Same model?"

"Yes," she answered. "Exactly the same like a twin."

"Did you get the plate number?"

"No. I thought I saw a ghost."

"How long was it here?"

"Less than five minutes. The car reversed back down the driveway and was gone. A minute later I heard a loud THUMP, saw flames inside the house and called 911."

"Thank you, Mrs.?"

"Terrabella. Molly Terrabella."

"You've been very helpful." Falk jerked his head in the direction of the car and Young followed.

Chapter 24

Tom Stewart made it official. Marco was now a paid informant for the DHS.

"You will only contact Agent Falk or me with any information you gather. Is that clear?" Marco nodded. "Any attempt to double cross or fabricate information will result in you being eliminated."

Marco sat in a molded red plastic chair opposite Stewart who had the remains of a submarine sandwich on the table in front of him. He sipped coffee from a Styrofoam cup. The meeting was in the snack bar of K-Mart Hollywood. Marco waited until the store announcement about a Blue Light Special ended.

"I get the protection plan I asked for and the money in a Swiss bank, right?"

Stewart nodded. "You have three months to earn your pay."

"I need money now, man. I'm gonna need *expense* money. I can't operate on air for three months."

"You lived okay before we met. Remember, every time we meet increases the risk of you being found out."

"People mail money. It doesn't have to be *handed* to me," Marco moaned.

"Never mail money, Marco. The dead letter office is full of mail that will never arrive." Stewart pushed his plate aside. "I'm going to give you a code word to be used only in an emergency. Place a call to the number I gave you and when someone answers simply say *ATLAS*."

Stewart slid a K-Mart shopping bag across the table. "There's a transistor radio in there. It's been paid for and the cash register receipt is inside. The radio has been modified into a GPS unit locked to a special frequency that is monitored 24/7. It plays AM/FM like an ordinary radio. You can switch to a special broadcast frequency by pressing the case between your thumb and forefinger on one side of the speaker. That will activate a signal and transmit your exact location. You'll be picked up in a matter of minutes.

"Remember. Call the number, say ATLAS and press the radio." Stewart shoved his chair back as two yelling five-year-olds rushed past and a harried mother laden with a tray of food searched for a table. Marco glanced at the kids. When he looked up Stewart was gone.

The stressed mother quickly hooked the toe of her shoe around the leg of the vacant chair, pulled it out and plopped down as the raucous brood rounded the snack bar and headed back toward the table.

Marco made a fast retreat. So ended his initiation into the dark and dangerous world of an informant.

"Why has the Department of Homeland Security taken such a sudden interest in a serial killer?" Massy asked. Her voice was muffled by the ski mask as she delivered coffee. She studied Koski as she drank.

Koski ignored the question, finished her coffee and asked for a second cup.

Smart-ass bitch is treating me like a waitress. "It's to your advantage to answer my questions. If you prefer, I can arrange for an interrogation expert to take over. It's up to you."

The cabin was dark, the windows blacked out. Only a thin shaft of daylight cut through the partially open hatch. Koski saw nothing but a small patch of blue sky. It was time to improvise. "I'm an assigned photographer from DHS investigating the Hollywood serial killings."

"Why is the DHS interested?" Massy repeated.

"Because the victims died by unusual circumstances."

"Unusual? What does that mean?"

Koski knew she had to answer questions but intended to say very little. "The method by which they were killed."

"DHS suspects some kind of terrorist affiliation?"

Koski shrugged. "First I've heard about it."

"Why else are they working with the police? That's not normal procedure." Massy took Koski's empty cup.

"DHS is ComCen now for all law enforcement agencies to cooperate with. Do I get a refill?"

"Part of the famous, 'We'll all be one big happy security force,'" Massy sneered as she started up the wooden steps. She paused at the top. "No refills." She climbed out onto the deck and slid the hatch shut.

Koski slumped against the bulkhead in total blackness, her mind racing. She knew Falk was looking for her. How could he find her when she herself had no idea where she was? Easing off the bunk, she cautiously crossed the cabin with her arms outstretched. She'd memorized the layout of the cabin during the short session with the masked woman. She knew where the galley was.

Perhaps she could find a knife or something to break a porthole and yell for help. She had to try.

Slowly she inched in the direction of the small galley until her fingertips touched a cupboard mounted over a tiny sink. Moving closer, she bellied up to the counter, then ran her hands lightly over the surface and along the leading edge until her fingers found a drawer pull. She slowly eased the drawer open, praying it contained something useful.

Koski lightly touched the items in the drawer. She was like a blind woman in a strange house. Suddenly she experienced a surge of hope as she touched a hard rubber object, grasped it firmly and withdrew a flashlight, her thumb resting on the slide switch. Covering the lens with one hand, she slid the switch forward and her fingers glowed red. She quickly doused the light.

She knew by its heft she'd found a six D-cell heavy-duty unit. It made a deadly weapon. Unmoving, she listened for the slightest sound from above. Satisfied, she turned on the light and shone the beam slowly around the galley.

All was neat and in place. On the wall next to a built-in, one-burner propane stove were three knives: a twelve-inch carver, a ten-inch serrated and an ivory-handled eight-inch paring knife. She removed the paring knife, pulled up the leg of her jogging pants and slid the knife down inside her sock. She thrust hard until the tip sank into the inner sole of her shoe allowing the blade to remain snugly in place against her ankle. Koski was tempted to take the carving knife, too, but decided not to push her luck.

Footsteps sounded on the deck. She snapped off the flashlight. The footsteps passed overhead and all was quiet. Not wanting to tempt fate, she eased back to the bunk, hiding the flashlight beneath the blanket, somewhat reassured in knowing she had some tools at her disposal. She would wait for darkness above before making any more moves.

"*She's* no DHS photographer," Jamul muttered, lounging in an easy chair in the penthouse as he viewed a liquid crystal flat screen, showing Koski on a closed circuit, infrared telecast system. "*That* woman's been trained for covert missions."

Massy asked softly, "CIA maybe?"

"Perhaps so, Doctor."

"I can have her unarmed."

"Not yet. We need to find out more about our adversary. What do we know about her partner?"

"I had him followed after he left his hotel with someone from the police. They went to the house on June Street and made contact with the property owner, then to the Hollywood station and back to the house. By then the place was in flames and our man long gone."

"Where are they now?" Jamul growled.

They both watched as Koski slowly crossed the screen and made her way back to the bunk.

Massy glanced at her watch. "I should be getting a report any minute." The soft buzz of her cell caused Jamul's head to turn. Massy flipped the phone open. "Go ahead."

Jamul raised his eyebrows when Massy, listening, nodded affirmatively. "Don't lose them. Bring them here to the Marina."

Chapter 25

"We're being followed, Victor. Two cars: a Jeep Cherokee and a Honda. They're playing swap off."

"Who's on right now?" Detective Victor Young asked as he made a sharp turn off Wilshire Boulevard and headed north on Fairfax Avenue.

"The Jeep," Falk said as his cell phone buzzed. "Falk."

"If you're looking for your partner, man, I know where she is." Falk recognized the voice at once. "Where is she, Atlas? Tell me."

"Slow down. Where are *you* right now?"

"Fairfax Avenue, heading north crossing Third Street."

"You're not even warm."

"Look, don't fuck with me, all right."

The Jeep was still in position three cars back. Falk couldn't see the Honda.

"You're being followed, man."

"Yeah, I know—two cars."

"They have orders to haul your ass in. Be careful. They're pros."

"Hey, communicate or I'll see your name gets spread around as an informer."

Marco obeyed. "She's being held aboard a forty-foot ketch in Marina Del Rey."

"I need a location." Falk glanced at Young, who nodded.

"'A' slip on Palawan Way. Park on Admiralty Way in the 1200 block. Walk south to Palawan. It's less than half a block. Turn left on Palawan. Four slips down on the left you'll see the ketch. It's white with blue trim named

Sea Note. She's aboard." The phone went dead.

Falk pocketed his cell. "DHS informant. How long to get to the Marina?"

"This time of the day we can make it in less than twenty-five minutes."

"First we have to shake them." Falk jabbed his finger in the direction of the parking lot of CBS Television City. "Quick. In there. Call for back up. Park wherever you can. We're going to make a switch."

The CBS lot was vast. The Jeep driver reacted quickly to Young's sudden turn and moved fast not to lose sight of his quarry.

"He's on to us," Falk muttered, watching the Jeep as it turned off Fairfax Avenue. Young had made contact with LAPD and was told there were patrol cars in the area heading for the lot.

"Back-up coming in from three entrances. They have a description of our tails." Victor rolled down the window, jammed a magnetic base flashing red light atop the car and stomped hard on the accelerator.

The driver of the Jeep made contact with the Honda. "He's turned into the parking lot at Television City. Where are you?"

"Heading west on Wilshire just passing the La Brea tar pits."

"Move it. We have to get them."

The Honda sped up. He could be in the parking lot in two minutes.

The first police car came in off Beverly Boulevard at the north end of the lot. The second radioed its position as it entered the crowded parking complex from the Farmers' Market, an open-air tourist attraction on Fairfax Avenue. Young acknowledged their call and gave his position. A third squad car radioed they were proceeding toward CBS through Park La Brea, a tiny section of high-rise and garden apartments south on Third Street.

"You guys see me yet?" Young asked.

"Affirmative. Where's the Honda? We see the Jeep."

Falk grabbed the microphone from the detective as they wheeled in between the rows of parked cars. "No idea on the Honda, but it can't be far away."

"Roger that."

The back window of Falk and Young's car exploded as it took a hit from a shooter in the Jeep. Falk updated the cops.

"We're under fire. They're using a noise suppressor." The words were hardly out of Falk's mouth when Young swerved violently to miss a woman and small child who walked out from between a row of cars. In doing so, he grazed the rear of a parked car, glanced off and had to wrench hard on the wheel to miss the petrified woman as she stood holding her youngster by the hand. Then she pulled herself and the child back between the rows as the Jeep roared past in a cloud of dust and grit.

"Victor, a chase through here will get innocent people hurt. Stay ahead then swing across his path. We'll bail and make a run for it."

Young nodded and stomped on the gas. One of the police cars was now close behind the Jeep with siren wailing, lights flashing. Suddenly, down one of the rows ahead, came a second black and white going flat out. If both kept up their speed they would collide at the next opening.

"Spin it *now* or we'll hit," Falk yelled. Young saw the cruiser at the same time he heard Falk. He had trained to make spins and turns in defensive driving; gas—brake—pedal—yank on the wheel. It had been years ago but it all came back to Young as he automatically carried out the difficult maneuver. He swung the cruiser so the driver's side was away from the oncoming Jeep then both men leapt from the stalled vehicle. With Falk leading, they vanished between the rows of parked cars.

The Jeep was unable to stop in time and rammed into the abandoned police car, pushing it twenty feet. It turned the vehicle into a ball of twisted metal before slamming to a stop against a red Mercedes, which immediately burst into a sheet of flame. The pursuing police car screeched to a halt and both officers ran toward the scene with their automatics ready. There was no need. No one moved from inside the battered and burning Jeep.

Young turned toward the wreck ready to join the two cops.

"No!" Falk gripped his arm and pulled him low to the ground between two cars. "Look." He pointed between the rows toward the Farmers' Market. The Honda was three rows away, heading toward the fire. Sirens in the distance alerted Falk it was only a matter of minutes before the area would be awash with emergency vehicles and onlookers.

The driver of the Honda swiveled his head from side to side trying to assess what had happened. Falk could see he also was talking on a cell phone. People ran toward the smoke and flames. The Honda driver was forced to a standstill.

"Let's take him out." Before Young could answer, Falk twisted his way through the parked cars. The detective followed until they were three cars from the stalled Honda.

"We'll take his car," Falk said. "Reverse out of this mess and get back onto Fairfax."

"What about him?" Young peered around the fender of a Chevy at the driver still talking into his phone.

"He stays...come on." They approached on either side of the Honda as people ran toward the wreck. Young was on the driver's side and almost at the door when the driver saw him. Young aimed his service automatic and squeezed the trigger. Click! A misfire!

The driver didn't panic. The other two police cars had joined in with the fire and ambulance and it was an impassable mass of officialdom. As Young tried to clear his weapon, the driver calmly removed a nine millimeter Sig Suer from a shoulder holster, tapped the automatic window button and leaned out. Falk, on the passenger side, took aim and fired a shot through the closed window.

The driver's head spun sideways. His dark, stringy hair splayed out in concert with his blood and brains as his skull exploded from the impact of a well-aimed nine millimeter Parabellum. Falk scooped up the ejected casing.

"Victor, let's move." Together they darted between the cars, moving away from the fire and confusion. "We'll steal a car, one closer to an exit, and then head for the Marina."

Young nodded, gasped his thanks and pointed across the lot. "We'll head for Beverly Boulevard. Follow me."

No one bothered them and within a few minutes they were beside a Subaru Outback. The doors were unlocked.

"This'll do fine," Falk said. "Hot wire it and let's go."

Victor Young wasted no time. Soon he had the ignition wires joined and the engine running. He drove sedately, not wanting to attract attention. Falk drummed impatiently on the dash as they exited onto Beverly Boulevard and headed west. He eyed the gas gauge noting it was down to a quarter of a tank.

"How far do we have to go?"

"About twenty miles."

Falk checked the side mirror. "Okay. When we get to the Marina drop me off on Admiralty Way. I'll walk down to Palawan Way. Stay far enough back to make sure I'm not being followed. I'll locate the boat and check it out."

Young turned the Subaru south on La Cienega. "We could involve the cops at the Marina. They'll know the area better than we do."

"Not unless I run into trouble. Right now all I want is to get aboard that boat and find Koski." Falk leaned back and wondered if Marco's information was for real or a trap.

Imminent Danger

Chapter 26

Koski was starving. She hadn't eaten for hours and decided to rummage around in the galley. She slid off the bunk and crept amidships, carefully shading the beam of the flashlight. Once in the galley area, she aimed the shaft of light at a hanging cupboard to the right of the sink and tugged the door open to find a few canned goods, an open box of soda crackers, a jar of strawberry jam with the top missing, and several slices of individually wrapped American cheese held down by a jar of horseradish.

She wolfed down three crackers, tore open a slice of cheese, wrapped it around a cracker, stuck her finger in the jam and wiped it on the cheese. It tasted like heaven. As she munched the last cracker, she heard footsteps crossing the deck. Clicking off the flashlight she returned to the bunk, licked her fingers, wiped her hands down the sides of her pants and waited.

Then the sound of voices caused her to investigate. Koski moved cautiously to the bottom of the steps beneath the hatch. She eased upward one step at a time. The conversation was barely audible but she was able to recognize the voice of the woman who had served the coffee.

"I received a call from the towers to be ready to move out of the Marina."

"Where to?" a male voice asked.

"Don't know. Orders are to be ready."

"What about her?"

"We go, she goes."

Koski knew if they sailed out of the Marina her chance of an escape was slim. She reached up and tried to move the hatch. It was closed tight.

It was early afternoon when Falk climbed from the stolen Outback and walked along Admiralty Way. LAPD Detective Victor Young drove off as arranged but kept Falk in sight and remained in the background.

A store, The Skipper's Locker, caught Falk's eye. A modern day ship's chandler. He quickly decided that a nautical appearance while scouting the Marina would be good cover. He crossed the street and entered. Electronic depth meters and navigational aids were stacked beside radio transmitters and hand-held GPS units. There was rope and line of all styles. Chrome and brass fittings, rustproof screws, nautical hardware for anything that sailed. He wondered what an old time sailor would have made of the place.

He headed toward a section devoted to the well-dressed sailor. Noticing the prices on various merchandise, he was reminded of the answer a friend of his had given when asked what it was like to own and operate a sailboat.

"That's easy, Joe. Just imagine standing in an ice cold shower in your most expensive suit and tearing up one hundred dollar bills."

Falk purchased a canvas carry all, the type with pull strings and easy to sling over your shoulder. He also picked up a pale blue zip front windbreaker, a pair of deck shoes, also light blue, and a navy blue cap with a golden anchor emblazoned above its shiny peak.

In a small dressing room, he packed his shoes, tie and jacket in the canvas bag, shrugged into the windbreaker and laced his new shoes. He checked in the mirror to make sure his shoulder holster didn't bulge, and placed his cap at a jaunty angle, making a mental note to dirty it up a little when he got outside. He didn't want to look like a complete rube.

He paid cash and was about to leave when he noticed an eight-foot aluminum boat hook with a paddle on one end and a hook on the other. The clerk happily rang up the sale. Falk slung the canvas bag over his shoulder along with the boat hook and almost whistled a sea chanty as he headed out the front door.

Once on Palawan Way, he curbed a natural urge to rush. Drawing attention was the last thing he needed. The layout of the various slips was his target. He passed one of the self-locking gates in the heavy duty chain link fence separating the public from the slips. He knew he had a problem.

He stopped in the pretense of tying a shoelace and quickly checked the lock. He relaxed. It was a standard type widely used in low security areas. On the dockside of the fence, a steel cover protected the twist lock, supposedly to stop anyone from reaching through and turning the security device. He'd opened similar locks with ease when he was a kid. To be sure, he pushed his hand through the fence and made a test run. His forearm had grown in the last thirty years and there was no way he could reach around the security shield. He even had a hard time removing his arm.

Damn it! He had to get down to the dock.

As he neared the gate of slip four, he saw the white and blue ketch. A burly man on deck seemed out of place. Falk felt certain he was security. In case he was questioned, Falk had prepared a cover story saying he'd promised to do a favor for a pal by cleaning the brass fittings on the vessel next to the *Sea Note*. It was a small sailboat with a blue tarpaulin tied down fast and pulled over the boom protecting the deck from the weather.

He toyed with the idea of calling down to the *Sea Note* to say he forgot to get the gate key from his pal. Yeah, right. Burly would tell him to go to hell. He was almost at the gate when a car pulled up and a young woman got out. She opened the trunk and lugged out an ice chest.

She called to the driver. "Don't forget to bring the cell phone after you park, honey." She slammed the trunk lid shut and the car drove off. The woman went to the gate, set down the ice chest and unlocked the gate.

Seeing his chance, Falk moved forward as she pushed the gate open. "Hey, let me help." Without waiting for an answer, he scooped up the ice chest and indicated with a nod that she go ahead. She smiled with Falk close behind her. For a moment he thought she was going to the *Sea Note* but she turned right at the bottom of the ramp and stopped beside the sailboat with the blue tarp. "Thanks. That was very kind of you."

There were only two boats in the dock. He had to come up with something fast. Burly now standing in the stern of the *Sea Note* watched their arrival with unguarded suspicion.

"Are you with the *Sea Note*?" the young woman asked as she began undoing the ties holding the tarp.

Falk looked around as if for the first time seeing the two boats. "No. I'm... I'm—this *is* slip four?"

"It is."

Falk continued his act. "Panay Way, right?"

"Oh, no. You're on Palawan Way. This is basin E. You need basin D."

Falk shook his head. "I feel like such a fool. I was supposed to meet my friend who has a boat in slip four. I'm not familiar with this Marina. Only been here twice and both times he drove. I better get going." Falk turned away and headed for the ramp when she called to him.

"Wait. My husband will be here soon. He has a cell phone. You can call your friend and tell him where you are. That's if he has a cell phone on board."

"That's a good idea. Let me help you get the tarp off." As he worked, he noticed the man on *Sea Note* had lost interest in their activity.

Falk had almost finished folding the tarp when the young woman pointed to a man coming down the ramp holding a canvas carryall. "Here's my husband now." She waved. "I bet he wonders who you are." Falk had no doubt he did.

"Hi, hon. Didn't forget to bring the phone, did you?"

The man shook his head and patted his back pocket. "It's right here." It was obvious he wanted to know who was standing on his boat with his wife.

"I said he could use our phone. He's lost." She turned to Falk. "Sorry. I don't know your name."

"Bill Moore," Falk answered quickly.

"Mr. Moore helped carry the cooler down to the boat then discovered he was at the wrong slip and the wrong dock."

Setting the carryall down, the man stuck his hand out. "Bob Curry. This is my wife, Jean."

Falk shook hands with them. "I know I must look a damned fool." Movement on the *Sea Note* caught his eye. A woman moved into sight next to the guard. They stood amidships near a hatch cover talking earnestly. The woman waved her arms as he spoke and pointed toward the twin high-rise towers across the basin.

Curry said, "Could happen to any of us. I have the same problem sometimes when I'm in a new Marina. I bet it happens often in one this size." He reached into his pocket and pulled out his phone. "Go ahead. Give him a call."

Falk tapped in numbers and two rings later Victor Young answered. "Jack, this is Bill. I've ended up on the wrong slip. I'm on Palawan Way. Yeah, I know, but I did get the boat hook you wanted. No. That's okay. I'll walk. How far did you say? Then I'll wait right here, slip four. You sure you don't mind? I'm with a couple that let me use their phone. I'm next to a blue and white ketch with two people on board." Falk turned away and spoke softly. "The woman on the ketch is just leaving and another man is going aboard."

Falk turned off the cell and handed it back. "He'll come and get me in the dingy; said it was a long walk." Falk knew Young picked up on the mention of the two on the ketch and would move in to give him cover. He could only stall for so long. Now she stuck her head out of the hatch and announced she was making coffee and would he join them?

Curry was forward of the mast securing a line as Falk said he'd enjoy a cup. Pretending to be on the lookout for the imaginary dingy, he kept an eye on the *Sea Note,* carefully checking the physical layout of both slips.

The ramp ran from the dockside gate to a jetty structure jutting out into the channel. Each slip notched into the jetty and a large storage box allocated to each vessel. There was room for the boats to maneuver and navigate into the main channel then head out to sea. From where he stood, he was less than twenty feet from the ketch.

It was a jump from the deck to the jetty, a short sprint and he could scramble aboard in seconds. Falk looked up to the road at the sound of an engine and saw the Outback. Its motor revved and slowed, making erratic progress along Palawan before coming to a shuddering halt opposite the two boats.

Young got out, opened the hood and leaned into the engine compartment. A minute later, he went to the rear, lifted the hatch back, rummaged under the tire well and returned with a handful of tools. Falk had his backup in position. Now it was up to him.

Koski had strained to hear snatches of conversation on deck. She climbed the stairs again. This time she pressed her ear against the hatch and was able to hear a few words. The woman was speaking.

"Keep an eye on the sailboat next to us. Take 'em out if they make any moves toward this boat."

Koski's heart fluttered. There was someone on a boat next to them! She knew that an inboard motor powered a boat as large as the one she was on. Grabbing the flashlight, she quickly moved back to the galley. The place to look for an inboard was below deck amidships.

The beam from her flashlight caught a quick glint high up on the bulkhead in the corner over the sink. The bastards had her under video surveillance! She killed the light and scrambled up onto the sink, reached into the cupboard and grabbed the jar of jam. She stuck two fingers of her right hand into the jar, scooped up a glob, and with her left hand felt along the edge of the bulkhead where it met the deck. There it was—a recess. Her fingertip felt the lens. After smearing a thick coating of jam across the glass, she eased back onto the floor. She turned on the flashlight and continued her search for a floor hatch to an engine compartment and bilge area. Within two minutes she found the hatch.

She grasped a metal ring, yanked hard and shone the light into the bilge area. The sudden stench of oil and dead air was a slap in the face. The beam of light fell on a sign in red paint with two arrows pointing in opposite directions. OPEN/CLOSE was stenciled above a black painted iron handle. Immediately she knew she must turn the handle to OPEN and the seacock would allow a flow of seawater into the bilge.

Aiming the light around the engine compartment, she located the inboard diesel. She was undecided whether to sink the boat. It would pose a threat to her life if someone didn't arrive before it sank. On the other hand, she could fill a can with diesel oil and rags, ignite it and cause black smoke to billow from below deck. That would gain attention. She decided to put the second plan into action. After all, there *were* people on the next boat.

Chapter 27

The antibodies transmitted by the biolog laser injector killed the CEO of Majestic Films instantly. He died on the back lot, crumpled in the dust of a western street set.

Grant arrived at the crime scene as the victim was being examined by the ME inside a cordoned off area. Captain Garvey was talking with several detectives outside one of the false fronted buildings.

"What happened, Captain? Who's the victim?"

Garvey grimaced slightly, remembering the words of the Chief about cooperation between the police department and the DHS.

Garvey sighed. "Head of the studio. He was inspecting the back lot with his security chief when he simply buckled and fell down dead. That was it."

"Sounds like a heart attack or stroke," Grant retorted.

"Yeah but at the moment he died his secretary was on the phone being told her boss would be killed on the back lot." Garvey paused. "He was dead before she could contact him."

The medical officer straightened and walked toward them.

"The *killer called* to tell her what was going to happen!" Grant exclaimed.

"Evidently whoever it was wanted her to know it was murder, not a heart attack."

"Why would anyone do that?"

Garvey rubbed his chin as the doctor joined them. "Let's hear what the doc has to say."

The ME quickly reported his findings. "Can't find a mark on him. Might have been a sudden heart attack. That's all I can tell you at the moment."

"What about the phone call?" Garvey asked. "Whoever called knew he was going to die. That doesn't sound like a natural death."

"Can't help you there. That's your department, Captain."

"How long before we know how he died?"

"Seeing the DHS is involved, I'd say an autopsy will possibly be performed later today."

Grant pushed forward. "I'm from DHS, Doctor, and I want to be present at the autopsy. Any problem?"

The doctor glanced at Garvey. "None at all. See you there." He nodded to the Captain and headed back to his car.

Grant and Garvey watched as the coroner's men bagged and loaded the body into an ambulance, slammed the doors shut and drove down the western street and out of sight.

Grant gazed at the wooden sidewalks and false fronted buildings. "For a minute there I expected to see them load the corpse onto a horse-drawn buckboard."

"I know what you mean," Garvey said. "I'll go with you to the morgue. By the way, what happened to your videographers?"

"They're on temporary reassignment," Grant mumbled.

"She's found the camera." A scrawny individual in shorts and tee-shirt sat hunched in front of a television screen. A second man reading a magazine glanced up.

"How could she?"

"Dunno. Look for yourself." He pointed to a blurred screen. He picked up a phone and called Jamul, who immediately gave orders to get Koski off the boat.

The men on the ketch already had their hands full. A column of black smoke curled from around the hatch cover.

Burly saw the smoke first. "That stupid bitch set the boat on fire!"

Falk turned at the commotion and saw smoke and two men tugging at the hatch. He grabbed the boat hook and leapt from the small sailboat to the jetty. Within seconds he was on the deck of the ketch. "Let's try this." Falk jammed the boat hook under the edge of the hatch but one of the men shoved him back and Burly started to pull out an automatic.

Falk quickly whirled, bringing the eight-foot pole hard against the side of Burly's head, knocking him senseless to the deck. The second man, shocked at the sudden deadly action, hesitated a split second too long. Falk rammed the oar end into the guard's stomach. The impact drove him backwards across the deck where he teetered for a second at the rail before vanishing overboard.

Wasting no time, Falk pounded on the hatch with his pole yelling Koski's name. He jammed the pole under the edge of the hatch and started to pry. The smoke continued to curl from below deck as he worked. Suddenly someone was beside him with an axe.

Bob Curry swung the axe into the center of the hatch, twisted the blade and repeated the action several times until he had a gaping hole. Falk dropped to his knees and yelled into the dark, smoky gap. He saw the can of burning rags and knew at once what Koski had done to attract attention. Falk called her name again and was suddenly relieved to see her dirty, smoke-grimed face peering upward toward him.

She quickly unhooked the storm locks and Falk pulled the damaged hatch onto the deck. She reached up, took Falk's hand and was yanked up into the fresh air.

Flinging her arms around Falk's neck, she kissed him long and hard before saying, "I knew you'd come."

He scooped her into his arms and carried her to the side of the boat. Curry jumped to the dock and held his arms up to take her. Once ashore, Jean appeared with Falk's ditty bag slung on her shoulder and handed a bottle of water to Koski. She took a fast swig then urged Falk to get everyone off the dock and up onto the road—FAST.

Victor Young's voice boomed from the road telling them to hurry.

Burly, still flat on the deck, crawled under cover of the thick black smoke pouring from the hatch to where his automatic lay. Young had the engine running as the four ran up the ramp to the road. Burly grabbed his weapon, got to his feet, squinted across the dock and opened fire. Rounds zipped into the ramp as Falk pushed everyone through the gate and into the car while a great sheet of yellow flame ripped skyward from the *Sea Note*.

"What in the hell happened?" Curry exclaimed.

Koski replied, "It's okay. The boat'll sink before the fire can spread." Turning to Falk she said, "When I heard you call out 'Down the hatch', I lit a match and touched it to a trail of paint thinner I'd laid from the galley to the bilge. I found the thinner when I was looking for the sea cocks."

"Sea cocks!" Falk echoed.

"Yeah. I also scuttled the boat."

"The U.S. government will cover any damage to your sailboat," Falk assured the Currys as Young drove them back to their car.

Chapter 28

Rita Massy slumped in an easy chair, gazing through the picture window of the penthouse. The spiral of smoke from the ketch slowly diminished, swirled by an onshore breeze. The wind did little to diminish Jamul's anger that he hurled at the unfortunate man reporting what they had discovered when they arrived at the slip.

"None of you went down to the boat? No one went aboard to see if anyone was there!" His voice grew louder and his black face, if it was possible, seemed blacker.

"The Coast Guard showed up. Then a fireboat and cops were arriving." The nervous man tried to explain. "We got the hell out."

"I told you to bring back the woman, not to get the hell out." Jamul turned away in disgust. In his heart he knew they had done the right thing. No way did he want to become involved in anything that might lead him to become part of any type of investigation.

Massy's voice was calm. "I'd say someone beat us to it, Jamul. Whoever it was no doubt rescued the woman and fled."

"Yes, Doctor, and I'll be ridiculed as a fool for not foiling the rescue."

Massy smiled. "Perhaps not. We can make the incident work to our advantage."

Jamul sat down. "Go on."

"We let it be known the escape was intended to happen. You planned the kidnapping as a means to test the ability and strength of DHS and its operatives."

"No one in the organization is going to believe that!" Jamul spluttered.

Massy lightly clenched her fist, extending her index finger skyward. "Let me finish. We now know the woman is *not* a DHS photographer. Neither is the man who rescued her. We have stronger and wiser adversaries to contend with than we thought—a more *unorthodox* agency, an enemy who uses tactics not unlike our own.

"Brasinov will identify them, whoever they are, and alert al-Qaida of their existence. You'll be a hero and stronger than ever. Trust me, Jamul. Everything will be ready by Sunday and then all of Islam will celebrate our latest strike against America."

"*Everything* better be ready, my friend," Jamul said as he rose and stalked from the room.

Chapter 29

The unexpected and forced detention in a house located on Rockledge Road, high in the Hollywood Hills behind the Hollywood Bowl, took Marco by surprise.

"You've been chosen for an important task, Marco. You were recommended as a man with smarts, who wishes to get ahead in life. Is that correct?"

Rita Massy asked the question sitting opposite Marco, a long oak table between them. The high beamed ceiling and oak paneled walls reflected the Spanish décor so popular in fine homes in Hollywood during the 1920s and 1930s. The afternoon light seeping through the lead lined windows was fading fast.

"Who wants to know?" Marco muttered.

"Who I am matters not, young man."

"Why was I brought here?"

"Instructions," Massy purred. "You and selected members of your gang are to become landscape workers. You will remain here each day after work until our task is complete."

A door at the far end of the room opened. A man entered and switched on an ornate floor lamp casting a yellow glow through its tasseled silken shade.

"You're aware that when any member of your gang is assigned to carry out an order we expect complete compliance. Disobey and the punishment is swift."

"Yeah. You kill them," Marco said softly.

"In your case I've been assured you are a man with ambition and leadership qualities, right?"

Marco nodded.

"For the next few days you'll be working with a landscaping crew in the Hollywood Bowl, preparing the grounds for the Easter Sunday Services. Each worker will be cleared by security and issued a pass.

"At the end of each day, a truck will return all workers to the landscape company headquarters. Your crew will be transferred here to stay overnight and return to the company each morning for the trip to the Bowl."

"What do we tell our families?"

"Say it's a job out of town, nothing else. Each of you may bring a change of clothes and a few personal belongings. Advise your compatriots this house is heavily guarded. They'll be shot if they attempt to escape."

Massy pushed back from the table. "There's a car waiting to return you to the Barrio." She gave an icy smile and walked from the room, high heels rapping the hardwood floor.

Marco watched her leave. His hands were clenched on the tabletop. He'd be sure he had a small AM/FM radio among his personal items. "Bitch."

Chapter 30

On the drive from the Marina to the hotel, Koski removed the paring knife from her shoe then curled up on the back seat and fell asleep.

"Hell of a gal," Young said, nodding at the knife. "What was she going to do with that?"

"Don't ask," Falk replied. "We should get our stories in synch about what just happened back there."

They decided that Young's report explaining their exit from the parking lot fiasco on Fairfax should include Falk receiving a tip saying Koski was a prisoner aboard a boat in the Marina. The resultant blaze and sinking of the boat shouldn't be part of the report. Falk took responsibility for any repercussions by saying it had been in the interest of national security.

Koski had showered, eaten a steak dinner delivered by room service and was now on the same page as Falk.

"The only person I talked to on the boat was a woman in a ski mask. She brought me a cup of coffee and asked questions."

"Anything about her voice?" Falk questioned.

"Educated, knew I was with DHS. Later I tried to listen in on a conversation up on deck discussing something about a penthouse. I got the impression they were waiting for someone to come to the boat to interrogate me. I also was under surveillance on a hidden, infrared closed circuit TV."

"What did you do?"

"Smeared jam over the lens."

Falk grinned. "Interesting."

"I wondered if they'd got you, too, Joe."

"They tried." He quickly brought her up-to-date on the events leading up to the Marina rescue. Falk got up from the table. "Whoever these people are, they've got state-of-the-art equipment. Time to relocate. I'll update Stewart."

Koski knew in cases like this it was standard operating procedure for Cerberus to send a couple of doppelgangers. They were operatives with similar physical appearance, who'd stay at the hotel, allowing them the opportunity to move on.

Falk finished his conversation with Stewart.

"Where're we going?" Koski asked.

"The Marina. Stewart says there's a Taswell 43' all weather Raised–Saloon cutter tied up next to the Coast Guard station. It belonged to a drug cartel, was seized and is now government property with modern *everything*. The Coast Guard is waiting to pipe us aboard. It'll be our temporary base of operations."

Koski blew out her cheeks. "Oh, boy!"

For security reasons, they made the journey to the Marina in the back of a laundry truck Stewart had sent to the service entrance of their hotel.

It was dark when they walked up the gangplank and were met by a Coast Guard lieutenant, who snapped a salute.

"Welcome aboard. I understand this will be your office for awhile."

"Correct, lieutenant," Falk replied.

The officer gave them a familiarizing tour of the cutter's layout. "We have a skeleton crew to take care of maintenance and security. They've been informed of your arrival and will stay out of your way."

Returning to their starting point, he pointed to the lighted windows of the Coast Guard station less than a quarter mile away. "You're hooked into our communications center. Here's a card with phone numbers and radio frequencies in case they're needed."

"Thanks. We're going to need a car. Can you handle that?"

"Already taken care of, sir. Mr. Stewart said to tell you there'll be a black Ford Mustang dockside in an hour."

"Thank you, lieutenant."

"Goodnight, sir, ma'am."

As a brisk wind blew up the channel, Koski huddled her arms across her chest. "Let's get warm." Falk slipped his arm around her waist and led her across the deck and into the salon.

"Nautical and nice," she remarked, taking in the décor and comfortable surroundings. "A lot better than the last boat I was on."

Falk said, "I'm going to take another tour around the boat to be sure I know the pointed end from the blunt end, okay?"

"Fine, and remember, I can show you how to sink her if you like."

Imminent Danger

Chapter 31

Shortly before 11 p.m. a cab dropped Martin Pease off at the home of Paul Horn in Pacific Palisades, a well-heeled community overlooking the ocean. Horn lived alone in a rambling house far too big for him. His wife had left him three years earlier for a younger and richer man. Horn had married late in life and his young wife had promised she'd love him forever then changed her mind.

Horn answered the door, holding a snifter of brandy. He was amazed at the sight of Pease on his door step.

"Relax, Paul. Let me in. I need a drink."

"Martin! I thought you'd..."

Pease pushed past and entered. "Well, you were wrong." He held up his right hand as if stopping traffic. "I wasn't followed. No one knows I'm here."

Somewhere in the house a clock chimed midnight as Pease finished telling Horn everything that happened since he left Pegmanti Industries.

Horn whispered softly, "If your formula does what you claim, al-Qaida isn't simply gaining another tool in its 'Arsenal of Evil' but a weapon it will embrace implicitly."

"Money and power, as usual, *are* the all-embracing commodities in this case, Paul."

"Enrico believes you could reproduce the germinating acceptance genes now if you wanted."

"He's right. He has no idea, however, what else has developed from my research. Only two others know the full capabilities."

Horn sipped his brandy. "Why are you telling me?"

"I need someone inside Pegmanti Industries I can trust."

Horn's eyebrows arched. "And you trust me? How touching."

"I don't trust you. I never did but I know your weakness for money."

"What kind of money are we talking about?"

"Put it this way. I'm giving you the opportunity to remain alive. If I were to inform a certain person that you knew about this weapon you'd be dead within the hour.

"We'll discuss money after I find out how much you're worth to me on the inside. Now listen carefully. This is what you tell Enrico."

Rita Massy sat alone in her car parked on Mulholland Drive, staring down at the lights of the San Fernando Valley twinkling like scattered diamonds. She needed quiet and time to reflect on the last few hours.

She was back in favor with Jamul due to her successfully arranged murder of the studio head on his own back lot. The autopsy showed no indication of foul play. Marco and his crew were safely under the control of al-Qaida by day and secure in the safe house at night.

It was almost midnight. She started the engine and turned up the heater. March could be a cold month in California. The radio murmured the late news as she eased the car onto Mulholland and toward her destination—the house on Rockledge Road.

The meeting would be pivotal to al-Qaida continuing as a leading presence in the terrorist world. The deaths of Saddam Hussein and Osama bin Laden, and the continuing relentless pursuit of their followers by U.S. and U.K. forces, caused al-Qaida to lose influence and control in many Islamic communities, along with others in the world who used the evil powers of terrorism for their own agenda.

Massy knew the day was fast approaching when the world would know that al-Qaida could still make the Western world reel. The Easter Sunrise Services at the Hollywood Bowl was a multi-religious ceremony designed to unite the world by showing respect to every religious sect.

The gathering of clerics from around the globe would represent every religion. The Governor of California and representatives of a dozen other world governments would stand as one in the white domed amphitheater. The soft dawn light of an Easter Sunday would slowly cast its pink glow across the thousands of souls packing the Bowl as countless millions around the globe watched on television. There was even the possibility the new Pope would be present—his first visit to California.

Security would be tighter than any other time in the Bowl's history. Massy slowed the car. She took the sharp downhill turn toward the Tudor stone house on Rockledge and moved toward a single light shining from a window overlooking the curved gravel driveway. The car crunched to a halt and a dark-suited valet opened the driver's door.

"Good evening, madam." Massy stepped from the car noting two armed men standing in the shadows. She nodded and walked up three wide stone steps to the double door entrance that swung open as she approached.

Once inside, she handed her coat to an attendant and was led across a parquet tiled reception hall. The servant opened a tall, ornate door and with an upturned palm indicated Massy should enter.

A huge stone fireplace at one end of the long oak-paneled room held a log fire burning brightly. Two high-backed armchairs framed the hearth and mantle. As Massy walked toward the fireplace, a voice from one of the chairs greeted her.

"Good evening, Rita."

Massy stopped beside the chair and softly replied, "Good evening, Mr. Pegmanti."

"Please, sit down." Enrico Pegmanti motioned to the chair beside him. "We're the early ones. We get the best seats in the house."

Massy settled into her seat, feeling the warmth from the fire glow around her. She had been to the safehouse several times before but never to one of their meetings. She wondered how many times Pegmanti had chaired secret enclaves in the fine Tudor mansion high in Hollywood Hills.

Massy had known for years that Pegmanti Industries made millions supplying various terrorist groups with chemical warfare poisons. As far as Enrico was concerned, money was money no matter where it came from.

"How are your Mexican American friends, Rita? I hear you have a bright young man by the name of Marco working for you. Didn't one of his friends have to be eliminated not too long ago?"

It never failed to amaze Massy how much knowledge Enrico amassed. It was seemingly endless.

"Yes. Marco and the others are kept here every night and assigned each day to the Bowl gardening staff making preparations for the Easter Services."

Enrico shifted in his chair and stretched his thin white hands toward the flames. To Massy, they seemed like vulture talons reaching for dead flesh.

Enrico stared into the flames. "What assurances do you have that he won't attempt some sort of retaliation for his friend's death? I understand Mexican culture leans toward revenge for such deeds."

"He's well aware that if he makes the slightest wrong move he and everyone else will die."

"Perhaps he's been smart enough to take advantage of that possibility."

Massy bristled. "What do you mean?"

"It's possible he already made arrangements with the police to be a paid informant. It happens."

"Do you know something I don't?" Massy was startled at the suggestion.

Enrico lowered his hands and rested them on his knees, continuing to gaze into the flickering fire. "I think you should be very careful. Test his loyalty. If you have any doubt, kill him."

If it had been anyone but Enrico Pegmanti talking Massy would have dismissed the idea of Marco being a possible informer. "How can we be sure?"

"Take this Young Turk aside and give him misinformation he might feel important enough to reveal. You'll know soon enough if the information leaks to the police. I'll leave it to your active imagination as to what you tell him."

A murmur of voices and the sound of others entering the room stopped any further conversation. A group of men approached the pair at the fireside. Several servants quickly arranged chairs close to the warmth.

Jamul, imposing in a scarlet hooded robe that emphasized his tallness, took a dictatorial stance facing the assembly. Feet apart, the glow from the fire radiated like a holy aura around him.

Brasinov was grim-faced and still stinging from the abortive attempt to kill Falk in the CBS parking lot and the loss of two of his men. He clenched his fists as he listened to Jamul.

"Welcome to you all. Tonight we formulate the final details of a long-anticipated dream for the nation of Islam; an occasion that will be forever burnt into the history of the Western world as an apocalyptic event."

Imminent Danger

Chapter 32

Millions of dollars sat waiting in Martin Pease's Swiss bank account. Nevertheless, secretly finding a way to leave the country was difficult due to tough airport security and customs. Both were formidable barriers even to those with nothing to hide. Pease had little doubt his passport information was already a "no go" in the international computer systems.

An analytical person, he reasoned the only one he might trust was an old acquaintance, Doctor Jack Wolf.

Pease waited until Wolf finished a lecture at UCLA and was walking back to his office, then fell into step beside him. Pease spoke softly. "Good afternoon, Jack."

Wolf spun around. "Martin!" He was genuinely surprised to see his old friend. "What the devil are you doing here? It's been years since we've seen each other."

Pease indicated a bench at the side of the path. "Sit with me a moment, Jack." He touched the edge of Wolf's sleeve.

"Let's chat in my office," Wolf glanced at the sky. "It's getting chilly."

"No. Here is better for us both. Please sit down, Jack."

"What is it, Martin? Are you ill?"

"Nothing like that." Wolf seated himself next to Pease.

"My life has been threatened."

"Good lord! Threatened by whom and for what?"

Pease glanced around before answering. "My formula. I suppose you know I'm no longer with Pegmanti."

"I heard you retired."

"I suppose I did in a way. I was given the golden handshake."

"Why?"

"Enrico Pegmanti believed I was stalling on my research, holding back until he died so as to claim all the fame and resultant monetary rewards."

"Were you?"

"The thought *had* crossed my mind. I decided against it when I discovered my research was going in a different direction than my original stem cell experiments."

Wolf forgot the coldness of a late March afternoon. "Different direction?"

"It was quite by accident. It was during a test on cell division and transplant. I took cells from a ferocious Rottweiler and transplanted them into an old, rather arthritic Golden Retriever that was expected to die at any time. Next morning, the Retriever was energetic and snarling at its keeper to a point where she could not approach the animal."

"Obviously a reaction to the transplant," Wolf replied.

"That's what I thought at first. Nevertheless I continued with transplants from aggressive animals into placid subjects. It became obvious it was possible to pass aggression and placidity back and forth, similar to brainwave synchronization experiments."

"You were able to calm an aggressive animal by transplanting cells from a peaceful one?"

"Exactly, but that's not all. Over months of in vitro experiments I developed a serum from the cells. Through a simple injection I obtained the same results as a complete Yigal transplant."

Wolf felt as if an electric shock had gone through him.

"Martin, you sound light years ahead of us here at the university."

"Working for Pegmanti Industries I was sworn to keep my discoveries secret."

"Surely you're free to share your research now?"

"Let me finish." It grew colder and a chilling wind began to cut across the campus. "I went further. It's not widely known but the company also has been experimenting with laser ray systems. I became friendly with a bright

114

young scientist several years ago when the laser lab was first established. I was frustrated having to sedate an aggressive animal prior to the injection.

"I didn't want an opiate or anesthesia to dilute the effectiveness of my serum. I needed a method to safely inject a savage animal. That's when I learned of the young scientist's discovery. He'd developed a delivery system far improved over a regular injection syringe. His system is why my life is in jeopardy."

Pease moved a little closer to Wolf and lowered his voice. "Thanks to the laser system, my altered cells have the ability to kill and leave no sign of an entrance wound or cause of death."

Wolf heard the thud of his own heart. "How's that possible?"

"The cell serum is delivered to the target by a means never before used. Laser technology combined with what I call a biolog laser injector or BLI. I discovered I can transmit any other biological monoclonal antibody drug over a quarter of a mile."

Wolf was stunned. "How?"

"Jack, trust me. It can be done."

"You're playing God, Martin! If your discovery falls into the wrong hands, bioterrorism could be the end of the world as we know it. What about this laser scientist you were working with?" Wolf's mind was racing. He had to get Martin Pease to Stewart.

"He left Pegmanti three months ago, recruited by Laser Research Labs. Rita Massy has a prototype of my delivery system and has used it to demonstrate its lethal ability to an Islamic group. My latest model is even more effective."

Wolf exploded. "Have you contacted the authorities?"

"No."

Wolf couldn't believe what he was hearing, "Why not, man?"

"Enrico Pegmanti and his daughter would be murdered."

"And Doctor Massy has your BLI model!"

Pease glanced around, startled by Wolf's outburst. "The prototype model. I have the latest BLI safely hidden. I'm the only one who knows its location."

Wolf had to get Pease to Stewart. "Doctor Rita Massy involved with terrorists! Martin, you can't just leave it hidden. Someone is sure to find out. Look man, I'll get you governmental protection. You can collect the BLI and keep it out of the hands of terrorists."

Removing an automatic from his pocket, Martin pressed the barrel into Wolf's side. "No. I need a safe place to hide *now*. Sorry, Jack. Let's go."

Chapter 33

The Department of Homeland Security was rife with problems. None of the merging bureaucracies, including the CIA and FBI, owned computer systems that could speak to each other. There was no mandate or funding in the nearly 500-page Homeland Security Act to change that. The DHS was originally designed to unify law enforcement agencies nationwide under the direction and guidance of a federal security tsar.

Nevertheless, infighting between various agencies, differences between trade unions, and leadership questions continued. Once acclaimed as a major tool in America's fight against terrorism, it was turning out to be a bureaucratic nightmare.

Shortly after 1 a.m. Chief Bradbury was slumped in the back seat of his chauffeur driven car on the way to Parker Center. Falk and Koski were off the DHS team. Grant had a broken leg. Three more deaths in the Hollywood area and the city politicians were putting the squeeze on the Chief.

Bradbury had called an emergency meeting of his top people at 3 a.m. at his Parker office. He had contacted Garvey, asking him to be there a half hour ahead of schedule. He wanted a one on one.

Garvey sipped hot coffee from a thick thermos mug when he arrived at police headquarters. It was 2:35 a.m. when he entered the main entrance, flashed his ID and headed to the elevators.

Bradbury's secretary, seated at her desk in the anteroom outside the Chief's office, looked up. "Go in, Captain. He's expecting you."

Seeing the secretary signaled to Garvey this was going to be an all-stops-out operation.

"Morning, Howard. Come in and sit down. I see you have your coffee already."

Garvey raised his mug slightly. "Never leave home without it."

Niceties over, Bradbury got down to business. "When the media get the news of the latest deaths—and the now non-existent DHS team—they're going to raise hell." Bradbury leaned back in his chair, the incandescent glow of the desk lamp accentuating the dark circles under his eyes. "What do we have on the latest vics?"

"Medical examiner's report shows no outward signs of cause of death. I'm awaiting updates from the morgue."

The Chief grunted. "The early killings showed a pinprick entrance wound, now, nothing. I'm getting feedback saying the perp is possibly testing a new killing device."

"I know. It's a refinement on the Bulgarian umbrella technique."

"A *hell* of a refinement," Bradbury muttered.

Garvey stared into his coffee cup. "I've got my best people working around the clock."

"That ruckus in the CBS parking lot included one of your men, right?"

"Yes, sir. Detective Young was assisting Agent Falk in a search for his missing partner. Young's report stated Falk received a tip to proceed immediately to Marina Del Rey while they were in the lot."

"Did that call result in the boat fire at the Marina?"

Garvey shook his head. "Nothing in his report to that effect."

"Have Young verbally update you on every minute he spent with Agent Falk; where they went, who they spoke to, everything."

"Young's due to return to Rampart division today."

"Not any more. He stays with Hollywood until this thing is over. Team him up. Get him out on the street and keep tabs on him at all times. Damned DHS."

Garvey was already mentally matching Young with Gully.

"Right, Chief."

A wall clock chimed three. "C'mon. Let's get to the meeting room. I gotta chew ass."

118

Chapter 34

Falk paced the deck of the cutter, mulling over the events of the last few days. He'd passed Marco's tip about Jamul on to Stewart, who advised him Cerberus was aware that Jamul, like numerous Hollywood personalities, leaned toward peace and aid to the under privileged, no matter what their political views toward American policy were.

In his own mind, Falk felt the information from Marco carried a message, a warning that more than friendship and understanding of other people's plight was at stake. Stopping in the stern, he gazed toward the lights of the twin Marina towers. One of the penthouses housed Jamul and he intended to seek him out.

Koski looked up as he entered the warm salon. "I thought you were going to stay out there all night."

"Come on. We're moving. Dress warmly. We'll be gone awhile."

The pungent smell of burnt wood and plastic still hung in the air and a thick fog rolled in across the Marina. Falk quickly opened the gate and nodded to Koski to go ahead down the ramp.

It was well after midnight and the opaque fog sucked light from the street lamps. They could still make out the faint outline of a mast and part of the deck jutting from the wreck of the *Sea Note*.

Falk nudged Koski forward toward the Curry's sailboat. "I've a key for the hatch."

"What if they come back?"

"They won't. They mentioned they were going up to Lake Tahoe for the weekend."

"How'd you get the key?"

"There were two spares hanging on a key board in the galley. I'll lift the tarp and you crawl under." He passed her the keys attached to a floatation device. "It's the red one. The green is for the gate." Koski vanished under the tarp. He heard her fumbling to unlock the hatch. He lifted one corner.

"Don't turn on any lights when you get into the cabin." She finally got the hatch open and slipped inside, felt for the edge of a bunk and sat down, thinking this was getting to be a habit. A few seconds later Falk scrambled in beside her.

"We took all our stuff onto the cutter, Joe. All we have is what we're wearing."

"We're still armed. I've a hunch we were watched going aboard. It's only a matter of time before they come after us."

"We had Coast Guard security and a skeleton crew. So what do we do now?"

"Get some rest and wait for Wolf to call me back."

Falk had left messages with Doctor Wolf's exchange before leaving the hotel. Wolf, however, had made previous arrangements with Stewart. As long as he was active in the ongoing investigation, they should have a safety signal between them. Stewart was to call his cell every night at midnight. Wolf was to answer "wrong number" and hang up. If Wolf failed to answer, Stewart would know the doctor was in trouble.

Three minutes later Falk's phone buzzed. He answered immediately. "Doctor Wolf?"

It was Stewart.

"Tom, what's up?"

"Doctor Wolf's missing." He filled Falk in on the nightly signal arrangement. "Intelligence reports indicate something big brewing in the Los Angeles area within the next few hours."

"Yeah," Falk said. "Easter Sunday service at the Bowl. It's been a security nightmare for months."

"DHS is running security. Your job is to find who is responsible for zapping homeless people and studio heads and why."

"Any word from Marco?" Falk asked.

"No, and FYI Greg Grant's in the hospital with a compound fracture of his right leg. You and Koski are still at the Marina, right?"

"That's affirmative."

"Good." Stewart's phone cut off.

"Why didn't you tell him we'd left the cutter? Stewart will find out when the USCG updates him."

"No need for him to know yet. Grant's in the hospital with a fractured leg."

"When did that happen?"

"Don't know. Didn't ask."

"That'll cheer up Bradley."

"If I know Grant he'll be back one way or another."

Falk had blacked out the windows and made sure no light was showing. Now he sat at the small table in the galley and tried for the fourth time in an hour to reach Marco.

Koski glanced up from a paperback she'd found in a small mesh hammock hanging beside her bunk. "He could still be out playing a gig. Nell said he played most nights."

"He has to take a break sometime."

"Maybe she knows where he is."

Falk pushed a set of plastic salt and pepper shakers around in a circle. His face was set in deep thought.

"Yeah. She said she worked late on her book." He quickly made a call. "Nell? This is Agent Falk. Remember me?"

Nell was wide awake. "Absolutely. What's happening? Are you going to give me my interview?"

"Not now. I called to see if you might know where Marco might be. I've been trying to contact him."

"I haven't talked to him in a week. Anything I can do?"

"Maybe. From what you told us about your sporadic gigs around town, I thought you might pick up some info here and there."

"I play and listen, pick up pieces of this and that. In fact, I earn a dollar or two as a stringer for a columnist here in town."

"I can't offer you money, Nell."

"I didn't mean it that way. I just wanted you to know I have contacts."

"What we need might be a bit out of your line."

"Try me."

Falk brought her up-to-date on Dr. Wolf—who he was, where he taught and that he'd vanished. "You still have my cell number?"

"Next to my heart," she said brightly.

Falk smiled. "If you come through you'll have an exclusive interview."

"I'll have fresh batteries in the tape recorder. Bye."

Falk disconnected and glanced at Koski. "What's that you're reading?"

"*The Saint Steps In*. It's about a guy named Simon Templar."

"Great. Get some sleep. We're going to be leaving the Marina before daylight."

Chapter 35

Enrico Pegmanti watched as Paul Horn paced back and forth in front of his desk. "Sit down, for God's sake, man. Security is equipped to protect our secrets. They have for years. Why should it be any different now?"

Horn, hollow-eyed and pale, turned to Pegmanti. "If Martin's formula gets into our competition's hands, it'll cost us millions." He lowered into the Chippendale chair and it creaked under his weight.

"You've no idea who phoned you last night?"

Horn shook his head. "Other than it was a man, none whatsoever," he lied.

"Tell me again what was said."

Horn leaned back and fluttered his eyelids closed. "The call came in around 11:30. I was just getting ready to turn in. At first I thought it was a wrong number. The voice was hesitant. He mentioned Pegmanti Industries and called me by name. I asked him who he was and what he wanted. That's when he said someone within the Pegmanti organization was about to sabotage our stem cell research program. When I asked how he knew the phone went dead."

"That was it?"

"Yes. I think we should alert the DHS."

"Don't be a fool," Pegmanti snarled. "We notify those bastards and they'll be all over us. We'll take care of our own security. If it'll make you feel better, you can work with the head of security to be sure everything is handled to your satisfaction. I'll give orders you have total clearance in the labs." Pegmanti dismissed him and informed his secretary to have the chief

123

of security see him at once.

Falk and Koski left the Marina before dawn. They drove northbound on the 405 Freeway until they reached the Sunset Boulevard off ramp, then headed east toward Hollywood.

"I could use some breakfast. How about you?"

"Soon as we collect Nell," Falk replied. "We'll treat her to breakfast." Koski shrugged and hunkered down deeper into her seat. If she had her way, the car heater would be up all the way and she'd have her coffee by now.

The sun highlighted the top of the Hollywood sign as they reached Nell's house.

"Stay in the car. I'll get her." Falk headed up to the front door and rang the bell. He rang three times before she answered.

Nell looked surprised. "Good morning, Agent Falk. Something wrong?"

"Plenty. That's why I thought we'd get an early start."

"Come in."

"No time. Get dressed. We're taking you to breakfast."

Nell took a sip of coffee. "After you called me last night I made some calls. No one knows where Marco is but you said the doc who went missing teaches at UCLA, right? I have a friend who works in maintenance. Those guys know everything that goes down on campus." She checked her watch. "He should be arriving at work about now."

Traffic was heavier now as Falk drove to UCLA. Nell talked. "He works out of the science building. He's not a floor sweeper any more. Sam's graduated to electrical lighting. He keeps the fluorescent lights glowing night and day."

After finding a parking place and walking along what seemed to be miles of corridors, they arrived at a cubbyhole office deep in the bowels of the building.

Sam was unpacking a box of fluorescent tubes. He looked up in surprise at the sudden appearance of the trio and then recognized Nell.

"Hey, Nell. What's happening?" He glanced at Falk and Koski with suspicion before engaging her in a hip-hop handshake.

Nell told Sam the agents needed help tracking down Dr. Wolf.

"I saw Doctor Wolf walking with a guy late yesterday afternoon."

"How late?" Falk questioned.

"Later than usual. I get off at five but yesterday I didn't get out until almost five forty-five."

"Can you describe the man with him?"

"Old like the doc, medium height. They walked toward the faculty parking structure. I didn't take too much notice."

"Anything unusual?"

Sam thought for a minute. "Come to think of it, the guy walked real close to the doc."

"Did you see them get into a car?"

"No."

"Do you know what make of car the doctor drives?"

"Dark blue Volvo. He keeps the car in good condition, uses a dust cover when parked in the lot."

"Thanks." Falk gave Sam his card. "Call me if you hear anything about Doctor Wolf." The trio left Sam with his light fixtures.

Falk asked, "Which way to the faculty car park?"

Nell pointed. "Over there. Come on. I'll show you."

"You know your way around the campus pretty well," Koski remarked.

"I should. I spent four years here getting my degree."

"In?"

"Master of Arts in Film/Television and Digital Media," Nell chirped.

Falk gave a low whistle. "Plus writer/musician and a stringer for a Hollywood columnist. You're a busy woman, Nell. What other talents do you have?"

"I do great interviews." Nell pointed. "That could be his car."

They approached a vehicle shrouded in a dust cover. Nell lifted a corner and peered under. She was right. It was a dark blue Volvo with doors locked. Falk had a door open in seconds. He and Koski quickly checked the interior.

"No sign of a struggle," Koski muttered as Falk rummaged through the glove compartment. "Whoever was with Wolf decided on a different mode of transportation."

Stewart called Falk as they drove back down the hill after dropping Nell off at her house.

"One of Doctor Wolf's associates suggested we contact a Doctor Martin Pease, head of research at Pegmanti Industries. Wolf and Pease worked together years ago. Contact him and see what you can find." Stewart gave the address. "Why did you move from the cutter?"

"Developments, sir."

The phone clicked off.

Enrico Pegmanti instructed his security chief that Horn was to have free access to the research laboratories. He also expected a daily report on all of Horn's daily activities. Pegmanti leaned back in his chair and created a steeple of his long bony fingers then rested his chin gently at the apex. Paul Horn had to be eliminated.

Chapter 36

Rita Massy attached the latest biolog laser injector beneath her forefinger. "Good work, Paul. Where did you get this?" Massy was impressed with the lightness and balance of the compact weapon.

"I checked every outside contractor doing work for Pegmanti," Horn said. "It was a long and arduous task but it proved fruitful on my twenty-second phone call. It was in storage at Celeste Castings in Torrance."

Horn discovered that Dr. Pease had arranged to store a metal box in their warehouse. Horn lied to Celeste Castings, explaining that Pease and the lab needed the contents of the box to continue with an important experiment. It arrived special delivery.

"It cost a bundle to run that baby down but I'm sure your people will reimburse me."

"No problem." Massy, with forefinger outstretched, sighted across Horn's living room. "You have the nomenclature on this weapon?" Massy took a handwritten manual Horn passed to her. Once she'd read it and made a few trial tests they'd be ready for the service.

"You did a great job, Paul. You'll be paid well. The difference between the two weapons is amazing. Let me show you." Massy opened a case containing the original prototype. "Just look."

She passed the device to Horn who held it awkwardly, not knowing what to do. "This looks like a large penlight to me."

Massy took the weapon and placed it in its case. "Go sit in your chair and I'll perform for you."

Horn obediently crossed the room and lowered into his upholstered armchair.

"Now, say I was going to point at that oil painting above your head." Horn looked worried. "Relax, Paul. I won't harm the painting." Massy gestured toward the artwork.

"Now it looks as if I'm simply pointing at the picture, right?" Horn nodded. "Good. Attached beneath my index finger and snugly hidden in the palm of my hand is the new micro mini weapon. If I were to fire it there wouldn't be any sound or indication I had done anything except point across the room." Rita Massy narrowed her sea green eyes as she studied the artwork. "That's a nice painting, Paul. Should I know the artist?"

Horn slowly stiffened in his chair. His eyes widened with fear.

Massy turned and pointed directly at Horn and clenched her fist. Her finger was still pointing at him as a recessed trigger in the body of the device activated the laser. A split second later Horn slumped forward in his chair.

"I said I wouldn't harm the painting." Massy gathered up the original prototype and opened the door. She glanced back at Horn's crumpled form, paused a moment, then walked back to the body. Less than a minute later she closed the door softly behind her.

Paul Horn's housekeeper discovered him early the next morning. Tom Stewart contacted Falk on his way to Pegmanti Industries.

Finishing the phone conversation, Falk glanced at Koski. "Paul Horn, an executive of the Pegmanti Empire, has been found dead in his home with no apparent signs of how he died. Let's go."

Koski turned up her coat collar and rubbed her hands together. "Southern California is supposed to be warm. It's almost April and we're down at the beach. Go ahead and turn the heater up."

Nell received a call from the Hollywood columnist, tasking his stringer to investigate a story about a DHS agent who broke a leg in a fall at the city morgue and was now in St. Vincent's Hospital. Nell immediately thought of Agent Falk!

Carrying a towel-covered tray and dressed in floral scrubs, Nell looked cute as she entered the room. There were three beds, two of them empty. Grant lay with a stack of pillows behind him, his leg in a splint suspended by pulleys. Nell had expected Falk and her face dropped upon seeing the scowling countenance of Grant.

"Whatever you've got on that tray, I don't want it. Get out of here."

"I thought this was Agent Falk's room."

Grant's eyes narrowed. "Wait a minute. Come here." Nell moved closer. "I was told there was a DHS agent in here with a broken leg and I thought..."

"You thought what?"

"I know Agent Falk and wanted to say hi."

Grant's investigative reporter instincts kicked in. "When did you meet him?"

"He and his partner were investigating a murder and I mentioned I'd like an interview." She paused. "I'm not really a nurse. I'm a writer and wanted some inside information about the DHS for my book."

"Did you get your interview?"

"Not yet."

Grant knew he had a winner. "What would you say if I told you I'm his boss? If you'll work with me, I'll give you an in-depth interview that *TIME* magazine would die for."

"What do I have to do?"

Grant didn't intend to screw up his first assignment. He couldn't strut his stuff with a broken leg but he sure as hell could get around if he had an electric scooter.

Grant called a medical rental supply company and ordered an electric scooter. Then he signed himself out and assigned Nell as his personal assistant.

Twenty minutes later he zipped through the corridors of St. Vincent's on a bright red scooter with Nell trotting to keep up.

Greg Grant was back on the job.

Imminent Danger

Chapter 37

Despite the many security procedures put into effect across the United States since 9/11, there were still numerous gaping holes in the system. Bridges and dams, airports and docks teemed with bureaucratic experts claiming their program was foolproof. Some used words such as watertight and impregnable.

The sad fact was most of the posturing related to protecting their jobs, an action 180 degrees counter to what the nation needed. America fell over itself in its desire to become terrorist proof. In doing so, they knocked large gaps in their hastily organized security screens, a case in point, the Hollywood Bowl.

Preparations for the Easter Sunday Services were ongoing. Every vehicle checked in and out—no exceptions. No one was permitted to enter the area without a thorough security check and every worker carried an official ID.

Marco, hands stuffed deep in his jacket pockets, stood with the other workers in the back of an open truck. Nonetheless, Marco, alone the last few days, had unknowingly hidden six bombs in the roots of trees in and around the stage area where the dignitaries would assemble.

The truck inched slowly forward into the nursery zone at the rear of the huge acoustic shell. A large part of the re-landscaping project had included planting new saplings. Unknown to anyone, and cunningly hidden in the root ball of each sapling, lay a small and powerful plastic bomb wrapped in sacking. Each passed through stringent hands-on security checks and electronic wands. They never registered a flicker on the security equipment.

The sniffer dogs were foiled by the addition of agricultural composts, chemicals and soil surrounding the roots.

When triggered, the deadly devices would hurl ball bearings at waist level into the audience. At the same moment, the biolog laser injector, with laser accuracy, would zap celebrities on stage. A second assassin, using the original prototype weapon, was primed to fire airborne bacterial laden shells set to burst over the audience as the tree bombs exploded.

Marco climbed down from the truck and stamped hard on the ground to restore his circulation.

"Hey, Marco. How many more trees we got to plant, man?" one of the gang members asked.

Marco shrugged. "When we're finished we go back home, okay?"

Marco carried the radio Stewart had given him and increased the volume of a Spanish music station. He always carried it, even going through security. So far, not one security guard bothered to examine the cheap-looking radio. To them, if it played it was a radio. Marco eyed a pile of new saplings stacked against a wall of the nursery, estimating at least two hundred and two days until Sunday.

Massy watched the crews receive their assignments. She decided this was a good time to test Marco's loyalty.

Feeling a sharp tap on his shoulder, Marco turned quickly. "You won't be digging holes today, Marco. You're working inside the nursery. They're a man short."

Marco's street smarts immediately went into overdrive but he remained silent.

"You're getting an opportunity to prove your worth to us."

"Meaning what?"

"Keep your eyes and ears open. The Department of Homeland Security has added a command center inside the nursery as part of the security coverage. I need to know how many people are on duty at all times. You'll report to a man named Fred and be watched every minute. Now get going."

Marco had gone only a few feet when Massy called out. "One other thing, I notice you carry a radio everywhere you go. Leave it with me. Fred doesn't like Spanish music."

Massy drove out of the Bowl, stopped at the corner of Hollywood and Highland, picked up a male passenger then continued toward the Santa Monica Mountains overlooking Malibu. Forty minutes later they arrived in a lonely, boulder-strewn canyon. Massy parked the car and swept her gaze over a rugged landscape of sparse vegetation and a few stunted Manzanita trees dotting the hillsides. Satisfied they were alone, Massy switched off the ignition.

"Let me have it." The passenger obeyed and she snapped the device under the forefinger of her right hand. "You must be totally familiar with this weapon before Sunday. Follow me and bring the cages."

Massy's companion walked quietly beside her toting two wire mesh cages, each containing two cats. He'd been called on in the past to complete assignments requiring a certain talent not easily found. This one would prove to be difficult.

"I've no doubt you'll master this weapon within a few hours." Massy held her right hand up beside her face, palm outward. The plastic object was clearly visible attached snugly under her forefinger.

"A friend of mine, trained by the British Army during WWII, told me that during pistol training they fired at wooden dummies designed to spring up as they walked the firing range. Soldiers were taught that when a target appeared to simply point and shoot."

"I've heard that one before. I still prefer the Weaver Stance," her companion said.

"I'm sure you do," Massy said silkily. "Forget that when using this weapon. You're going to be using one never seen outside of the laboratory where it was designed."

The duo was now a half mile into the canyon. Massy scanned the harsh terrain. Her shooter must learn to use a piece of equipment unknown even to the U.S. Armed Forces.

"There'll be no sound or recoil. Once you get the hang of it you'll feel as powerful as Zeus hurling his thunderbolts."

Her cohort remained silent as he watched Massy walk forward and point toward a boulder jutting from the side of an outcropping. "See that odd shaped boulder?" He nodded.

"Set one of the cages on top. Leave one cat inside, put its companion in the other cage and keep it with you."

The man trudged up the rocky slope, set the cage in place and glanced back down to Massy.

"That's fine," Massy called. "Get back down here." When the man returned, Massy asked, "How far away would you say our target is?"

"I'd guess about fifty yards."

"Good." Lightly clenching her right hand into a fist but with the forefinger extended, Massy pointed toward the cage, tightened her clenched fist and then lowered her arm. "Bring me the cat. Leave the cage where it is."

The man hiked back. He could see the cat through the wire mesh as he approached. When he reached the boulder, the cat was apparently unharmed, seemingly fast asleep.

Officer Robert Gully opened the cage door and removed the animal. It didn't move. Gully stared at the still feline. The damn cat was dead. It was at that moment Gully realized the immensity of the situation. He was about to use an instrument of death that would soon allow terrorists to wield unprecedented power in political assassinations worldwide.

"We don't have all day, Gully," Massy shouted. "Get back down here. Today's Friday. Unless you're perfect on Sunday you'll be a dead man. You still need a lot of target practice."

"Damnedest looking weapon I've ever seen," Gully muttered.

Massy watched Officer Gully, the man she had chosen to commit an act of terrorism against his own country, examine the BLI. Over the next few hours, Massy explained in detail the workings of the biolog laser injector.

Finally, in late afternoon, Massy was satisfied with the skill and accuracy Gully had attained in such a short span of time.

"You've excellent control of the weapon, Gully. I suppose I have to thank the LAPD for the hours of extensive weapon training they give their officers."

For the first time since he'd agreed to be the shooter, Gully felt a shiver tingle his spine. He'd sold his soul for promised riches. Anger and frustration had turned him into a hired assassin.

It all began when Gully wrote up his partner, a rookie fresh from the Academy. During an investigation the rookie had inadvertently handled a piece of crucial evidence that later ruined any chance of a conviction.

His partner's error also ruined Gully's long-awaited promotion. As officer in charge, he failed the system by allowing it to happen. Gully protested, saying the man was incompetent. His captain advised Gully that charges of racism might possibly enter in if he protested the outcome. The rookie was a young black man.

Gully swallowed his pride and remained with the force. Less than ninety days after his transfer, Massy contacted him and painted a picture of riches if he considered becoming an informer.

Gully received a huge amount of money upfront. The agreement videotaped without his knowledge. Two days later, Massy played Gully the tape, advising him the video might show up at the DA's office if he ever decided to change his mind and stop obeying orders. Now, almost two years later, he stood in a rock-strewn canyon, learning to use a weapon of frightening possibilities. Will what he was about to do go into the history books along with past traitors who had caused world wars through their actions?

The bodies of four cats lay stretched on the ground. Massy nudged one with the toe of her shoe. "Can't see any marks. Not even a veterinarian can say how they died. You see, their own body killed them the instant the frequency transmitting the chemical particles penetrated their system. It works the same with any living body. Biocomplexity. Death is instantaneous. No apparent internal damage and marks on the body. It's a perfect killing tool."

Massy remained silent on other features of the weapon, such as the ability to project mind-altering drugs or other dedicated opiates. Giving too much knowledge to an assassin was never a good idea even when you had decided he'd die at the scene.

The shadows grew longer and a salty Pacific breeze snaked through the canyon.

Massy snapped, "Come on. Get the cages back to the car."

Gully's Easter Sunday assignment was LAPD security—helmet, goggles, and gloves. As he lugged the cages back to the car, Massy instructed Gully to modify his right hand glove to accommodate the biolog laser injector.

Marco stacked the last hundred pound sack of potting soil onto a wooden pallet and stepped aside as the steel tusks of a stubby yellow forklift hoisted the load skyward. It spun around and wound its way across the concrete expanse of the indoor nursery. It was almost quitting time.

"Learn anything, Marco?"

Massy stood beside him, face slightly tanned, wearing scuffed and dusty hiking boots, her usually clean fingernails dirty.

Marco nodded. "Yeah. It's easier digging holes out there than hauling sacks of horse shit in here."

"There's more to learn in here." Massy nodded toward the security area in the far corner of the warehouse.

Marco grunted. "I couldn't get within fifty feet of that place. A couple of guys at lunch said the entire Bowl is swarming with security, night and day."

"Tomorrow's Saturday. It's our last chance to gather information."

Marco shrugged. "Boring as hell in here. Let me have my radio. I won't play Spanish music. I need something to keep my mind off dried horse shit, peat moss and potting soil."

Massy shook her head. "I'll keep it until our work here is done."

Chapter 38

Like most of the homes they passed on the drive up the steep twisting roads, the mansion was equal to the best. It was a three-story Tudor, gray slate roof tiles and two sets of twisted red brick chimneys. Grant's second call from the hospital was to his friend in Beverly Hills who had arranged for a handicapped-equipped van to be waiting outside. Nell brought the van to a crunching halt on the thick gravel driveway and turned to Grant.

"You've got rich friends."

Grant nodded. "Old money. Lower the tailgate."

Nell opened the back doors and pressed a switch unhinging the tailgate from a vertical position down to the van's floor level. Grant had already moved his scooter to the back of the van and smoothly inched forward onto the elevator. Nell pushed another button lowering him to street level.

"C'mon. Let's get inside." Grant switched on and whirred toward the front entrance.

The entrance hall was huge. A black and white checkered marble floor and wide, curved staircase led to the upper floors. Nell walked beside Grant across the entrance hall and into a cavernous room furnished with heavy antique furniture. Thick damask drapes were pulled closed across leaded windowpanes. A deep seated couch covered in umber colored satin was in sharp contrast to the bright blue dress of a small, wizened woman seated demurely at dead center.

Grant swerved to a halt in front of the couch. "I'd like to introduce my new personal assistant, Nell Fynn with a Y. Nell, this is my aunt, Ms. Agatha Coleman."

Agatha looked to be in her late eighties, white hair and piercing blue eyes that still sparkled with a zest for life.

"What's he got you doing, my dear? He's not to be trusted. Ditched college and broke his mother's heart. Went off to be a newspaper reporter."

"Investigative journalist," Grant said. "Now I'm with the DHS."

"Even worse," Agatha said. "He's been staying here with me while looking for murderers. Now he's driving around with a broken leg on a senior citizen's electric scooter. Tell me. What exactly is a personal assistant anyway?"

"I'm not sure yet. I just started today."

"She's going to keep me up-to-date. Nell has contacts and I think I can make use of them."

"What sort of contacts?"

"Skills and contacts," Grant replied. "Nell's also a writer."

"Well! With those qualifications she might even solve your case, Greg."

"I'm doing all I can to get two of my agents back who were transferred from my team. Nell's in touch with them."

"And what are you going to do confined on that contraption with a broken leg?"

"Run the show from here using the wonders of electronics and Nell on the outside."

Agatha turned to Nell. "He's turning you into a remote controlled private eye. You'll end up like that young woman in the detective novels. What's her name? She's in those books with a single capital letter for a title."

Nell laughed. "Oh, you mean Sue Grafton's Kinsey Millhone. I should be so lucky."

Chapter 39

Martin Pease called a cab from UCLA that took him and Dr. Wolf to spend the night in a Westwood Motel. On Saturday Pease rented a car and drove east on Sunset as Wolf's mind worked overtime trying to think of a means to contact Stewart.

The local news was on the car radio and Pease suddenly reached over and increased the volume. "Listen."

The reporter said, "Paul Horn, an executive with Pegmanti Industries of Southern California, was found dead in his home early this morning. The police are treating the death as a possible homicide..."

Jabbing the off button, Pease shouted, "*Now* do you believe me?"

Wolf had never doubted him. He remembered Massy from the short time, years ago, when he worked for Pegmanti. Massy had befriended the young Englishman upon his arrival at the company. Perhaps even back then Massy saw Pease's potential.

"For God sake, Martin. A terrorist cell with a futuristic delivery system *you* designed!" He must contact Stewart immediately. "I can get you help."

Pease gave a harsh laugh. "Who? Someone with the government?"

"A person I've known for a long time."

"He can get me out of the country?"

"Yes."

"You can reach him by phone?"

"Yes."

"Here's my cell. Call him."

Wolf quickly tapped Stewart's number. "Tom, this is Jack. Yeah. I'm okay. I'll be at your place in twenty minutes. I have someone I'd like you to meet."

Falk drove north on the Pacific Coast Highway heading to the Pegmanti address when his phone chirped. "Falk. Okay. We're on our way." Checking his side mirror, he made a screeching U-turn.

"What's up?" Koski grabbed the armrest as Falk pushed the car way over the speed limit.

"Stewart. He wants us back at his hotel. Doctor Wolf's with him."

Forty-five minutes later they entered Stewart's suite.

"You both know Doctor Wolf." Wolf raised an arm in greeting and Koski saw how tired he looked. "And this is Doctor Martin Pease."

So began the debriefing.

Two hours later Pease ended his story.

"Where can we find Doctor Massy?" Falk asked Pease.

"I don't know. She always contacted me."

"Koski," Stewart ordered, "contact Laser Research Labs in Pasadena. They'll know."

Koski had directory service give her the number. "This is Agent Susan Koski, FBI. Listen carefully and take down this number. Have someone in authority phone me back immediately. They'll be screened through by an FBI operator. Tell them Agent Susan Koski told you to contact her. You'll be routed to me at once. Do you understand? Good. Now do it."

The room was silent for what seemed like an eternity. In reality it was less than seven minutes before Koski's cell rang. Identifying herself, she asked where Doctor Rita Massy could be located. She listened, raised her eyes and stared at Falk. "You mean there is no way she can be reached? Yes. I understand. Thank you." She snapped the phone shut, "She's on a month-long sabbatical somewhere in the Amazon rainforests."

"Rubbish!" Pease snorted. "She's *here in town*."

"You've no idea where we can find her?" Stewart asked.

"No. We agree over the phone to meet in various places of her choice. I never know where until an hour before the meeting."

"We can get a warrant and search her house," Falk suggested.

"You'll find nothing," Pease said bitterly. "Rita Massy is far too smart to leave any incriminating evidence."

"Then where *does* she operate from?"

"I've no idea."

Falk wondered aloud if it were possible that Jamul had Massy as a houseguest during the planning stages of a forthcoming attack. Pease shrugged.

Stewart had assigned a surveillance team to Jamul's place immediately after Falk reported his breakfast meeting with Marco. The stakeout confirmed the fact that Jamul had a yacht moored at the Marina, which he also placed under surveillance. Having no information on Massy at that time, the watchers had simply videotaped everyone entering and leaving the building and the yacht.

"We have video on every person who went in and out of the towers and the yacht, right?" Falk asked.

Stewart nodded. "Yes. For two days."

Falk sighed. "Massy could be in the towers, on *Caviare* or any place in the Marina. If Jamul is involved he's keeping a low profile. I suggest we get technicians to go over the tapes, frame by frame, with a picture of Rita Massy beside them."

Imminent Danger

Chapter 40

Falk and Koski scrutinized Massy's employment files at Laser Research Labs in Pasadena. Falk came across a black and white photograph attached to a company security document taken several years earlier. He passed the form to Koski.

She matched the picture with a blowup from video surveillance. A small frown creased her brow. "That's the woman who interrogated me on the boat!" she said softly.

Falk looked over her shoulder. "You said she wore a ski mask."

"She did. It's the eyes. I'll never forget them."

Falk flipped through the background information in the dossier. Education degrees, publications awards, hobbies. "Says Massy's hobby is sailing," he read aloud.

"And I'm sure she was in the Marina when I was being held," Koski grunted.

"Call DMV. If she does have a boat registered they'll have it on file."

Koski phoned, using the same procedure she used when contacting Laser Research. Within five minutes she had the information. A Dr. Rita Massy was the registered owner of a Grand Banks 46 Classic.

"DMV doesn't have any information on individual slips but they have the registered owner's home address. Massy's is 2109 Avondale Road, San Marino," Koski said quietly.

"Let's check it out," Falk replied.

San Marino is an upscale conclave of mansions and historic homes sedately set amid trees, half-acre lawns and security walls. It's backed by a police department dedicated to the serenity of its residents.

Built at the turn of the century by powerful industrialists, politicians and other movers and shakers of the time, the area was designed for the rich. Today, their descendants retained the same lifestyle.

"Massy must have been doing well to live around here," Falk muttered as he drove along Euston Road, passing the Huntington Library and Art Gallery.

Koski, engrossed in her map book, looked up. "Yeah. Hang a right on Woodstock."

The Avondale address turned out to be a large, two story Spanish hacienda with the customary red tiled roof. It sat back from the road behind a pair of ten-foot high decorative iron gates. It was secured by a thick chain and a padlock the size of a dinner plate. Two infrared security cameras covered the approach to the gate.

"Wait here." Falk inspected the padlock, brass, old-fashioned but effective. He turned quickly when Koski tapped the horn and a police car rolled up beside him.

"Anything we can do, sir?" a polite but commanding voice asked.

"Yes, officer. We want to talk with Doctor Massy." He indicated the padlock and chain. "Seems she's not at home."

The officer slid from behind the wheel. His partner was already out and watching Koski. "Keep your hands where I can see them, sir." The officer removed his automatic and held it at his side. "Slowly remove your ID." The cop held his weapon away from his leg.

"We're from the Department of Homeland Security."

"That's fine, sir."

Falk removed his ID and held it to view.

"Tell your partner to hand her ID through the window." He jerked his head toward the other cop.

"Do as he says, Koski."

Satisfied with the IDs, both cops relaxed. "What does the DHS want with Doctor Massy? She's been away for almost a month."

"We need to talk to her."

"When she left, Agent Falk, she informed the station she'd be gone for six weeks. We keep a close watch on property when any of the residents around here leave."

"We'd like to get in and look around," Koski said.

"You'll need a search warrant."

Falk had no time to waste. "Fine." He put away his ID and returned to the car. "Call Stewart. Bring him up-to-speed and tell him we're going back to the Marina."

Koski nodded and transmitted.

Falk and Koski entered the Harbor Master's office in Marina Del Rey. After a brief explanation and ID presentation, they waited in a pleasant room overlooking the main channel.

"I can see the cutter we almost spent the night on." Koski said, craning her neck for a better view of the large craft.

A middle-aged woman entered the room. She carried a thick leather book and angled into a chair facing them. She thumbed the pages without saying a word. Satisfied, she marked the page physically with her right hand and closed the cover. "We don't usually give out information like this."

"We understand," Falk responded.

"Seeing it's for the DHS the Harbor Master is making a concession."

"Thank you."

The woman tilted the book toward her chest as if afraid they might see something they shouldn't then slid her hand from between the pages and read aloud.

"Doctor Rita Massy, Grand Banks 46 Classic, slip number 1443 Bora-Bora Way, Basin A."

Koski had swiftly jotted down the information.

"Thank you, ma'am," Falk replied. "The agency requires me to advise you it's against the law to disclose that the Department of Homeland Security requested this information. If for any reason the person we're seeking is given any indication that could in any way be detrimental to our investigation, that party will be charged with breaching the Securities Act in a time of war. Any questions?"

Wide-eyed, the woman whispered, "I understand."

Upon leaving the Harbor Master's office, Falk said, "We'll cut through Fisherman's Village and check out Jamul's boat. It's too long for a regular slip."

Once through the collection of shops and restaurants and onto the walkway adjacent to the main channel, Falk pointed. "There she is. Wow! Looks like something Onassis might have owned."

They leaned on the walkway rail like tourists watching the activity of the crew working topside, scrubbing the deck and polishing the shiny teak rails and brass.

"Check out the helicopter," Falk said, indicating a bright blue Bell 206B.

Koski shaded her eyes and scanned the far side of the channel. "According to the map on the wall back in the Harbor Master's office, Bora-Bora Way is directly across from where we're standing."

"It is," Falk agreed, "but right now I want a closer look at *Caviare*."

Jamul had boarded his yacht Friday night under cover of darkness. Now, seated at a custom-built console of electronic wizardry, he could observe any part of the yacht on a large flat screen monitor. The equipment enabled him state-of-the-art satellite send-and-receive capabilities. The sophisticated equipment, under the guise of business use for his worldwide interests, used an especially designed code that was cunning yet simple. He used words and phrases widely accepted in show business jargon but with different meanings when matched to the decoding manual.

A smaller screen beneath the monitor flickered to life. Massy's image filled the screen and her whispery cold voice filtered through concealed speakers.

"The woman who sank the boat is standing dockside accompanied by the man who rescued her. Two of my men followed them when they left the Harbor Master's. Send backup from the yacht. We'll take them out."

"I'll have them ashore at once," Jamul rumbled.

Massy nodded as the image faded.

Mikhail Brasinov's first venture to the U.S. as a skilled Islamic warrior had been a complete failure. So when Jamul suddenly ordered him and another man ashore to go after Koski and Falk, he was determined to prove his worth.

Brasinov's reputation was well-known. He had no need to be concerned. He had killed many and disrupted dozens of the NATO troops' plans to bring peace to Bosnia. Many lauded Brasinov's claim that NATO and U.N. troops had hidden all the dead bodies and that had been their only means of keeping peace.

His present assignment to the cell chosen to represent Islam's next blow against the U.S. on American soil was a great honor for a young man born to peasant stock in Eastern Europe. Growing up with war and hatred, he quickly learned to kill or be killed. He'd made the choice. His future was with radical Islam.

Imminent Danger

Chapter 41

Jamul knew nothing must disturb tonight's black tie affair. This was a pivotal part of the overall operation. Easter Eve vigil would begin at sundown and be celebrated aboard the *Caviare*. A grand gesture on Jamul's part, designed to show his deep concern for world peace and his embracing of all religions. The idol of millions, however, still had important duties to carry out to remove him from any suspicion of being associated with a planned terrorist attack.

He closed down the console and shrugged into a flight jacket. He flipped on a baseball cap and tugged down the bill, went topside and walked aft. Two mechanics were finishing their final flight check on the Bell as Jamul put on dark glasses and climbed up to the helipad.

"All ready?" Jamul asked, knowing the aircraft had been standing by for at least twenty minutes. Assured all was in order, he eased into the Perspex cabin, settled in the pilot's seat and began his pre-flight check.

Jamul was a skilled copter pilot with five years experience. He glanced at one of the mechanics and twirled his right hand in the sign for takeoff. The rotors came up to speed. The mechanic's overalls fluttered from the down draft as the helicopter slowly lifted from its pad. It hovered over the main channel for a few seconds, swooped left, climbed and headed toward Hollywood.

He was flying to the Bowl to supervise final preparations of the audio and lighting systems. As usual, he was in charge, as he would be Easter Sunday morning. He would be standing center stage as the sun rose, leading a massed choir in singing Handel's *Messiah*. Audiences worldwide

149

traditionally rose from their seats at the first stirring notes. Tomorrow the powerful hymn would be his signal for the violence to begin.

"Two on our tail," Falk whispered as he glanced back toward the Coast Guard station.

Koski looked toward the *Caviare* and spotted two men running down the gangplank, darting glances as if seeking someone. "Make it four." Seconds later the small blue helicopter clattered skyward from the fantail.

Falk grabbed his cell from his jacket pocket. "We're aft of the *Caviare*. Okay, make it fast. We'll fake a medical emergency." He closed the phone. "Okay, Koski. Faint and stay down."

She responded as if cued by a film director. A small crowd started to gather and Falk quickly ordered them back.

"Give her air." Glancing over the knot of onlookers, he saw that the Coast Guard had responded to his call. Three Coast Guardsmen, one pulling a gurney, ran toward them from the nearby USCG office.

"Step back please. Nothing to see here," a commanding voice ordered as a corpsman knelt beside Koski. Falk scoped the area to see if he could spot the followers. They'd vanished.

The medic rolled Koski onto the gurney and Falk fell into step with them as they carried her back to the Coast Guard station. It had worked...for now at least.

The same lieutenant who showed them around the cutter was on duty when they arrived.

"Welcome aboard." He grinned. "Good ruse."

"Yeah, but we're going to need a way to leave here *without* being followed." Falk tapped Koski's shoulder. "Oscar winning performance."

She got to her feet. "Thanks."

"Seeing you're such a good actor," Falk quipped, "I've an idea on how we can expand your role."

Chapter 42

Rita Massy had been gone less than ten minutes when two men walked up and hustled Marco from the nursery building into a waiting car and drove him to the safe house. No one spoke on the short ride. Now, handcuffed and sitting on the floor of an empty room on the top floor, Marco felt dazed by the sudden change of fortune.

Twilight filtered through a grimy window at the end of the room. He struggled to his feet and shakily crossed to the window. He leaned against the frame and stared down to the grounds, aware that they were swarming with unseen guards.

Enrico Pegmanti, assisted by the butler, shrugged out of his thick overcoat as he entered the safe house and demanded, "Is he here?"

"Yes, sir," the butler answered.

"Bring him to me." Pegmanti walked through to the same room where he and Rita Massy had met. He lowered slowly into a chair beside the fire. He was already wearing his tuxedo for the black tie event aboard the *Caviare* later in the evening.

A log in the hearth flared a gas plume of sapphire blue. Pegmanti watched it with a childlike fascination. The house was silent except for the soft hiss of the burning wood. It seemed to soothe the old man until the sound of a door opening broke the spell. Pegmanti continued staring into the flames as footsteps came closer to his chair and stopped.

Pegmanti cast a sideways glance at the man and Marco at his side. "Leave us alone," Pegmanti ordered.

The man nodded. When the door had clicked shut, Pegmanti indicated a chair opposite him. "Sit down, young man."

Marco had no idea who the old man was but knew instinctively he was in the company of a man of power. Slowly he folded himself onto the edge of the chair. Still cuffed, he sat stiffly, his arms pulled behind him.

"What caused you to become a traitor, Marco?"

Marco was stunned. What had he done to cause suspicion?

"I'm not a traitor."

"You don't consider working for a group of foreigners determined to overthrow the American way of life not traitorous!"

Marco blinked rapidly. The old man was talking about the Arabs, not him being an informer. Quickly his mind spun into action. "I did it for the money."

"Were you born in the United States or Mexico?" Pegmanti asked.

"I was born in East Los Angeles."

"Even worse, Marco. You sold your birthright *and* you're a traitor." One of the logs burnt through and fell, sending a shower of tiny sparks spiraling up the chimney.

"Many years ago I also became a traitor, not by selling out to the enemy but by leaving my country in 1931 when it needed every able bodied man." He turned his head and looked at Marco. "Like many other Italians, I came to America a penniless immigrant. I was seventeen." Pegmanti paused and rubbed his left hand over the top of his right, as if trying to increase his circulation. "Over the years I made a fortune and tripled it during World War Two," his voice almost a whisper. "Then I became a traitor a second time. Hearing about you has changed my mind."

"Why me?"

"You're aiding a terrorist group. The same as I've been doing. I'm an old man looking for forgiveness. I've decided to make amends on this Easter Eve, the great vigil before Easter Sunday morning."

Marco tensed. Why is this old guy telling him anything? "Who are you, mister?"

"It matters not. I ordered you killed."

Marco sat straighter on the chair edge and swallowed hard before asking, "And now?"

"Admit that you'll agree to work against these people and I'll see you leave here alive and you can complete your mission."

Marco knew the old man could have him killed, the same as they killed his best friend. "I joined for the money. I don't care what the Arabs do."

"You'd make a lot more money if you gave the government information that could break up a terrorist cell." Pegmanti reached into his jacket pocket. "I believe this is yours. I'm told you don't go anywhere without it." He switched on the radio and a music program was in progress. Snapping it off, he continued. "I know what this really is, Marco. When I tripled my fortune during the war, part of my company was manufacturing such devices for the government, perhaps not as sophisticated back then, same idea though."

Marco was defiant. "All I can tell anyone about this job is I've been digging holes and planting trees."

Pegmanti nodded slowly. "Very well...now listen carefully."

Imminent Danger

Chapter 43

After several phone calls, one of them to Chief Bradbury, Grant had gathered enough information to decide the best place to begin looking for Koski and Falk. He was determined to get back into the action. That crazy dame had sunk a boat in Marina Del Rey and now they'd been seen snooping around in the Marina again. That was all he needed.

"We'll dress as medics," Falk said crisply. "I'll need a volunteer to replace Agent Koski on the stretcher and a USCG ambulance to drive to Daniel Freeman Hospital. Once the 'patient' is delivered to emergency, Koski and I will walk through the hospital and out the front entrance. A car will be waiting to take us to Bora-Bora Way, slip number 1443. Any problems, Lieutenant?"

"Can do, sir," he answered.

"Then let's do it."

Daniel Freeman Hospital was less than two miles from the Marina. Upon arrival, Koski and Falk rushed the gurney into the emergency entrance. They turned everything over, including the scrubs they'd worn, to two Coast Guardsmen who had gone on ahead to await their arrival. Then they vanished into the hospital corridors.

Koski, slightly out of breath, walked across the main lobby and out the front door.

"Good plan, Joe."

"Keep moving."

A Coast Guard vehicle rolled into view and they quickly crossed the sidewalk and ducked into it. The lieutenant was at the wheel and quickly pulled out onto Lincoln Boulevard and headed back toward the Marina.

"Next stop Bora-Bora Way," announced the lieutenant. "We'll have to go all the way around to the other side of the Marina. It won't take long."

"What do you know about the large sloop docked near Fisherman's Village?" Falk asked.

"The *Caviare* belongs to the pop singer, Jamul. We don't see him very often. The sloop sits there most of the year with a skeleton crew. Waste of money if you ask me."

"There's going to be a big party on board tonight. A bunch of bigwigs, politicians and foreign visitors are gathering before the Easter Sunday Services at the Bowl. I guess you'll be part of security."

"Yes, sir. Absolutely. We received orders to increase our presence along the dockside near the *Caviare*. Show the flag and make everyone feel safe and sound. Main security will be undercover DHS."

Koski caught a glimpse of a street sign as the car turned left onto Admiralty Way.

"Almost there, ma'am," the officer said. "Any place in particular you'd like to be let off?"

"Basin A, slip 1443," Falk answered.

"Okay. That's on the south side of Basin A. You want me to wait?"

"No. We'll be okay. I've got the USCG phone number in my cell if we need assistance."

"Fine. Here we are."

Meanwhile, Jamul had completed his preliminary checks at the Bowl, visited with and instructed his stage crew, joshing with them in his usual breezy manner. He made sure as many people as possible saw him at the Bowl then made ready to return to the Marina. He headed back to the helipad, assuring everyone he'd see them early Sunday morning.

Once Falk and Koski were out of the car, they looked down into Basin A and the neat rows of boats. Koski pointed across the channel. "I was right. We're directly opposite the *Caviare*."

"She sure looks pretty all lit up," the lieutenant remarked. "Take care now." He turned the car and headed back.

Falk stared across the channel toward the yacht. Light bulbs strung from stem to stern added a festive touch.

"I think I see Massy's trawler, Joe."

Falk followed her pointing finger. "I didn't know you were an expert at recognizing boats."

"I'm not. There was a boating magazine in the Harbor Master's waiting room and it featured a Grand Banks on its cover."

"Point out a couple of other boats so it's not obvious we're looking for a Grand Banks trawler. I'll go down and check it out." They both tested their communication equipment, adjusting the earpieces and testing the mikes.

"Hear me okay?" Falk asked.

"No problem."

"Stay down and cover me."

Walking in the shadows, he headed toward the dock gate. One or two lights glimmered from a few boats. The trawler was dark. He glanced up as the reverberation of an incoming helicopter shattered the stillness. It swept low across the channel, approached the stern of the *Caviar*e and settled gently onto the helipad.

At the dock gate, Falk removed the key he'd taken from the Curry's and quickly opened the lock and started down the ramp toward the Grand Banks. One gate key fit all.

There were no lights showing and Falk needed to be certain there was no one aboard. The design of the trawler was such that it was easy to see into the top cabin from dockside. He kicked off his shoes and stepped aboard. Then he padded across the deck to the channel side, bending low, making himself less noticeable from the road. If not for the sound of lapping water and the ping-ping of wire halyards strummed by a light wind as they tapped the aluminum masts of nearby sailboats, it was dark and silent.

He checked the cabin door—locked. He quickly used a lock pick and within seconds was inside. Street lamps cast enough radiance to enable him to see without a flashlight. Moving forward to the bridge, he checked the controls and quickly familiarized himself with the layout.

Falk was experienced with powerboats and knew many of them had similar controls. He crossed to a set of steps and went below into the main salon area. Nothing out of place. If Rita Massy lived aboard, she was a fastidious housekeeper. He checked the sleeping area, same thing, neat. His earpiece came alive as he entered the main cabin. "Joe," Koski whispered. "Someone just parked up on the road."

"Are they still in the car?"

"Yes." Falk left the cabin, scooped up his shoes, jumped ashore and swiftly hunkered down behind one of the large storage bins assigned to each boat. Then he heard the sound of the gate opening and footsteps descending the ramp.

Rita Massy had intended to go directly to the *Caviare* from the penthouse communications room after warning Jamul. When she learned they had lost sight of Koski and Falk, she remained in the control room, monitoring communications and hoping they'd report finding the duo. Finally, fuming at their escape, she opted to return to her trawler and dress for the party.

Falk watched Massy board and go below.

"I'm going back aboard," he hissed into his mike. "Stay where you are."

Koski's voice whispered in his ear. "Be careful."

Chapter 44

Officer Robert Gully rolled down the window of the police car, allowing a stream of air to enter as they cruised down Hollywood Boulevard.

"Jesus. I'm whacked," Gully grunted.

"You volunteered for Special Services."

"After my demotion I went out for the special squad 'cause of the extra pay."

"You've been acting kinda strange, too."

"What do you mean, strange?"

"Edgy," Victor Young said. "Anything bothering you?"

"Nothing's troubling me, pal. Just tired is all."

"After the Bowl we can go home and get some sack time."

Gully felt a sudden surge of adrenaline run through his body. This time tomorrow he'd have committed the act.

Rita Massy began to change into her dress, hurrying, wanting to be across at the *Caviare* before the main guests arrived. Facing a mirror, she made a third attempt to get her hair exactly right. Suddenly, halfway through her task she stopped and listened. Someone was on deck.

She backed away from the mirror and eased the cabin door open. Every nerve was alert for the slightest sound. It could have been a seagull or perhaps the wind. She opened the door a little wider until she could see down the short corridor. No one there. She left the door ajar, went back to where her black satin dinner jacket was hanging, reached into a cunningly designed holster built into the inner lining, and removed a Glock 17 with a loaded magazine.

She kicked off her black pumps, slipped into a pair of rubber soled deck shoes and moved into the corridor.

Falk knew he'd accidentally banged against the wheelhouse and could have been heard. Quickly opening the wheelhouse door, he entered and eased it shut. He crouched between the Captain's chair and the control panel and waited.

Chapter 45

Marco sat opposite the old man and knew his only chance of remaining alive was to go along with him.

As he started to speak, Pegmanti held up his thin bony hand. "You're wondering why I'm offering you a chance to live. Correct?"

Marco nodded.

"I've discovered there is a plot to kill my wife and daughter." He stared at the flickering flames in the hearth. "I'm not concerned about me. I deserve to be killed after the life I've lived." He turned toward Marco. "But not my daughter."

Pegmanti shifted his frail body in the chair and continued. "There is an assassination plot to kill the pope along with other religious leaders from around the world. It will happen during the Sunrise Service. I want you to get the message to whomever it is you work for."

"How can I? I'm a prisoner in this house."

"When I leave you will come with me. My driver will exchange places with you. When he's found, he'll say that you overcame him and forced me to go with you."

"No one will believe that."

"I think they will when they find my driver tied up and unconscious." Pegmanti slipped a cell phone from his pocket. "I've contacted him. He knows what to do."

"Does your driver always come inside the house when he picks you up?"

"Of course not but he will today. I told him to bring me a thick scarf I left behind. I've had a nasty cold and don't want to catch pneumonia."

Marco was impressed. So the old bastard had it all figured out. "When's he coming?"

"In a few minutes. We have to be ready."

Five minutes later the door opened and the driver entered carrying a thick woolen scarf. Placing the scarf beside Pegmanti, he crossed to the drapes, removed a tasseled cord and placed it on a chair. Then he went to Marco and unlocked his cuffs. Next he removed his peaked chauffeur's cap and coat and turned his back to them.

Pegmanti ordered Marco, "Tie his hands behind him with the cord. Make them secure and hurry."

Marco obeyed and within seconds had the driver securely tied. Pegmanti handed Marco a leather sap.

"He must look as if he was attacked." The driver looked at Pegmanti and nodded.

Marco took the weapon and quickly carried out orders. The driver slumped to the carpet without a sound.

Pegmanti arched his thick white eyebrows. "You've used one of those before, young man. Put on his coat and cap and hurry. Turn up the collar and stay at my side until we're at the car then open the rear passenger door. Once I'm in, close it, get in and drive away. Don't speed. I don't want to raise suspicion." Pegmanti wound the scarf around his neck.

Marco shrugged into the coat, pulled on the hat, tugging the peak low, took a deep breath and stood at Pegmanti's side. "Let's go."

No one saw them as they walked to the front door. Outside, one of the guards nodded as they went down the stone steps to the car. "Good night, sir."

Once behind the wheel, Marco had to restrain himself from tromping on the gas as he drove away from the house. Once through the gate he turned and headed down Rockledge Road, headlights sweeping through the curves.

"When we get to Sunset, I'll give you directions to my home in Bel-Aire. I shall remain in hiding until I'm certain you have contacted your superiors and I know my wife and daughter are safe."

Pegmanti reached into his pocket, removed Marco's radio and leaned forward. "Keep your eyes on the road and reach back and take this." The radio went from hand to hand. "Many lives depend on you, Marco. Don't fail."

Imminent Danger

Chapter 46

Grant and Nell arrived at the Harbor Master's office. Grant, in his usual swashbuckling manner, threw his weight around flashing his badge despite being seated on an electric scooter. He demanded to know if any of his agents were asking questions.

The woman who gave Falk the information about the location of Massy's boat was ashen-faced. "I can't tell you anything. I was warned I would be committing a federal offense against the Securities Act in a time of war."

Grant looked at her in utter amazement. "They told you that?"

"Yes."

"*I'm* in charge of the DHS task force. They work for me."

"I still can't discuss our conversation, sir."

"There will be trouble if you don't."

"Not as much trouble as having a federal charge against me in a time of war."

"Oh for God's sake, woman..."

The woman glanced across the room as the door opened and a ruddy complexioned man entered. "What's the problem, Marge?"

Marge moved closer to the newcomer. She quickly updated him.

"I'm the Harbor Master and what this woman told you is true. She reported the entire meeting between the two agents to me."

"Fine. She's seen my credentials and I want to know what they wanted and where they were going after leaving this building. You can call Washington and verify who I am."

The harbor master was a tall, well-built man who eyed Grant with a withering look. "I did twenty-five years in the Navy, young man. I know what it is to disobey orders or federal regulations."

"Then pick up the phone and call this number."

Grant reached into his pocket, removed a calling card and handed it to the harbor master. "Make it fast. A lot of people are in imminent danger of a terrorist attack. We don't have time to waste."

The harbor master heard the harsh tone of urgency in Grant's order. "Marge, call this number and let me know when you get through." She took the card and scurried from the room, happy to be away from the argument.

Grant drove the scooter to the window and glared out across the channel.

In less than five minutes Marge and the HM were back in the room. "Washington wants to speak with you." Marge handed the phone to Grant.

"This is Grant. Who's this?" Grant's face tightened. "Yes. I understand, sir." He listened to his boss bring him up-to-date on who Koski and Falk actually were.

The voice in his ear continued. "Allow them to continue whatever they've arranged regarding this case and for God's sake give that woman a written note telling her she won't be prosecuted by the government." There was a pause and Grant heard a sigh. "I heard you had a broken leg and were in the hospital. What the hell are you doing at the Marina?"

"I have an electric scooter, sir, and I wanted to get back on the job."

"Your entire handling of this operation so far has been a cock-up, Grant." His boss hung up.

This was Grant's debut assignment for DHS, and his boss was all over him. He considered his operation a complete failure. He *had* to make some good points…and fast.

Jamul exited the helicopter. Seething, he went directly to his suite. He'd been unable to raise Massy on the radio and it was almost time for the first guests to arrive. Rita Massy was the official greeter, allowing Jamul time to make his grand entrance.

He called her cell phone again. Still no answer. Jamul was not only angry, a tinge of fear entered his thoughts. He must remain calm. There was too much at stake. He contacted the yacht's captain, instructing him to be prepared to greet the guests and continue as host until Massy arrived.

On the other side of the channel, Koski watched the trawler intently for any sign of movement. She knew Falk had gone back on board after Massy. Moving a little closer but still hugging the shadows, she gazed across the channel at the lights of the *Caviare*. Her main task was to be sure Falk was okay. A slight crackle in her ear indicated Falk had switched on his phone. She waited for his voice—nothing. Koski tensed then realized his phone was open. He was broadcasting to keep her up to speed. Falk was in trouble.

Massy crept closer to the wheelhouse. She pressed back against a wall when a commanding voice told her to drop her weapon. Throwing herself to the deck, Massy fired three shots toward the voice and heard breaking glass.

"Unless you want to bleed out on your boat, lady, throw your weapon up here." Falk could dimly see a darker mass down in the salon.

Massy obviously had no intentions of dying. "Don't shoot!" She tossed the Glock into the wheelhouse and heard it clatter across the wooden planking.

"Stay where you are, Koski. I'm okay," he whispered. He knew she'd heard the shots and was already down on the dock next to the boat. He saw her crouching beside one of the lockers. Her eyes never left the wheelhouse.

"Okay, Doctor. Come out with your hands on your head," Falk ordered as he eased up from behind the helm controls.

Massy crawled into view, her hair still a mess.

"Over there." Falk indicated with the barrel of his automatic. "Back against the wall. Keep your hands on your head." He checked her for any other weapons. "We're going to the Coast Guard station. You have a lot of questions to answer. But first, you're going to clear our lines and if you try anything I'll drop you on the spot. Understood?"

Massy nodded. She went out the door onto the deck. Falk followed close behind. She jumped to the dock, went forward, let off the bowline, turned and went aft for the stern lines.

Falk watched every move as he heaved the lines onboard. "Okay, back onboard and make it quick."

In the seconds it had taken Massy to go to the forward line, Koski had nimbly crossed the dock and was on deck in seconds, crouched behind a hatch.

"Nice work. Stay out of sight." She smiled and readjusted the earpiece. Falk had seen her.

"You did well, Doctor Massy. Now get over here and start her up."

Massy fired up the engines and started to flip toggles.

"Forget the lights," Falk ordered. "Move across the channel and find a mooring close to the Coast Guard station."

"We can't cut across the channel without navigation lights. Marina Del Rey takes a dim view of breaking the rules of the road."

"I'm sure they do but we're going to break them now so move out."

Massy spun the wheel and eased the boat away from the dock. Falk picked up a pair of binoculars and focused in on *Caviare*, secure in the knowledge he had Koski as backup. He could see guests on the deck sipping drinks and enjoying the evening.

Massy thrust the throttles forward. She spun the wheel, causing the boat to heel to starboard and knocking Falk off balance. At the same time she kicked him at the base of his spine.

Koski leapt into the cockpit and slammed a karate chop into Massy's carotid artery. She staggered across the deck, hit the rail and went overboard. The trawler was now under full power and churned out across the main channel. It streamed a phosphorus wake and narrowly missed a sailboat heading up channel.

Yells from the sailboat were lost in the roar of twin diesels as the boat continued an out of control rampage across the channel. Falk clawed to his feet, grasped the helm and fought to get command of the bucking vessel. At the same time, he desperately reached into the darkness for the throttle controls.

Chapter 47

A flashlight beam swept across the control panel and Koski's voice called out, "Back off the throttles, Joe."

"They're jammed. They won't move!" Koski was at his side in seconds. Together they attempted to pull back on the controls but they remained locked at full throttle. Pounding across the channel at full speed with no lights was akin to taking a chance driving the wrong way in the fog on the interstate. Falk reached for the ignition key and turned off the engine. The sudden silence after the roar of the motors and the slowing of the forward movement was sweet. The Grand Banks slowed to a wallowing motion in mid-channel.

"Get that beam on the panel, Koski. Find the light switch before we get run down." Koski located the switches and a second later the cabin and navigation lights came on. Red and green never looked so good. Falk realized they were closer now to the *Caviare* and that people had watched the mad dash across the channel and the sudden stop and were crowding the rails wondering what was going on.

"Hit every light switch you can find. Get below and turn on the main salon. Light this boat up."

Koski quickly carried out the order as Falk called the Coast Guard station.

Nothing happened. He redialed. Still nothing. The phone was useless. He yelled to Koski. "Something's wrong with my phone. Could have happened when I fell. Let me have yours."

She tossed him her phone.

"This is Agent Falk. Put the lieutenant on and make it fast." Within seconds he was speaking with the officer.

"We need your help, Lieutenant. We could do with a tow, two scuba diving suits and double tanks for both. I'll fill you in when you arrive."

Passengers on the sloop found the trawler a point of interest. The excitement grew when a searchlight from an approaching USCG cutter stabbed through the darkness as it neared the drifting craft.

It was more than excitement that surged through Jamul's body when he recognized Massy's trawler. Returning to his quarters, he snapped on a two-way radio and tried to raise Massy. No answer. He could see the USCG cutter going alongside, lines thrown across the decks as several men jumped aboard. Damn! What happened to the fool? This was the last thing he needed. Grabbing a pair of binoculars he focused in on the action and saw the boat was about to be towed in.

Each of Jamul's trawlers was fitted with a self-destruct system. Despite the thoroughness of security on each craft, there was always a possibility that some forensic evidence could lead back to him. If someone had boarded Rita Massy's boat, it had to go.

Jamul dialed a preset frequency on his radio to trigger the explosive device system that would disintegrate the vessel and everyone aboard with a touch of his finger. He had to be certain the USCG hauled the boat far enough away from his sloop before triggering.

He watched as the crew got the trawler in tow and headed back toward the USCG dock.

Passengers on the *Caviare* lost interest as the boat moved away. Jamul watched; his finger hovering above the switch that would obliterate Massy's folly. Jamul had a perfect view of the port side of the Grand Banks up-channel twenty feet behind the cutter. What he didn't see were the two scuba divers who slid into the water from the starboard side and dove deep as the doomed boat wallowed its way to eternity.

Koski's phone rang continuously as it sat on a bunk next to her clothes in the cabin.

Tom Stewart cursed, tossed his phone aside and addressed Wolf. "I can't reach Falk or Koski, Doc. We have a problem."

Imminent Danger

Chapter 48

They came for him as he knew they would. He was ready. A small suitcase sat on the floor next to the front door. When the bell chimed Pegmanti opened the door himself.

Two men stood at the top of the steps. One of them showed his ID and asked, "Mr. Pegmanti?"

"Yes." He picked up the case. "My wife and daughter...?"

"They're safe, sir. Come with us."

Enrico Pegmanti walked down the steps, stopped and looked back at the house, wondering if he'd ever see it again. Shaking his head, he turned toward the car, an agent's hand on his elbow. His wife and daughter were safe. He'd made his decision. There was no looking back. It was time for his last confession.

One of the agents held open the passenger door and the other took his suitcase. Suddenly the sharp crack of a high-powered rifle seemed to make the world stand still. Two more shots fired from the direction of a group of trees near the house hit Pegmanti in the face and neck.

Enrico Pegmanti, a man who had lived his life on his own terms, died without a sound.

After calling for an ambulance, one of the agents called Stewart. "He's dead, sir. Sniper—happened in a matter of seconds. Pegmanti had a small suitcase with him."

"Bring it in right away," Stewart snapped.

Deep below the icy channel, Falk glanced at the luminous dial of his wrist compass. He swam ahead of Koski as they headed for Jamul's sloop.

Koski, to his right and slightly behind, followed in the wake caused by his flippers. The water was inky black. Falk had requested the lieutenant send the compass as part of the scuba equipment along with an innovative piece of underwater hardware, a multi-node miniature transmitter. It was smaller than a pack of cigarettes and designed to attach to metal by a powerful magnet.

The transmitter emitted a signal to allow a receiver ashore to log an exact location up to a distance of several hundred miles via satellite hook-up. Perhaps its greatest asset was that an onshore operator could activate the receiver section of the underwater transmitter any time, sending a mega-high frequency signal through the metal of a ship's steering mechanism, disturbing all electronic flow on board. This totally disabled the electrical system. Controlled by an onshore operator, it was equal to reaching out and cutting the boat's main power switch.

They weren't using flashlights in case someone on deck noticed a glimmer of light beneath the surface. Koski moved in beside Falk as he located a site on the *Caviare's* metal rudder. He'd arranged with Koski that he would signal when the time came to back away from the vessel.

Swimming as a team was standard operating procedure and in many cases had proved to be a lifesaver. Now, Koski was close enough to make out his shadowy presence as he clamped on the electronic device and tested it to assure it remained in place. He was turning; ready to give the signal to follow him back to the dock where the Coast Guard lieutenant had promised to be waiting with the car.

Koski saw Falk's signal and turned. Suddenly a rib crushing THUD and a water amplified concussion wave flung them both hard against the side of the sloop. Ten feet beneath the waters of the channel, they were swirled like dolls. Koski's mask ripped from her face and for a few seconds she didn't know if she was facing up or down. She was totally disorientated by the violent turbulence. The swirling darkness and the need for air caused her to grab wildly for her mask and mouthpiece.

Falk fought hard to remain upright, knowing Koski was in trouble. She had been close enough when he gave the signal to move out. Suddenly she cartwheeled past, her mask and mouthpiece torn from her face.

Frantic he reached toward her but she wasn't there! Ignoring the mind-altering ringing in his ears, he dove even deeper. His arms and hands were outstretched in a desperate attempt to find her.

On the surface, those on the deck of the *Caviare* were shocked to see the Grand Banks trawler suddenly erupt in an orange fireball. The stern lifted high out of the water as the shattering roar of an explosion rent the quiet evening.

Jamul watched the trawler, now blazing from stem to stern, roll onto its side, spewing black clouds of oily smoke. Within minutes it slid beneath the waters. The tow cable from the Coast Guard cutter thrashed the turbulent waters like a hungry sea serpent. Fast action by one of the Coast Guard crew in cutting the cable saved the cutter from going under.

Jamul remained at the porthole. No one would find anything in the remains of Massy's boat. He left his cabin and went topside to share his supposed shock with his guests.

A fat man with a drink in his hand stood at the rail amid a crowd of nervous guests as Jamul walked up beside him.

"What in the hell happened?" the man asked. "Was it a terrorist attack or something?"

Jamul shook his head. "I doubt it. An engine room explosion I'd guess."

"You'd think the Coast Guard would have known something was wrong before towing the vessel," the fat man said indignantly.

"I think they were as shocked as we were." Jamul didn't recognize the man but knew he was doing the right thing, mixing and acting as mystified as the others. Then he saw the mayor plowing towards him. This man he did know.

"Jamul," the mayor rasped. "We were almost blown out of the channel. What's happening?" The mayor's fat face was gray with fright and he licked his thick lips with every other word he uttered.

"Good evening, Mr. Mayor. Glad to see you're okay. Seems the craft the Coast Guard was towing blew up in mid-channel. We're lucky they weren't any closer to us. It could have caused major problems."

"We need better security, damn it. If this is any example of the security being supplied by the DHS to a group of people like us tonight, I have little trust in them."

"We can't blame the DHS, Mr. Mayor," Jamul stated.

"We can and I do. You have some very important people aboard your yacht, Jamul. DHS is going to hear from me and I'm not the only one aboard who will raise hell. I've already considered contacting the President and cancelling tomorrow's Sunrise Service."

"But Mr. Mayor, it's a long-standing tradition. We can't let something like this cancel tomorrow's event. Think of all the dignitaries who have traveled from around the world to stand together; so many religions showing a unity never before known. The world will think they don't have the faith to pray together."

Jamul laid it on thick and the mayor, his political mind tuned to every word, nodded in agreement. "Perhaps you're right. Nonetheless I will insist that security at the Bowl be doubled."

"A wise decision, Mr. Mayor," Jamul purred as he moved toward another group of VIPs on deck. The majority of his guests acted calmly although he knew many were worried. Acts of terrorism had become a way of life no matter where you went.

"Was that a terrorist attack, the explosion out there?"

Jamul turned to see an elderly woman point across the channel with her champagne glass as she looked up at him from under a mass of white curly hair. He recognized her as one of the city council members but her name escaped him.

"Of course not," Jamul said. "Rest assured we have the best security on and around the boat. I can promise you the evening won't be spoiled in any way."

A tall, gaunt man joined them. "Gussy, I'm sure Jamul will see that we remain safe here tonight and tomorrow."

Jamul recognized Assemblyman Jason Grainger and his wife. Jamul immediately took over. "There you are, Mrs. Grainger. Your husband knows I will do everything in my power to see that you and everyone aboard tonight have a wonderful time, and a safe and memorable Easter Morning Service.

I've heard there's a possibility the Pope himself will be present."

Gussy smiled demurely and with practiced skill deftly lifted another flute of champagne off a passing tray. "I suppose so but in my position on the council I have to be sure all goes well."

"I assure you it will. Now you must excuse me. I have to be certain all is ready for our dinner below."

Mr. and Mrs. Grainger sipped and smiled as Jamul headed across the deck.

"What a wonderful man," Gussy sighed. "I knew from the first moment I met him, he was just what we needed in this city. I told the mayor..."

Jason nodded. "Yes, yes, dear. I'm sure you did. I see someone over there I have to say hello to." He moved away from his wife, leaving her standing on the deck with a faraway smile, trying to see where the waiter and the drink tray had gone.

Imminent Danger

Chapter 49

Koski quit trying to claw for her mask. She knew she was going to drown. As a young girl, she overheard an aunt say that drowning was a peaceful way to go. Now, with her lungs seeming ready to burst through her rib cage, she knew her aunt was wrong.

As Koski sank deeper into the numbing ice cold water, she lost the will to fight. She wanted to open her mouth, suck in and speed up the inevitable. Her downward drift stopped abruptly and a hand clamped her nostrils shut. Something pushed into her mouth and life-restoring air rushed from Falk's breathing apparatus in a cloud of bubbles. He wrapped one arm around her waist and kicked hard for the surface.

She breathed again and automatically kicked toward the surface. Falk quickly removed the mouthpiece, sucked air and returned it to her. He dove deep to get her and they'd have to share his air on their assent. The darkness and uncertainty of how many feet he had to cover before getting to safety depended on his self-control and strength.

After what seemed an eternity they broke the surface. He gratefully breathed in the night air, shaking his head to clear his vision and settle the nausea rising in the pit of his stomach. They were several hundred feet behind the *Caviare's* stern and close to several small sailboats at anchor. The boats afforded them shelter from the lights along the walkway of Fisherman's Village.

Koski gasped as Falk removed her mouthpiece and pulled her into the shadows of a dingy tied behind a sailboat.

"You're okay. Spit it out. You're okay."

179

Her face was deathly pale and her short blonde hair plastered to her head. She opened her eyes, sputtered and coughed. "I thought I was dead."

"Few more seconds and you would've been."

"I'm so cold, Joe."

"First, help me get you into that dingy. Can you do that?"

She nodded weakly. He pulled her to the side of the craft and passed her a rope running from the boat. "I'll go aboard from the stern so I don't tip the boat then I'll haul you in. You okay?"

Koski's teeth chattered. "Yeah, but hurry."

Falk was in the dingy in seconds. Even the heavy tank and equipment hadn't slowed him. He turned and reached for Koski. He yanked her into the boat and covered her with a piece of tarp he found stuffed under the wooden seat. He slipped off his tank and laid it beside her, placing the mouthpiece in her hand.

"Take a drag as you need it. I'll be fast as I can."

She nodded. Falk squeezed her hand, slid over the side and swam silently to the dockside to locate a ladder. He was fully aware that suddenly climbing out of the channel in a wetsuit after an explosion was cause for one of the many security people around the area to shoot first and ask questions later.

When Pegmanti's suitcase arrived, Stewart snapped it open. Dr. Wolf was at his side.

"Let's see what he was carrying," Stewart said as he took out a thick manila envelope and laid it on the table before removing an old cigar box. Stewart tugged the envelope open and removed a sheaf of typewritten papers. "Business correspondence between Pegmanti Industries and some of its customers." He thumbed through the pages quickly.

Wolf looked over Stewart's shoulder. "Yes. I recognize some of the company names. Why was he carrying those?"

"We'll know soon enough. I'll have a team go through them at once. Go ahead, Doc. Check out the cigar box."

Wolf released a small metal clasp and lifted the lid. A plump human finger with a diamond ring attached lay on a blood-soaked paper towel.

"My God," Wolf whispered.

Stewart peered into the box. "Paul Horn's ring finger was amputated. The police haven't revealed that fact. It's part of the ongoing investigation."

"You think it was sent to Pegmanti as a warning?"

Stewart nodded. "Yeah and the motivating factor that made him decide to use Marco as a means to escape."

Wolf looked up. "Where is Marco?"

"I don't know. I'll have to get in touch with this Nell woman."

Despite repeated attempts, Stewart was unable to reach Nell or dig up any information from DHS in Washington on the whereabouts of Agent Grant. He hung up and the phone rang at once. "Stewart." It was Grant's boss in Washington.

"I'm calling to give you a heads up. I had a call from Agent Grant. He has a broken leg and is trying to operate from a goddamn electric scooter. Haul his ass in."

Stewart grunted. "Where is he?"

"The Harbor Master's office in Marina Del Rey."

"Give me his number. We'll get right on it. In the meantime, tell your people working security for the *Caviare* to evacuate everyone. *Right now.*"

Falk located ladder rungs built into the dock wall so boat owners could access their small craft. He slipped off his fins and hooked them onto his equipment belt and then carefully started to climb. He used the glow from the dockside lights as a guide and carefully raised his head above the dock's edge. All clear. He was about to complete his climb onto the walkway when he heard someone coming. He remained motionless as the sound of footsteps grew closer. He had to get help for Koski. If he suddenly appeared on the dock a trigger-happy security guard might shoot him. The footsteps stopped a few feet from the top of the ladder. Damn!

He gripped a rung with one hand and unhooked one of the fins, took a deep breath and hurled it far out into the channel. The splash caused the person above to immediately turn toward the water and lean forward. Falk, moving with the speed of a striking viper, grabbed the man's leg.

The man reacted in terror. Something coming out of the darkness was the last thing he expected. Falk was up and over the edge of the dock. One fast blow with the side of the remaining heavy flipper into the security officer's neck was all it took.

Falk dragged the unconscious man into a darkened entranceway of one of the stores and waited. He heard the distant sound of music coming from the sloop. He slipped out of the scuba equipment. He removed the guard's uniform, secured the man with his own handcuffs and pulled on the uniform. He made sure the guard's nine millimeter automatic was cocked and loaded then strode toward the *Caviare*.

Chapter 50

"Sorry to break up the party early folks." The voice of the officer in charge of security came over the speakers of the *Caviare*. The music stopped. Jamul was dumbstruck. No one had informed him of any impending announcement. Standing beside the mayor there was little he could do except listen.

"Due to safety precautions we must ask you all to leave in an orderly fashion. No need to panic. Members of the Coast Guard and Department of Homeland Security are standing by to assist in your departure. Thank you."

Jamul excused himself and went topside. Once on deck he was shocked to see so many armed security personnel. The dockside was swarming.

Jamul approached one of the ranking officers. "This is an outrage. Who authorized this? I'm entertaining very important people."

"Direct from the President, sir," the officer replied.

Jamul began to speak but the officer cut him off. "Sorry, sir. Orders." Jamul was fuming. He didn't intend to let tomorrow morning's event turn into a failure.

The security personnel and the passengers leaving the sloop made perfect cover for Falk. Within minutes, he was in the Coast Guard station arranging for assistance for Koski. Two medical corpsmen left at once.

Falk stood in the deep shadow of a building close to the sloop as the passengers filed down the forward and aft gangplanks. Now that Koski was well cared for he moved forward. He walked up one of the gangways with a group of security personnel. It was the perfect chance to check out the sloop.

"You three guys." Falk turned as an officer ordered, "Get below. Be

183

sure everyone's off this boat." Falk didn't need a second invitation. As he followed the two men ahead to a companionway, he saw a tall black man in an argument with a security officer. He recognized Jamul immediately. Once they were below, the two security men stayed together and went forward. Falk went aft seeking the captain's quarters.

As Falk clattered below with the other two men, he missed seeing Agent Greg Grant carried down the gangplank. His scooter was hauled off between two security men while his assistant, Nell, followed. Grant tried unsuccessfully to assure the two burly guards that he was from the DHS as he reached for his ID. Once off the ship, he found himself plunked dockside. The two guards turned and went back aboard, thinking whoever it was must have been nuts.

"Nell, back to the Coast Guard station," Grant fumed. "This is ridiculous." She had to trot to keep up with him as he recklessly drove along the dockside through the crowds leaving the sloop.

Color slowly returned to Koski's cheeks as she sat wrapped in a red blanket, sipping a mug of hot chocolate in the Coast Guard station. She heard raised voices in the vestibule. She recognized Grant's voice immediately.

"I was carried off the boat. I insist you let me back onboard. I'm investigating a very important case."

Koski leaned forward, not wanting to miss a word. The lieutenant's voice cheered her to no end.

"The order came from the top to evacuate the boat, Agent Grant. Orders are being carried out." He paused. "Are you *sure* your superiors know you're working with a broken leg and riding an electric scooter?"

"Yes, damn it, they do."

Koski opened the office door. With the blanket draped around her shoulders, mug in hand, she made an imposing figure. "Greg! I thought I recognized your voice. Nell! What are you doing here?"

Grant glared. "Where's Falk?"

"It's a long story." She held up her mug. "Either of you want cocoa?"

Nell shook her head. "Koski, you look pale."

"I just got hauled out of the channel…"

"You were on the boat that blew up?"

"We got off before it actually exploded."

Greg wheeled in closer. "So where's Falk?"

Koski knew he'd keep badgering her until she told him. "On the yacht is my guess," she said calmly.

Greg's eyes narrowed. "It's being evacuated. No one's allowed aboard."

Koski shrugged. "Then I suggest we stay here until we get updated."

"Not me," Grant growled. "Come on, Nell. We've places to go. Let's move it."

Koski took a swig of her hot drink then peered over the rim. "New job, Nell?"

"I'm his aide, part-time." Nell was quickly discovering that being this guy's aide was crazy. She seemed glad when the lieutenant told Grant he wasn't going anywhere.

The area below deck was tight. Falk moved aft with caution. The other two guards going forward gave him the perfect opportunity to check Jamul's quarters.

"Can I help you?" Falk spun around. Jamul was standing behind him.

"Security. Orders to clear the yacht," answered Falk.

"I heard the orders, officer."

"Agent, sir; DHS."

Jamul's eyes flashed. "Excuse me, agent?"

"Captain, I have orders to be certain the ship is clear of passengers and crew."

"Fine. I'll accompany you but first I need something from my cabin." Jamul led the way to his quarters. Falk followed, somewhat surprised at the unassuming manner. A few minutes earlier he'd seen him arguing with a deck officer.

Was this tall, gregarious man truly a born again Muslim, craving to be instrumental in arranging an opportunity for world religions to come together or was he a major player in a terrorist plot?

Jamul stopped, unlocked the polished mahogany door of his cabin then waved Falk inside. Jamul sauntered in behind him, headed to a built-in wardrobe and removed a leather flight jacket. "There are so many details and so little time."

Falk stood in the large cabin and eyed an amazing array of electronic equipment.

"My hobby, Agent Falk," Jamul drawled. "Modern day equivalent of Ham Radio. Electronics have come a long way since those days." He nodded toward the wall. "Transmitter-receiver, television-radio and computer technology all combined. Worldwide satellite capability, too, of course." Jamul smiled, opening his arms wide. "Show business tools of the twenty-first century."

Falk studied the array. "Captain, we're due topside. Once you're ashore DHS can finish its sweep of the sloop."

Jamul nodded. "Of course and I must fly to the Bowl and oversee last minute details."

Falk remained silent as he followed Jamul out of his cabin.

Chapter 51

Koski was edgy as she watched the passengers and crew stream past the Coast Guard station windows in full evacuation.

"Why is everyone being taken off?" Nell asked. "If the boat is in danger and we're this close don't you think we should be moving out, too?"

"Precautionary procedure," Grant muttered. "We'll have to wait here for a heads up." Grant's boss had instructed the USCG that Grant remain at the station.

Koski had no idea where Falk was. She knew he'd made it to shore and arranged for her to be picked up. Was he on the yacht? She craned her neck to get a better view. There were no more passengers going down *Caviare's* gangplanks. The vessel had an empty look. Why would he remain behind? Something was wrong. She had to locate him.

Koski casually mentioned she had to go to the ladies room.

"I'll come with you," Nell said. Koski gritted her teeth.

"Don't take too long, ladies," Grant called as they went out the door. "We may have to move at a moment's notice."

"How do we find the washroom?" Koski asked.

"First door down the hall, on the left," replied a young Coast Guardsman.

Once in the bathroom, she turned to Nell. "Stall for me. I don't want Grant to know I'm gone."

"Gone where?"

"To find Falk," she said softly. "Stay here as long as you can. If anyone asks, make up a story. Give me as much time as possible."

Arriving topside, Jamul located the officer in charge and informed him he was flying to the Bowl to check out last minute details and security. Jamul's lips were set in a grim line as he lifted the copter off. He glimpsed the last of his evacuated guests shuffling back to their waiting cars.

At the foot of the gangplank, Koski flashed her badge and security gave her clearance to proceed. She caught sight of the Coast Guard lieutenant and called, "I'm looking for Agent Falk. Have you seen him?"

"I just came aboard. I was dockside overseeing the evacuation. What makes you think he's aboard?"

"A hunch I guess." Koski's face brightened. "Hold it. There he is." She moved swiftly across the deck to where Falk was speaking with the deck officer who told Jamul to obey orders and leave the boat.

"Hey. You're supposed to be recouperating in the Coast Guard station," Falk said.

"I've recouped, Joe."

Falk put his arm around her shoulders. "This is my partner. She's supposed to be on light duty."

"Nice to meet you, ma'am," the officer replied, touching the peak of his cap.

"We were discussing Jamul," Falk explained. "He's taken off for the Bowl. I was with him in his cabin."

Koski nodded eagerly. "And?"

Falk shook his head. "Other than seeing his array of electronics— zilch."

"Security is checking them out as we speak," the officer added. "Everything's normal."

Falk rubbed his chin. "I suggest every piece is checked out closely. Haul everything over to the Federal building in Westwood. The Feds have the tools and personnel."

"We'll get on it right away," the officer replied. "Nice meeting you, ma'am." He turned and headed aft.

Chapter 52

A debriefing by an expert is a harrowing experience. Marco blew out his cheeks and sighed. "Man! I've answered all your questions. What more do you want?"

"You're doing great."

A wooden table and a plastic cup of Coke separated Marco from his inquisitor. The agent finished his cigarette and stubbed it out in an overflowing ashtray. "I must be sure you haven't forgotten any small detail about Enrico Pegmanti that might help us."

"Unless you have a new stack of questions, man, I've said it all. I was with him less than an hour, including the drive to his home."

The agent looked up as he lit another cigarette. "I do have a few more. Once we're through you'll see Mr. Stewart." Marco watched the man studying his notes. He wondered if telling Stewart he could gather information that would break up a terrorist cell had been such a good idea. He sipped the Coke, glad he was still alive. He knew, however, that things would never go back to what they were.

The phone rang and Marco's interrogator answered, "Agent Martin." Glancing at Marco he said, "Almost through." Hanging up, he started the tape recorder beside him again.

Tapping his notebook he said, "When you've answered these you'll be on your way."

Gully was ready. He'd practiced for hours concealing the plastic bio weapon he was going to use at the Sunrise Service. No word from Massy. Not that he expected any. That bitch was a stone killer. If anything went wrong tomorrow, he knew he would be among the first to die.

Now, standing before a full-length mirror in his bedroom, he repeated the movements. He raised his arm and pointed at a crucifix on the wall, making sure the plastic weapon remained hidden in his gloved hand out of sight. He nodded back at his reflection. Perfect. This time tomorrow he'd be on a plane winging to Rio with enough money to live the rest of his life in the sun.

The house on Rockledge was no longer useful as a safe haven. The Marco and Pegmanti escapade had seen to that.

Jamul's helicopter tilted a 180 and headed out over the coastline toward Catalina Island. Jamul's destination was a small souvenir shop in Avalon named Catalina Curios. For over twenty years it had served tourists, creating a steady stream of customers. It was easy for anyone to enter and exit without suspicion. A perfect set up, run by a husband and wife who'd lived on the island for as long as they had owned the shop.

The community knew them as a friendly couple in their late sixties, spending their twilight years on the island. In reality, their income came from a Syrian cartel in Damascus.

Jamul leaned back, clenching his jaw tightly as he thought how the centers of control in the Middle East had shifted since the Iraqi conflict. American presence had shaken the once complacent regime of various terrorist organizations worldwide, from the green countryside of Northern Ireland to the desolate mountains of Afghanistan and Iran and across to the shores of Gaza, Lebanon, Syria and beyond.

Tomorrow's operation *must* go perfectly. It would show the world that al-Qaida could still select a target and carry out the plan despite the boasting of Americans at home and abroad. This attack was meant to make the highly touted Department of Homeland Security look inept. It also would rekindle a flame in the breast of Islam, igniting like a band of fire around the Arab world.

The helicopter began its descent and Jamul concentrated, guided by a single light below. There was a car waiting for him. He allowed himself an hour, less if possible, to make the visit and be back at the Bowl before two a.m. The soft thud of landing skids on grass announced his arrival.

Three Middle Eastern men sat in a small back room office of Catalina Curios. They looked up as Jamul entered, escorted by a bodyguard.

"Welcome, Jamul." A small, wizened man rose from his chair at the table. "Allow me to introduce my friends."

"Thank you," Jamul's deep voice rumbled. "That won't be necessary. It's better if I know as little as possible. You understand."

The man smiled. "We understand." Nodding to the guard the wrinkled man indicated a chair be placed at the table.

Jamul slid onto the seat and folded his arms. "There have been problems at the Marina. We might have to cancel the event."

The men straightened and a murmur of disbelief rose as Jamul continued. "I assure you it will be a last resort if such a thing were to happen. Nonetheless, too many unordinary occurrences over the last few days have alarmed me."

"We arranged the deaths of Pegmanti and Horn. No suspicion will fall upon you, Jamul."

Jamul shook his head. "Doctor Massy's boat was hijacked and her with it. I was able to destroy the boat before the Coast Guard searched it."

"That's very good, Jamul. You did well."

Jamul grimaced. "Perhaps, but I have no assurance that Doctor Massy went down with the boat. She may have been picked up. She could be questioned…"

The man slid the cuff of his jacket back and checked his watch. "We're only hours away from an enormous display of strength; a strike against the infidels that will demonstrate to the rest of Islam that we are not beaten. We will never stop. Despite whatever worries you have, we must go forward, Jamul. It's too late to stop. Go now. The safe house here on the island knows to expect you after the attack. Continue your work for our cause and may Allah shower his blessings upon you. Allah Akbar."

Jamul was aware that the Imam sitting before him could be the next President of Iraq. He could be voted in by popular demand and sanctioned by the United Nations. He also was aware that the cell on the island would continue to be a secret place to plan future attacks against America. He had his instructions. It was time to leave.

Chapter 53

Jamul landed the helicopter in an area designated for the LAPD skywatch copters. The police aircraft would continuously circle the Bowl throughout the service. Jamul had previously arranged with the mayor to have his aircraft use the landing pad. The city was always gracious to those who helped fill the coffers of commerce.

Now, stalking across the helipad, Jamul waved to the guards, who grinned and returned the salutation. He had given out over a thousand of his latest CDs to key personnel in the last two days. Everybody loved Jamul.

Arc lamps shone harshly across the stage, reflecting the white arch of the domed shell. Stagehands and technicians swarmed. They were pulling cables and calling orders, moving electronic equipment in one last effort to have everything in place.

Jamul watched from the seated area where in a matter of hours hundreds of worshippers would take their seats. He turned, scrutinizing the hills behind the last seats in the massive amphitheater. Few lights glowed, indicating the remoteness and seclusion of the homes.

Security constantly patrolled the Bowl. Jamul was aware that, despite the number of guards in the area, there were infiltrators. Massy's walking zombies, thoughtless obedient monsters of Islam. Armed and programmed to use their bio-lasers, they lay motionless in the darkness beneath special gauzy black cloths. They waited for their moment to kill before their transition to hell.

A chilly wind stirred through the Cahuenga Pass from the San Fernando Valley, rustling the leaves of the newly-planted saplings. The

193

bombs, cunningly nestled amid their root balls, awaited the transmitted signal to detonate.

Jamul planned on remaining at the Bowl for the rest of the night. He'd keep busy with last minute details. He planned to greet the famous as they arrived, pay homage to church leaders and curry favor with the various religious clerics. After opening the service as lead singer with the massed choir from all nations, he'd fade into the background before the assassinations and the dreadful roar of exploding bombs. Then he'd reappear and rush to help those in need.

Jamul moved toward the feverish activity on stage. A smile creased the edges of his lips as he recalled the words of Massy when she last reported on the serum's progress.

"They will walk among their own—unsuspected—infidels killing infidels. What more can we ask for?"

"Hey, boss, everything's ready for a final check." A brawny man in blue jeans sporting a gray ponytail waved from the stage.

Jamul returned a mock salute. "Be right there, my man."

Koski and Falk returned to the Coast Guard station with the lieutenant. Falk said, "We're going to need a car, lieutenant."

"Agent Grant's SUV is in the parking lot."

"He's here?" Falk exclaimed.

Koski interrupted. "Joe, I was going to tell you…"

"That's okay. Let's get the vehicle. Lieutenant, I'd appreciate it if you don't mention who took it."

The officer led them to the SUV. "Wait here. I'll get the keys." He was back in a few minutes and gave the keys to Falk. "I told Grant we had to move it. It was blocking another car."

Falk slipped the ignition key off the key ring and handed the ring back. "Let's hope he doesn't miss the key until later."

"I'll stall him as long as I can."

"Thanks, Lieutenant. You've been a great help. I'll see it gets reported to the right people. One more thing." Falk scribbled a phone number on a piece of paper. "Have someone keep calling this number. When they get through, tell him to meet me at the Hollywood police station."

The officer nodded. "Good luck."

Falk turned on the ignition and headed for Hollywood.

Imminent Danger

Chapter 54

A little past three in the morning and activity at the Bowl was still intense. Jamul went about his usual routine before a concert, checking everything on stage, yet his mind kept returning to the *Caviare*. Was he under suspicion for his fast departure? Was he being watched?

He signaled the sound technician that he wanted a test on the main mike. He watched as it lowered toward the stage. It stopped at a predetermined spot where he would be standing when leading the choir. He beckoned to his soundman and gave him new orders. The man nodded and returned to his controls. Some workers noticed and stopped their activity as Jamul stood center stage, head tilted and eyes staring into the darkness.

The first tremulous note of an organ sounded. It was reed-like at the beginning then grew in tone and tenure, filling the massive speakers, swelling and expanding as the first bars of the opening hymn rippled through the night.

Then the organ stopped. There was a crash of silence as Jamul's mellow-toned voice picked up the note the organ left in midair and took it to a new dimension of a solo performance. Each word of the hymn was clear, sweet and amplified. Spreading out across the seating area, it caused guards at the very back, close to the hill behind the Bowl, to stop and listen in awe.

The workers on stage remained rooted in place. When he had finished they rewarded him with applause.

The test had relaxed him. He felt more in charge, more self-assured. The orders he'd given his soundman were to record the opening hymn, then, if need be, play it back in case of any last minute hitch that might keep him off stage. Already preparations were underway to let in the early arrivals. In a few hours the sun would begin to rise.

Stewart, Pease, Wolf and Marco had gone directly to the Hollywood station after the call from the USCG lieutenant. Now they were studying a large-scale map of the Hollywood Bowl with Falk, Koski and Captain Garvey. Garvey jabbed a stubby finger in its center. "I have men throughout this area, here, and going all the way around the Bowl's parameter. The DHS has their people and the FBI. Any unusual movement and we'll have them."

"Captain," Stewart's voice had a hard edge. "Our intelligence reports that the danger may already be in place." Hours of debriefing with Marco and Pease had intensified the realization they were up against an imminent danger that could cause worldwide repercussions.

"We can cancel the service," Garvey said. "Instigate another massive search, bomb squads, sniffer dogs, the works."

"This is a gathering of religions from around the globe, Captain. Perhaps for the first time in history so many diverse religions have agreed to come together and participate in a religious service. We blow the whistle and cancel this, America becomes known as the devil's handmaiden. Besides, as long as Jamul is there and we keep an eye on him, I think we still have a chance."

"I hear you, Tom but there's no guarantee Jamul will be there. Trust me. We should take him out—now." Falk spoke the words passionately.

"I know how you feel, Joe. We pull Jamul off the stage before the service starts and it'll be called everything from racism to an anti-religious, capitalistic sentiment by the rest of the world."

Falk remained silent before turning to Marco. "Marco, tell us where you were in the Bowl every day when you were working."

Marco waved his hand over the map. "All over. We were assigned different jobs when we came in every morning. I worked on a crew planting saplings and in the nursery stacking bags of steer shit. Things like that."

"Were you ever working on the stage, near it, under it, close to it?"

"No. Just hard labor, man. Lifting, digging, hauling stuff around outside. Like I said, only time I was inside was when I humped manure."

"Show me on the map the area you and the other guys worked in."

Marco stared at the map, walked around the table and squinted at it from a different angle. "That's the stage, right?" Falk nodded. Marco traced his finger around the side of the structure to where the nursery yard was located. He tapped his finger. "In and around there. We'd collect a bunch of saplings, load them onto flatbeds and haul them out to the job."

"Where was the location?"

"Different each day. We started there." He tapped the map again. "We worked our way back up the side of the Bowl, on the other side of the seating area—over here." He ran a finger in a circle. "We had to dig every hole with a post digger. Hard slow work."

Falk nodded. "I'll bet. How many did you plant each day?"

"Twenty of us on the team. We each planted about ten or fifteen I guess."

"Notice anything about them?"

"They were trees, man. That's all."

Falk rubbed his chin slowly. "Planted all along this side of the Bowl, right?"

"Yeah, and down along that side, across the back and down here."

Falk watched Marco trace an arc beyond the last row of seats then back toward the front of the Bowl."

"That's a lot of trees, Marco."

"Tell me about it."

"If your team each planted ten a day that's two hundred trees!" Koski exclaimed.

"We were told we were planting a new forest that one day would be a living monument to the Easter Sunday when the world came together and prayed."

Falk slapped his hand down hard on the map. "Let's move, Marco. We're going to dig up..."

"Joe, what the hell..." Stewart cut in.

"Those trees could be part of the plot. They surround the audience on both sides and at the back, possibly booby-trapped to detonate by remote radio transmission."

"So where does the mind-altering serum come in? What about the so-called zombies, Joe, and the Hollywood murders? How does all that fit in to the Hollywood Bowl?"

"I don't know. But we've got to check those trees."

Martin Pease spoke for the first time. "Someone will be out there with a biolog laser injector—possibly several of them."

Chapter 55

Falk, Koski and Marco flew to the Bowl in a police helicopter. Martin Pease had brought everyone up to speed on the chemical weapons most often used if any terrorist action was to take place. Upon landing, security led them to a small office next to the amphitheater.

The head of security, a tired-looking man in his fifties, pored over a detailed map of the Bowl with three DHS personnel. He looked up as the door opened. "Agents Falk and Koski." He eyed Marco. "Who's he?"

"Special witness, sir," Falk replied gruffly. "He's been cleared by Stewart."

"I'm Bob Sorenson. Glad to meet you." They shook hands.

"We have very little time, sir." Falk said.

"Yes. Stewart filled me in. He said your special witness helped plant the trees." He looked directly at Marco. "Were certain trees rigged?"

Marco shook his head. "Don't know. They all looked the same to me."

Sorenson cursed. "There are hundreds of trees and no time to start digging them up. Besides, they could be booby-trapped."

Falk's mind raced. Scores of bombs exploding simultaneously would kill hundreds, plus there would be others slain by biolog laser injectors. It didn't make sense. Why would Jamul remain on the stage if that was about to happen? The Pope and other church leaders would also be on stage. If any of them became casualties it could ignite a worldwide religious war. An incident of such massive proportions occurring on American soil would make the United States an international villain, responsible for any repercussions that might follow.

Falk spoke up. "We have to close the Bowl, Sorenson. The service must not go on, no matter how many religions we upset."

Sorenson spun around. "Special tactical teams plus my people are in place. DHS security and LAPD are covering every possible angle. We take control of any tree bombs. We can carry on."

Marco interrupted. "When we were held each night at the house on Rockledge, I could see the entire Bowl, the seating area, the amphitheater, everything."

"Go on," Falk said.

"I also got to see other things."

"Like what?"

"A bedroom full of electronic equipment, radios, computers and stuff. I got talking to one of the house cleaners and she told me it was an amateur shortwave station. Belongs to the owner. But it wasn't."

"How do you know?"

"My cousin, José, is a Ham operator. Been doing it since he was a kid. I knew him and his equipment. What I saw at the house was state-of-the-art digital."

"And they could transmit a signal to detonate bombs in the root balls, right, Marco?"

"I guess, but today you can detonate an explosive device from a cell phone."

Falk nodded. "True. Nonetheless, we're going up to the house. Sorenson, I suggest you assign several of your men to be with Jamul at all times, plus some he doesn't know about—just in case."

"Okay. I can spare a couple of men to go with you."

"Thanks. That won't be necessary."

Chapter 56

The house on Rockledge was dark. An air of emptiness hung about the place as Falk slowly drove past. "You said the grounds were patrolled at all times, right?"

"All the time," Marco answered. "There were lights on in the house and grounds 24/7. We had lights until ten then it was lights out for us."

Falk turned the car around, switched off the headlights then started slowly back along the road. "I don't see any sign of light in the house or on the grounds."

"Maybe they've gone," Koski whispered. "They'd have no need to hang around after the attack."

"I can take a look," Marco said.

"Wait. You and your crew were locked in the attic every night?"

"Like a jail," Marco snapped.

"Stay in the car with Koski. I'll check out the house."

Koski opened the glove compartment and removed a flashlight. "Take this."

"Go around back," Marco hissed. "There's a window next to the kitchen door that's easy to open, old-fashioned lock."

"You don't miss much, Marco."

"It's a hobby of mine, man."

Falk grunted and vanished into the darkness.

A sallow-faced man quietly sipped coffee in the attic. The only light was a dim glow emitting from a shielded dial light on a portable transmitter. His assignment was to detonate the tree bombs.

From his vantage point, he could clearly see when the first streaks of dawn glowed in the east over the Hollywood Bowl. When the lights dimmed and the sun crested the hills, he would open the window and listen to the strains of the opening bars of the organ followed by the voice of Jamul. Then the choir would merge into the famous Hallelujah Chorus. When the hymn ended and the religious dignitaries walked on stage, Jamul would slip away, and that would be his cue to detonate.

After the explosions, mass panic would grip the survivors. Gully would eliminate the VIPs on stage. Jamul would then appear heroically through the smoke and carnage to aid the wounded and dying. He'd be seen on worldwide television as a brave and caring person.

The man smiled thinly and poured a second cup of coffee from a thermos. Unlike Officer Gully, who would fly to Rio, he would remain in Los Angeles, where he'd retire and continue living in the small house in Silverlake. Maybe he'd buy the place. He would have enough money. He nodded and sipped. Yeah, he'd buy the house…like he and Jenny had once dreamed.

The memory of her voice floated in his mind, soft and sweet. "Take care of yourself, Vic." Just the way she used to when he left for work each day.

Chapter 57

Marco was right. The window slid open with little resistance and Falk climbed into a large, old-fashioned kitchen. He stood motionless. Except for an occasional drip-drip from one of the taps over the sink, all was silent.

He removed his shoes and set them on the windowsill. Next, he snapped on the flashlight, shielding the beam to a mere slit with his fingers. He carefully crossed to the door and pushed it open.

Moving with caution along the wooden planked corridor, he headed toward the front of the house. Where was the stairway? He paused, tilting his head from side to side, listening for the slightest sound. The building might be empty now but someone may return at any time. He picked out the outline of a banister and the lower steps of the staircase, carpeted in thick pile. He had the advantage of moving silently.

He carefully made his way to the second floor landing, stopped, paused, before turning right and softly opened the first door he came to. A bedroom, everything in order, as if it had recently been cleaned.

He checked three other rooms. Each was neat and clean. He looked into the remaining rooms. The fifth was different. Heavy drapes hung at the windows. Falk quickly closed them, making sure no light leaked out, then shut the door and switched on the light. At once, he saw the room was a workshop. Coils of electrical wire lay on the floor in a corner. A toolbox and soldering iron along with several schematics were piled next to it. Whatever had been there was long gone. Falk rapidly checked the rest of the room but found nothing significant.

Victor Young drained the last of his coffee from the thermos into his cup. It wouldn't be long now. He was dressed warmly. Nonetheless, the cold had crept into his bones. He needed to go down to the kitchen and make another thermos of coffee. He had time.

As he opened the attic door, Victor Young thought he heard a sound. Sliding a suppressed nine millimeter Colt from a shoulder holster, he stood on the landing. It might have been the wind, but he had to be sure. His investment was too great.

Young had lost his ambition when Jenny died. From that moment on he simply went through the motions of living. The police psychologist had worked to help him deal with his loss but sometimes, no matter how much assistance someone gets, he simply gives up.

Officer Young had given up. It then he'd been approached to become a stringer, an informer, someone who knew the inside workings of the LAPD. That included everyday procedures carried out by uniformed personnel. He'd been told the feedback was for an author wanting information for a book.

Young agreed. He realized he was going nowhere within the department and began to feed back bits of information. It was two years before he was informed whom he really was reporting to. By then it was too late.

His sudden assignment with Falk was a worrisome time. He wasn't about to let anything get in his way. The cell looked after their own. Each person was unto themselves, each a separate unit taking orders but never knowing the other members.

He had no idea that his friend, Officer Gully, was destined to be a featured part of the morning's horrors. Like many throughout history, two men had decided to betray for pay.

Young crept down the stairs, one hand holding the thermos, the other his nine millimeter. He stopped on the second floor landing and listened. All was quiet. It must have been the wind. By the time Victor reached ground level Falk was slipping on his shoes and sliding out the kitchen window.

Less than thirty seconds later Young turned on the kitchen light, crossed to the sink and filled a kettle with water. He set it on the stove and turned the heat on high.

Chapter 58

The blow that Koski administered to Massy on the trawler hadn't carried its full effect. The boats pitching and tossing had everyone off balance. As a result, the chop sent Massy reeling back against the rail and over the side. The moment she hit the water it was swim or die. A lifelong swimmer, she kicked off her deck shoes, struck out for the dock and merged into the darkness.

Fifteen minutes later, she dragged herself onto the dock a few yards from where they'd set sail. She lay shivering, gasping in great gulps of air. Finally getting to her feet, she staggered along the dock to her stowage locker, retrieved the hidden key from its place under a nearby ledge and opened the lid.

After drying herself as best she could on an old piece of rough canvas, she rummaged deeper among the collection of miscellaneous items that had gathered over the years. An old pair of blue jeans and—best of all—a thick, woolen, paint-splattered sweater. Quickly she shrugged it on then pulled the jeans on over her dress pants. No shoes, no problem. Her car was parked on the road. A spare key in a magnetic tin box was tucked under the front fender.

A thunderous roar and a vivid flash of flame abruptly lit up the dark channel. Massy shaded her eyes against the sudden glare. She knew at once that Jamul had triggered the doomsday switch on her boat. So much for the two meddlesome bastards from DHS.

Live-aboards on nearby boats came out on their docks and huddled in groups discussing what happened. Massy kept to the shadows as she made her way back to her car.

Once in the vehicle, she watched as the flames finally flickered out and the wreckage of her boat sank from view. She started the car and headed onto Bora-Bora Way.

Massy was aware that Jamul knew she'd gone to her boat to dress for the evening aboard the *Caviare*. Yet the bastard had triggered the doomsday switch. Hatred for Jamul swept through her as she gripped the wheel. Jamul was an upstart compared to the work she'd carried out over the years for the cause. *She* should have been the one chosen to head the West Coast cell, not a crazy jumped up pop singer. She was well aware that Jamul was chosen because of his popularity with his millions of fans. He was a man who worked unsuspected behind a facade of adoration. It was then that she made up her mind to kill him.

She drove toward basin E near Palawan Way. Her intention was to board one of the other Grand Bank trawlers Jamul kept docked and ready for an emergency. She'd have no problem boarding. She'd simply tell the guard she was on a special assignment and needed to change into dry clothes before heading to the Hollywood Bowl.

Dressed and possessing a somewhat soggy, laminated security pass she'd retrieved from her dress pants, she was ready to enter the Bowl. The guard waved her through. Once inside she'd locate Gully and assign him an extra target—Jamul.

Massy had made herself well-known to most of the security and DHS personnel at the Bowl when the trees were being planted. She knew where Gully and the special security squad were assembling. Glancing at the dash clock, she knew they were already in place. She had one stop to make before going inside.

Falk was only a few yards from the house when Young flicked on the kitchen light. So there *was* someone in the house! He hugged the wall and eased back toward the lighted window. Whoever it was didn't seem to care if anyone saw the light.

Falk could see a man in the kitchen, his back to the window, standing at a stove. The man moved out of Falk's vision for a moment. Falk watched until the he reappeared with a jar of instant coffee. With his back still to the window he scooped three spoonfuls into a thermos. He reached for a steaming kettle and filled the container, screwed the top on, flipped off the light and left the kitchen. Falk headed back to the car.

Koski rolled down the window when Falk tapped on the glass. "Marco, come with me. There *is* someone in the house. I need a guide. I'm taking no chances that whoever it is will get away. Stay with the car, Koski. We may have to move out fast."

Koski grumbled, admitting she would rather go with Falk but knew it made sense to use Marco's knowledge of the inside layout of the house.

"We won't be long," Falk said. "Keep the engine running."

Koski watched them disappear into the estate's grounds. Sighing, she sat back. It was getting cold. She turned on the engine and switched on the radio and heater; might as well be comfortable.

Rita Massy knew the house on Rockledge was empty except for Young. Now she was going to pay him a visit and change his schedule. The original plan was for Victor to trigger the tree bombs using three separate frequencies set one minute apart.

To be certain Gully had a chance at Jamul, she wanted the sequence changed to two frequencies one minute apart, a thirty-second pause then the third frequency. This would be unsettling to Jamul, whose timing would be off as to when to reenter the stage.

She also didn't have her cell to call Young. It was water-logged and she'd left it on the boat. She slowed the car and turned onto Rockledge.

Falk and Marco made their way down the side of the house and arrived at the now dark kitchen window.

"You first. Wait in the kitchen," Falk whispered. Marco nodded and quickly and silently opened the window and nimbly entered. Falk followed, closing the window partway behind him.

"I found the room on the second floor where you saw the radio equipment. Whoever's inside must be on the ground floor or the third floor."

"Or in one of the attics," Marco whispered. "There's four, two at the front and two in the rear."

"Do the back attics have a view of the Bowl?"

"Yeah. We were in one and I could see it."

"Kick off your shoes and follow me, Marco."

Massy was about to slow at the gate when she saw a car parked opposite. Immediately her adrenaline warned her of danger. She continued driving Rockledge, taking a quick glance in the car as she passed. It was too dark to be sure but it seemed there was someone in the driver's seat. To be certain, she drove a quarter of a mile along the road and pulled onto the shoulder and partway into a large growth of mulberry. Dousing the lights and killing the ignition she sat and waited. She removed a suppressed automatic from the glove compartment and opened the door. She'd been sure to arm herself while dressing. She stayed off the road and walked back along the grassy shoulder toward the parked car.

Chapter 59

Koski was listening to the radio when Massy's car swept past. She watched the taillights vanish around the curve ahead. What a desolate spot. She wondered why anyone wanted to live up here. Privacy, she supposed. She glanced at the dash clock and noted that Falk and Marco had been gone fifteen minutes. She grew edgy. Maybe she should go check. They both had cell phones. Falk would have called if there was a problem. She settled back in the seat.

The low sound of the radio, the hum of the motor and the warmth from the heater were too soothing for her to stay keenly alert. She turned off the heater and cranked the window down a bit.

As Massy neared the parked car, she realized the engine was running and there *was* someone inside. There could be more than one person. Crouching, she inched her way closer until she was sure the first shot would hit the front tire. Leaning against a tree for support she aimed and squeezed. Phutt...a muffled cough and the nine millimeter slug slammed into the tire. Massy waited motionless.

Koski felt the tire collapse then the car dipped its nose to the right. A blowout without moving! For a second she wanted to open the door and see what happened. Instead, her training and instincts made her quickly grab her weapon and snap off the safety.

Falk whispered, "Marco, are there any other stairs leading up to the attics?"

"Yeah. Back stairs from a yard. We had to use them every night. Didn't want us tramping mud through the house, I guess."

"Fine. Take me to them."

The house was from an era when there were live-in servants and the back stairs were typical of the day. Falk opened a door and shone his covered light onto the bottom step, uncarpeted.

"I bet they creak, right?"

"Never noticed. We were always talking and kidding when we came back."

"All the same, I think we'll go back to the carpeted stairs," Falk muttered. As he closed the door, he noticed an old-fashioned key in the lock. He removed it and put it in his pocket.

Falk waved a halt on the third floor landing. All of the rooms they'd checked were empty. Only the attic remained.

"Wait here. I'll call if I need you. Okay?" Marco nodded and Falk slowly mounted the attic steps with his automatic at the ready.

Koski, with her weapon cocked, suddenly realized a tire doesn't blow out on its own. Someone shot it out. Without hesitating she jammed into drive, stabbed the accelerator to the floor, skidded out onto Rockledge and barreled down the road on the flat tire. She fought to keep control as the car bucked against the rim on asphalt.

Massy was shocked at the sudden action. She pressed back into the bushes as the car's front right fender swept past her, missing by inches. The rear tires kicked up clumps of grass as it sped into the darkness with its lights off. It all happened so fast. Son of a bitch! She didn't even have time to shoot at the vanishing vehicle. It wouldn't get far with a flat. The driver had been waiting for someone and whoever it was was still in the house and had no way to escape. Massy quickly crossed the road and entered the gate.

Sparks flew from the front wheel rim as Koski wrestled the steering. She knew she had to stop or risk going off the road. She noticed a car pulled off to the right, parked almost out of sight in a stand of mulberry bushes. She had seen a car pass her a short while before the tire blew. Was there any connection? She pulled to a shaky stop behind the vehicle, got out, went to the front and felt the radiator. It was still warm. It could be the car. She tried the door. Locked.

Koski reached into her purse and removed a small wallet of lock picks. Ten seconds later the door swung open. Using a pen light from her purse, she swept the narrow beam around the car's interior until it landed on the glove compartment. She opened it and rummaged around until she found the registration papers. She gave a small gasp as the beam lit up the owner's name. Jamul. The address was the penthouse at the Marina. Koski slammed the car door shut and ran back toward the house.

Arriving at the gates, panting for breath, she stopped. No sense in barging into the grounds. She must catch her breath and be ready for anything. She was in peak condition. It took but a few seconds and she breathed steadily as she ventured toward the house. Remembering what Marco said about the kitchen window being an easy entry, she cautiously headed down the side of the house searching for it.

Falk was halfway up the attic stairs when he heard voices on the landing below. He stopped. Someone was talking to Marco; someone who seemed to know him. Easing down one stair at a time, he strained to hear.

Massy had silently entered the house by using a key at the front door. She heard voices on the stairs and with weapon drawn she started upward.

The voices stopped and Massy continued. In the graying darkness of the third floor she saw a shadowy figure leaning against the wall. Massy's hand slid along the wall until she felt her fingers touch the light switch. *Click.*

The sudden bright light caused Marco to cover his eyes for a second. When he lowered his hand, Massy exclaimed, "Marco! What are you doing here?"

Marco used all of his streetwise cunning. In a split second he answered, "I came to rob the house."

Massy stared at him in disbelief. "You kidnapped Pegmanti?"

"Sorry, lady. He fooled you. He used me to escape. It was a set up. I came back here with a friend. I knew there were some nice pieces I can sell."

"Who were you talking to?"

"My friend," Marco replied.

Massy looked around the empty landing. "Where is he?"

Marco nodded down the corridor. "He's checking out the rooms."

"Who was in the car?"

"Three of us. Two of us came in and José waited in the car."

Massy still held the gun on Marco. "José had a flat tire so you don't have a ride now, Marco. Tell your pal down the hall to join us."

Falk heard the conversation and knew he had to make a move.

Massy eased to the bottom of the attic stairs and called up while keeping an eye on Marco.

"Victor, get your ass down here. We have company."

Falk was stunned. If someone came down the stairs there would be no place for him to hide!

"Who the hell's down there?" Victor Young called.

"It's me, Massy. Get down here now!"

Falk waited until the footsteps were almost at the bend in the staircase, then ran down the stairs, leapt the last few and landed on Massy sending her crashing to the floor. Massy's automatic slid across the landing. Marco scooped up the gun while Falk threw all his weight into a punch to Massy's jaw. Her head snapped sideways and she went limp. Falk turned as Young came down the last few steps, his automatic spitting flame.

Dropping to the floor, Falk rolled behind Massy's crumpled form. She took all three shots in the chest.

Marco held Massy's gun steady with both hands and squeezed off three rounds before Young could re-aim. One in the chest, one in the throat and the third between the eyes dropped the man at the foot of the staircase.

Falk scrambled to his feet. In the last seconds before Victor fell, he'd recognized him. For a moment he thought everything had gone wrong. Falk winced at the sight of Victor. What caused a man like him to become a traitor?

Koski heard the shots and headed up the last flight, her gun at the ready.

"All over, Koski. Take it easy. Marco just saved my life."

Falk and Koski found the transmitter in the attic. Falk stared through the window at the lights down in the Hollywood Bowl.

"Perfect view from here," he said.

"Yeah. When the sun came up he'd have been able see every tree we planted," Marco whispered.

"We still have to get counterinsurgency forces to evacuate the early arrivals. No doubt they're already in their seats." Falk punched Stewart's cell number as he spoke.

Imminent Danger

Chapter 60

The darkness of night shifted to the dim grayness of predawn. Jamul was in his element, ordering people around, being important, needed and adored.

He crossed the stage to oversee some detail and happened to glance out across the seating area. A shock of adrenaline surged through his veins. There was a light on at the house, shining from the attic. The house was supposed to remain in total darkness. Victor Young's orders emphatically stated—the house must be dark.

"You okay, boss? You look like you seen a ghost out there." Jamul turned to see one of the electricians standing next to him.

"I'm fine. This historic event is going to be a great moment for the world." Jamul glanced over to the international and American television crews carrying out their last minute duties. "Over ninety-five million people will be viewing the service that will show the world that it is possible, with the right leadership, for all religions to come together in unity and harmony."

Jamul's mind raced. *Something is seriously wrong*, he thought. He could fly out in the helicopter and leave now, but then how would he explain his sudden departure before the massacre? His grandstanding act as an angel of mercy to the bomb victims would be gone. He paced the stage, pretending to be checking the directional microphones as he struggled with the new situation.

In a flash of genius, Jamul's unique ability to think under pressure kicked in. During his scheduled absence after the opening hymn, he'd make it to the landing pad, board the chopper and trigger the tree bombs from a pre-set back up transmitter on board. Then he would double back and re-appear

217

on stage as the angel of mercy after all.

The explosions would, as designed, signal the drug-injected, mind-altered zombies to use their bio weapons on the audience while Gully took out religious leaders on stage.

A feeling of elation swept through him. Everything was going to go as planned. Then, as quickly as the euphoria enveloped him, it vanished., replaced by a sense of cold reality as he saw columns of camouflage-clad soldiers, in full battle gear, trotting around the outer perimeter of the amphitheater. They stood in a line, shoulder to shoulder, M4/A1 rifles slung at the ready.

A group of civilians walked across the wide stage toward him. Jamul recognized the mayor and several city council members. "Mr. Mayor, this is an unexpected pleasure." Jamul was the genial host. He gestured toward the assembled troops. "I see we are to have tight security on top of the already tight security."

The mayor looked tired and pale under the lights of the arc lamps. His entourage was grouped around him. "The Department of Homeland Security canceled the service, Jamul. The Holy Father's plane has been rerouted to a military Air Force base where it will be refueled and return to Rome."

"That can't be true!" Jamul exclaimed. "The world is awaiting the greatest gathering of religions ever held."

"We have red alert. Imminent danger of a terrorist attack here in the Bowl. Everyone must be evacuated."

Jamul shook his head. "We can't allow a rumor to stop the service."

"DHS doesn't consider this a rumor."

Jamul's mind flashed back to the lights in the attic and the Army's sudden appearance. Soon there would be a mass evacuation of hundreds of early worshippers. He must prove that al-Qaida can attack even when a red alert is in effect. There was still time to cause damage.

"I understand we must obey the evacuation order, Mr. Mayor." Jamul's voice was calm.

"However, I feel it my duty to remain on stage and sing the opening hymn as the authorities conduct an orderly evacuation. On this Easter morning, it is the least I can do under the circumstances."

Perhaps they wouldn't be able to cause the catastrophic damage and death as planned. But if he moved fast he could get to the helicopter, trigger the tree bombs and start a chain of events that would show the world they could still strike. The television crews would waste no time in showing the damage to a world waiting to view a meeting of peace. Instead they would witness total disaster.

The mayor desperately wanted his city to appear in the best light possible under the most drastic of conditions. Millions of international viewers weren't going to see the religious gathering they hoped for or be able to listen to the choral groups singing the praise of Easter.

Jamul's voice would soar high across the Bowl. It would be a tribute to all who believed in freedom of religion and a perfect cover for his vanishing act.

Imminent Danger

Chapter 61

Falk pocketed his cell. "Stewart says the Bowl is being evacuated. The Sunrise Service is now officially canceled." He looked at Victor Young's body and shook his head. "Let's move."

Koski dropped to one knee beside Massy and started going through her pockets.

"What are you looking for?"

"I need her car keys, Joe."

"Why?"

"Our car is out of commission."

"What happened?"

"Long story. Here they are." She got to her feet and started down the stairs. Falk and Marco followed.

Koski filled them in about the blowout and her escape as they made their way back to Massy's car.

Highland Avenue was a sea of vehicles and crowds of people on foot. Horns blared and police bullhorns crackled. It looked like a riot.

"Damn." Falk pulled to the curb more than a half mile from the entrance. "We're going to have to hike in."

Two police helicopters circled overhead. Falk looked up at the persistent eyes in the sky and remembered Jamul had flown from the *Caviare* in his copter to the Bowl.

"Marco, do you know where Jamul lands his helicopter?"

"Not far from where we worked in the nursery area."

"Lead the way."

"You'll have to climb through brush and over some walls. We can get to the back of the nursery by cutting through the intersection of Highland and Cahuenga near the Hollywood Freeway."

"No problem. Let's hustle."

As in the earlier rehearsal, the giant organ played an opening chord that quickly changed to a sustained note of pure joy then flew high through the early morning air. Next Jamul's magnificent voice entwined with the now fading note until only his resonance filled the amphitheater. Outside and in, the crowds became mesmerized by Jamul's singing as it trickled through the assembled masses. Such was the power of his talented voice—even though it was a recording. People who moments before had been pushing and shoving, edging on the verge of panic, began to slow. Some even stopped to listen, unaware that Jamul was slinking through the shadows toward the helipad.

Falk and Koski exchanged glances as Marco led them through thick brush and high grass. She nodded, feeling her skin tingle at the sound. How could someone who sang with such amazing sweetness design plans of mass destruction and assist in carrying them out? She thrust through the brush wondering if sweetness was only a hair's breath away from evil as was genius to madness.

Marco pointed. "Over there. You can see the roof of the nursery building."

Falk nodded. "We go over the fence?"

"No," Marco answered. "Stay close."

Like an infiltration squad, the trio wended their way between trees, bushes, old crates, lawn mowers and coiled hoses. Marco held up a warning hand. "There's a hole in the chain-link fence. Follow me."

"Marco, the place is crawling with security," Koski hissed.

"They're busy with the crowds." They were in the nursery yard now with no one around.

"Which way to the helipad?" Falk asked.

"Just beyond the trees we planted."

"With bombs in the roots, right?" Koski muttered.

"So they say."

"Koski, you and Marco move around to the amphitheater. Stewart said he was near the stage. Tell him I'm going to cover the helicopter pad in case Jamul decides to leave early. Advise him to be watchful for anyone with a bio weapon. It'll be small and probably hidden in one hand. Anyone pointing in an aggressive manner could be a shooter."

When the organ music faded, it was the cue for the choir to sing as a unit, allowing the massed voices their own moment of glory. Jamul dreaded the moment. There wasn't going to be a choir. Everyone had been ordered to leave. The organ had faded when suddenly the sound of two clear and strong voices reached Jamul's ears. Looking back, he saw the young women in white cassocks slowly walking on stage.

Two more entered from stage right then three and four, singing and growing stronger in voice as the choir grew. They were coming back in groups, slowly getting into their position as a choir—defiant to any terrorist threat. The organ softly picked up the melody.

The television cameras jockeyed for position to air the dramatic scene. The announcers were excitedly telling the world what was happening. Their voices reflected the dramatic moment as the singers grew in numbers until almost the entire choir was in place singing like they never had before.

Koski and Marco watched the choir's amazing appearance as they walked toward the front of the stage.

"I thought everyone was ordered to leave," Marco said.

"They were," Koski mumbled as she saw Stewart waving to them to join him.

Stewart's first words were, "Where's Falk?" Koski brought him up-to-date. Stewart looked tense.

"Jamul's gone. No one can find him."

The first bomb exploded and earth and rocks rained down as people screamed and ran. The choir, who only moments before were blissfully singing, now crouched in horror as they shielded themselves from falling debris.

The roar of explosions turned hundreds of people into a pushing and shoving mob fighting their way out through the main entrances. Few noticed the zombie-like figures pointing randomly at the exodus as they triggered their deadly bio guns. Mind-altered and confused, not seeing their targets on stage, they blindly fired at anything that moved.

Gully, with the special police detachment, saw them and immediately knew what was happening. Their targets, the religious clerics, were gone, hustled out at the first warning. Gully knew he'd never be paid in full. He'd been abandoned, left to fend for himself. The pope had been his target.

More deafening explosions roared in rapid succession, shaking the Bowl. Those inside the amphitheater fell as shrapnel, rocks and pieces of trees scythed through bone and flesh. The result was far more devastating than had been expected. Rather than being a means to panic people while the mind-altered zombies took out the clerics, the bombs had created a massacre.

Falk was almost at the helipad when red and orange geysers erupted from the ground a hundred feet away. First the blast, then a furnace-like heat blew him to the ground. Jamul had made it unseen to the copter. He snapped on the back-up transmitter and triggered the last sections of trees then started the engine for takeoff. He planned to say he'd been forced at gunpoint by one of the terrorists to fly him out of the Bowl.

Falk shook his head, trying to clear his vision and the ringing in his ears, then staggered to his feet. The clamor of the blades slashing through the air and the whine of the engine spooling up told him Jamul was getting away. Sucking in drafts of cold morning air, he ran toward the helicopter as it started to lift. Quickly he leapt onto the landing skids and jammed himself into a position that allowed him to grasp a stanchion protruding from the underside of the cabin. Blade rotation increased. The sound screamed in his ears as the chopper rose, swaying slightly before gaining altitude then moved through the air with surging speed.

Falk looked back on the chaos below, praying Koski was safe.

Jamul banked the helicopter in an arc toward the coast. If Jamul was heading to his yacht, it was only a matter of minutes before he set down on the stern. If he decided on going further abroad, Falk knew he'd be in deeper trouble.

Chapter 62

Koski, Marco and Stewart had dropped to the ground as the first bombs exploded. Koski gazed skyward as a helicopter lifted off, already vanishing into the smoke from the explosions. If she hadn't been aware that Falk was near the helipad she might never have noticed it.

The semi-darkness made it impossible for her to see someone hunched beneath the cabin. Then the copter was gone, the sound of its engine diminishing as it vanished into the clouds of black smoke rising from the trees.

"That could be Jamul," Koski yelled to Stewart. "Contact the police helicopters."

Stewart squinted up. "Too late, Koski. They're on a secure frequency. By the time we got through he'd be long gone."

"He's already long gone. We have to do something. Joe could be in that copter."

Stewart realized she might be right. If Falk had gotten close enough, he'd have made every effort to board the aircraft. If he had, he'd have stopped Jamul from leaving.

"Let's get over to the pad," Stewart rasped.

After searching the area, they knew Falk was gone. "Jamul could have forced him on board at gun point."

"Jamul would have shot him like a dog," Marco said. "He's not the kind to take prisoners."

"Not unless he needed a hostage," Koski said quietly.

Stewart leaned more toward Koski's theory and quickly reached for his cell phone. Within seconds, he was in contact with the Coast Guard at the Marina.

"This is Stewart. Put me through to the officer in charge immediately." He looked back at the shattered ruins of the seating area and the medical teams at work. "Lieutenant, has the helicopter returned to the *Caviare*?" Stewart's face tightened. "*Caviare* sailed over an hour ago?" Clicking off, he turned to Koski. "Your theory could be right. You two follow me."

Fog hugged the Pacific and reached inland like a gray wrinkled blanket. They should be over the Marina by now. How would Jamul make a landing? Falk stared down at the thick swirling vapor. The copter stayed on course, not attempting to descend. Where was the damn fool going? A rendezvous at sea?

The chill factor troubled him. His grip was weakening and he had to concentrate every second to stay in place as icy numbness slowly crept through his body.

There was a break in the overcast for a few seconds and he glimpsed the Pacific and knew they had flown long enough to pass over the coast. There was only one place to head for in such a small aircraft—Catalina Island, thirty miles west of the Marina. He knew he couldn't hold on much longer, then he heard a sweet sound. The engine pitch altered slightly and he felt a change in speed. Jamul was preparing to land.

Seconds later they were in deep wet clouds. The rotors were swirling the opaque murkiness around him until suddenly everything became clear and the rising sun welcomed them back to normalcy. Below, Falk saw the top part of Catalina Island as Jamul swept over the western edge of the coast. It was a lonely stretch far from Avalon and the hustle of tourists and commerce.

A two-lane road ran along the edge of the island. No sign of life among the scrub brush. Jamul had chosen a deserted landing place. Gently, like a butterfly, the copter touched down without a shudder. Falk couldn't move. He wanted to roll off, find a place to hide. It was no use. He could hardly release his grip from the stanchion.

The rotor's blades wound down and he heard the cabin door click open. The whoosh-whoosh of the blades sounded like a giant scimitar twirling over his head ready to execute anyone in their area. Falk watched as Jamul's legs came into view, then stood beside the copter. He immediately dropped into a squat and stared at Falk.

"Enjoy the ride did you?" A nine millimeter automatic rested casually on his knee. "I don't think you can raise your hands so stay as you are. A car will be here in a few minutes and we'll take a ride into Avalon. I have friends waiting."

Imminent Danger

Chapter 63

Stewart led Koski and Marco back to the security point inside the nursery. Koski, trotting eagerly to keep up, reminded him of the equipment she and Falk had installed beneath the water line and attached to the sloop's rudder. "We can transmit and cut electrical power—stop her dead in the water."

"I don't want to stop her yet. I want the yacht shadowed." Stewart's cell chirped. "Stewart here. Right. Get a fix on the call. I'll get back to you." He pocketed the phone. "DHS received an anonymous call saying Jamul and an agent by the name of Falk were being held hostage."

"Held where?" Koski asked.

"They didn't say and we didn't have time to get a fix on the call."

"Trail the boat until they're in international waters then attack," Marco suggested.

"No. We can switch it off like a toy whenever we want," Stewart replied. Koski knew he was right.

"Jamul was tight with the Arabs, like I told you. Why take him hostage?" Marco asked.

"Jamul's tight with everyone from the President down to his fan clubs," Koski muttered.

Marco snorted. "It could be a trick saying Jamul's been taken hostage. How do we know? They could say that to give him an alibi, make him look like a hero. Hey, man, the world would rather believe he's a hostage than an al-Qaida terrorist."

"I like your thinking, Marco." Stewart slapped him on the shoulder.

"If the world finds out Jamul *is* part of al-Qaida his career is over," Koski added.

Stewart shrugged. "Maybe he's ready to receive adoration from a different section of the world. He still has money and power to hide anywhere, live unseen, like Bin Laden and others did. People like Jamul live only to cause problems in the name of Islam. We have to get them both back any way possible."

A car drove up the deserted coast road and stopped. Falk sat in the grass beside the helicopter. A man exited the car, moved quickly across the open ground and exchanged words with Jamul. He walked over to Falk and kicked him in the ribs. He pulled Falk's arms behind his back and snapped on a pair of handcuffs then calmly walked to the copter and climbed in.

"Go to the car," Jamul ordered. Falk got stiffly to his feet as the sound of the chopper winding up rattled through the air.

Jamul followed, covering Falk with his automatic, and opened the back door of the car. "Get in." Jamul entered the front passenger seat, the barrel of his gun aimed at Falk's chest. "Sit back and enjoy the ride."

Chapter 64

Koski paced anxiously in front of the security desk. Marco was slumped on a chair with his eyes half-closed. He opened them at the sound of Stewart's voice.

"When Jamul's helicopter took off, we know he headed west. That's all we know. Fog has socked in the coast. He could be anywhere."

"West could mean Catalina," Marco offered. "How far could he go in that little bird, man?"

"West also can mean any of the Channel Islands. He may have headed west then turned north up the coast. We have a full alert out for *Caviare* and the copter."

"That damn boat could be a decoy to make us do just what we're doing —tracking it—while Jamul and Joe head in another direction," Koski added.

"Understood," Stewart said edgily. "We'll have to wait."

Stewart earnestly updated Koski and Marco.

"Seemingly, the *Caviare* was infiltrated during the evacuation when security was recalled for duties at the Bowl, leaving only a skeleton crew. As it stands, the focus is on getting the dead and wounded out of the Bowl. No official word on Jamul's whereabouts yet."

"Are they going to say he was taken hostage?" Koski asked.

"Yes."

"I still think Jamul nailed Falk and hauled his ass off to Catalina," Marco muttered.

Koski turned angrily. "Agent Falk is not in the habit of having his ass hauled anywhere he doesn't want to go, Marco. Remember that."

"Yeah, well he might have this time. There's heavy fog over the coast. No sign of them since the fog lifted. I bet Jamul hightailed it to Catalina. As a hostage, he'll have the public on his side and rooting for him to be found. He lays low for a week or two then lets someone find him and it's welcome home, Jamul."

Stewart grunted. "I have a helicopter taking two DHS specialists to Catalina from the Marina to join others on the island. I've ordered they stop here first. I want you and Marco on board."

Koski brightened. "You know where they are?"

"No, but I agree with Marco. Catalina is a good place to start."

Marco cut a glance to Stewart. "I like the way you think, man."

The sound of a copter landing out on the pad stopped any further conversation.

"Let's go. That's them now," Koski said.

Greg Grant had raised hell at the Coast Guard station after his car was stolen. He phoned his boss in Washington, complaining of no cooperation in assisting him with his investigation. His boss told him he was off the case until fit to work. No way was he going to represent the DHS sitting in an electric scooter with his leg in a cast.

Nonetheless, Grant was determined to prove he wasn't going to fail on his first assignment. Now, with the carnage at the Bowl, he wouldn't give up. He pocketed his cell. No one would know he was off the job.

"Nell, I've been ordered to the Bowl to do whatever I can to help."

"We don't have a car," she reminded him.

"Tell me about it! You and that Koski woman go to the john, she leaves you locked in, my car's stolen and we're stuck here while the Hollywood Bowl is blown apart." He glanced out the window in time to see two uniformed security guards entering the building.

"Follow me." Grant wheeled out of the room to the front office as the men entered.

"DHS," Grant announced. "We're on special assignment and need transport to the Bowl. Can you guys help us?"

One of the men, a burly sergeant, looked surprised. Grant waved his

ID. "Check it out."

A Coast Guardsman came around from the front desk. "He's for real, scooter and all. She's his aide," he said, indicating Nell.

"Jesus! I've heard of walking wounded but this takes the cake."

"Well, can you help?" Grant asked.

"We've just been ordered to board a Coast Guard helicopter and fly to Catalina with one stop at the Bowl. You're in luck."

"Let's go."

Koski and Marco stood at the edge of the landing pad as a Sikorsky VH-60N chopper touched down amid a whirl of dust. The door slid open and a uniformed man waved, indicating for them to get aboard.

They ran across the concrete apron. Koski grabbed the soldier's hand and he hauled her inside. A second later Marco was on the floor beside her and the door slammed shut. Koski felt the aircraft shudder as it swayed upward. She shrugged into a safety harness, buckled up and settled with her back against the bulkhead.

When Koski finally checked out their surroundings, she couldn't believe her eyes. Lashed on the opposite side of the copter sat Greg Grant, an electric scooter beside him! Marco's eyes widened as he recognized Nell sitting a few feet away. The noise was too loud for them to converse. All four stared at each other in disbelief.

Imminent Danger

Chapter 65

Officer Robert Gulliver's only contact with the plan had been through Massy. Now, standing in the Hollywood Bowl amid the aftermath of the explosions, he knew he'd been a cop too long to think his part in the plan would be forgotten. He was a marked man. Marked by whoever had masterminded the Easter morning carnage.

The bio weapon attached to his finger felt cumbersome inside his riot glove. His squad had moved to one of the exits to oversee the exodus of those able to walk out of the Bowl.

Massy had treated him like a servant, overbearing and cynical of a cop who sold out. She had underestimated Gully's ability to uncover a few facts about her. Cops had means and he used them to his advantage. He learned the doctor somehow was associated with Jamul. She frequently visited Jamul's Marina Del Rey penthouse and owned a boat at the Marina. She'd get her money if she'd survived the bombings. If she didn't get paid she'd use blackmail. Celebrities hated bad press.

Jamul's car drove five miles along the coast road before it turned onto a narrow road and headed inland. A few miles later, it came to a stop in front of a decrepit house with a red tiled roof that had turned an ugly orange color over time.

Falk surveyed the place. "Hope that dump has a toilet. I've gotta go."

Jamul led the way through several nearly empty rooms to a kitchen at the back of the house. "Take his cuffs off," he told the driver. "Show the way. Stay outside and leave the door open."

Falk eyed a tiny window with a grimy cracked pane set high in the whitewashed wall of the washroom and knew there was no escape. He noticed a slither of dried up soap on the floor as he was washing his hands. He scooped it up and put it in his pocket.

When Falk exited the restroom, he was surprised to see a gray-haired Jamul dressed in a natty business suit.

"We're ready, Falk. You'll be in a wheelchair."

Brasinov pushed an old wheelchair toward Falk. "Sit down." They all left through the back door and walked toward a minivan parked behind the house.

"Cover his legs." Jamul tossed a blanket to the driver. "Snap these cuffs to the right-hand arm rest, down low." The driver obeyed and yanked Falk forward and to one side as the cuffs snapped low on the armrest, almost at seat level. With the rug covering any sign of the metal manacles, to a passerby he looked like a twisted cripple.

"We mustn't forget his hat." Jamul slipped a size large LA Dodgers cap onto Falk's head. It slipped down, resting on the bridge of his nose. "Perfect. Let's go, Mikhail."

Mikhail Brasinov moved forward, gripping the wheelchair handles, and followed behind Jamul.

Chapter 66

Catalina has only one airport. The Airport in the Sky was a quarter mile from the Sikorsky as it settled down onto a restricted pad located away from general air traffic.

As the rotors slowed and it became possible to hear, Grant yelled, "I can have you arrested for running out on me. You know that!"

"Yeah, right," Koski replied. "If I'd have known you were on this aircraft I'd have waited for another one." She turned to the two DHS men.

"Let him get off himself. He's on sick leave and a little out of his mind. If you take any orders from him you'll both be up for aiding an incompetent in time of a national emergency." She jumped down from the aircraft and Marco followed.

"Stay with him, Nell," Marco shouted over his shoulder. "You heard what she said."

As Koski and Marco left, they heard Grant bellowing threats at the top of his voice.

"Is what you just said true?" Marco asked.

"Don't know. I had to say something to keep him from tagging along."

A tall man, a major with the Army Corps of Engineers, walked toward them and touched his cap in salute. "Agent Koski?"

"Yes."

"Tom Stewart asked me to meet you and," he looked at Marco, "Marco, right?" Marco nodded. "Follow me. I have a car waiting."

The major brought them up to speed on the drive into Avalon. There was a security team at the airport checking all incoming and outgoing aircraft. The Coast Guard and local police were already checking every boat that was at anchor or tied to a mooring, and, following airport procedure, all incoming and outgoing sea traffic.

"This is going to be a time-consuming job as you might have guessed. Easter, the town is full of tourists and college kids, swelling the population by thousands. If the terrorists have landed on the island and are holding Jamul and Agent Falk hostage, it'll be difficult to find them."

Koski stared out the window. Catching a brief glimpse of the harbor, she saw what looked like a floating forest. If the authorities were going to check every boat they were in for a tough job indeed. As if reading her mind the major said, "As I mentioned, Easter is always a busy time in Avalon."

Koski motioned to the crammed harbor, "How do you expect to check every boat? There must be hundreds."

The major gave a short laugh. "Very carefully. And don't forget aircraft up at the airport."

"You think Jamul and Joe are being kept hostage here on Catalina Island, major?"

"No one knows. DHS is checking several other possible locations."

Viewers around the globe watched the televised reports from the Hollywood Bowl in disbelief as explosions gushed amid the exiting crowds with sickening detail. Vatican City announced the Holy Father's survival as a miracle.

The abduction of Jamul and a government agent from the Bowl by the unknown terrorist group and the declaration he was now a hostage mystified everyone. Why are terrorists holding a man like Jamul hostage? He was a recognized Islamic working closely with religions around the world to bring peace and understanding to all. The Easter Morning Sunrise Service was to have been his crowning moment in bringing the world together in an understanding of cooperation between Christian diversity. Nations wondered who had planned and carried out such an evil attack. Was Jamul alive or dead?

Jamul watched the television coverage with mixed feelings. It was not up to the cell's original expectations. Nonetheless, millions now knew that

America was still vulnerable to an attack, anytime, anywhere. Playing a hostage was perfect cover for his part in the deadly act. He planned to remain out of sight until he organized and staged a dramatic escape from his captors and emerged a hero.

Two weeks before the Bowl attack the cell had made arrangements for Jamul to enter a private convalescent home for the mentally impaired. This was an expensive retreat in the hills overlooking Avalon, where families of the rich and famous hid away their embarrassing relatives. Jamul's stay was to be in a lavish private section of the home.

Imminent Danger

Chapter 67

Officer Robert Gully was aware the bio weapon was worth plenty. He'd never see the other half of the money he was promised, but if he sold the weapon to the right people it would more than compensate the loss.

Gully, present when the bio weapons used by the "zombies" to fire the gas into the crowds were collected by the police, took a silent delight in seeing LAPD experts baffled about what they were. He stood among his fellow officers with the latest model of the biolaser strapped snugly under the index finger of his gloved right hand. He knew it was only a matter of time before the word got out about the new tools of destruction. Then they would remain under heavy guard in the LAPD weapons lab.

Certain people in the LA underworld would be very interested in a demonstration.

The major clicked off his cell as the car came to a stop outside the Coast Guard station. "No helicopters landed at the Catalina airport during the time Jamul's copter was hijacked. Authorities are checking the surrounding areas for possible sightings."

Koski nodded as she viewed the crowded harbor. The sun was up and the fog had burned off, heralding what promised to be a bright sunny day. Bright for some, she thought as she followed the major toward the office. In all the confusion at the Bowl, the helicopter could have gone in any direction. They might be miles from the landing place. The thought nagged at her as they entered the building.

Marco remained silent throughout the journey. Now he knew the reason Stewart went along with his suggestion that they check out Catalina. It happened during his debriefing with Stewart after the escape from the house with Pegmanti. He mentioned his conversation with Massy and the time when she refused to return his radio, saying he might be assigned to a place where the buffalo roamed.

Not until they were at the site of Jamul's vanished helicopter at the Bowl and he'd mentioned the copter might have headed for Catalina did he recall a school trip to the island. He'd seen a herd of wild buffalo roaming the hillsides. Marco had caught the sudden realization in Stewart's eyes when he mentioned Catalina. Now here they were.

"Marco, you look like you're going to fall asleep." Koski's voice brought him back to earth.

"Uh, yeah. I was thinking, that's all."

"Stay alert. We're going to a briefing."

A hastily arranged meeting room was set up in the Coast Guard station. Several people were already seated when the trio entered. Koski and Marco sat at the rear of the room as the major walked to a battered podium and introduced himself and the others.

"As you are all aware the country is on high alert. I've been sent to organize search parties to go through every water craft in the harbor." A groan of disbelief filled the room.

"I know. Naval personnel from Long Beach and Marines from Camp Pendleton will comb the hills and valleys of the island. Houses, stores and businesses will be searched by local police and a detachment of Military Police being flown in from the Embarcadero in San Francisco.

"DHS will also be working the same venues. The reason Catalina was picked as the most likely location of the terrorists holding Jamul and probably FBI Agent Joseph Falk is because of a clue received during a debriefing several hours ago. Nothing is for certain but it's the best we have to go on at the moment."

Koski leaned in to Marco. "*You* were debriefed by Stewart. Was it you?"

Marco whispered, "Later."

Koski glowered but kept quiet.

The major ended by saying they had a lot of ground to cover and no time to waste. He glanced at his watch. "We'll meet back here in one hour."

The major rejoined Koski and Marco. "Arrangements have been made for you two to stay at the Hotel Villa Portofino on the sea front. I doubt you'll have much time to spend there. When you do, you'll each have a room in which to catch some sleep. In the meantime, we can grab a bite of breakfast from the Coast Guard. C'mon."

Koski and Marco followed as the major fell in step beside a Coast Guardsman who led them to breakfast.

"Tell me what you know, Marco," Koski hissed. In the space of time it took to get to the mess hall, Marco filled her in. "That's a hell of a slim clue! I can't believe Stewart went for it," Koski muttered.

"It's all we have. If we didn't have that we'd be still wondering where to start."

Koski knew he was right.

Imminent Danger

Chapter 68

Falk was in the wheelchair, strapped in the back of the specially fitted minivan, unable to speak. He'd been drugged with a strong opiate after being loaded aboard. Jamul still acted the part of a white-haired old man as he sat next to the driver. The rear of the van was windowless. The drive took under an hour. Finally they came to a stop and the back door was flung open.

The driver operated an electric lift and lowered Falk to ground level. Jamul said a few words to Brasinov who nodded and shoved Falk up a ramp and through the entrance of a fine-looking old building. Falk was able to catch a quick glimpse of the harbor in the distance and a view of the famous casino near the harbor wall.

Two nurses dressed in white and a distinguished-looking man in a pinstriped suit, Dr. Victor Richardson, greeted them with much bowing and scraping. Immediately Falk knew they were in a very private, very expensive nursing home.

"Good morning, Mr. Rashantan. We are honored to receive you," Richardson gushed as he leaned over Falk. The nurses beamed their welcome, stopping just short of a curtsey.

Jamul quickly said, "Mr. Rashantan is lightly sedated at the moment. My name is Mr. Saba. You will communicate through me at all times."

"We have everything in order, Mr. Saba, as instructed by your people in Johannesburg," Richardson purred.

Jamul smiled, thankful that his friends at the curio shop had made the arrangements. The preparations demanded absolute secrecy.

"Mr. Rashantan and his party aren't to be disturbed under any circumstances. Mr. Rashantan is here in the United States for top-secret government meetings that are to take place later in Washington, D.C. The layover on Catalina was designed to keep the media out of the picture and the need for top security."

Dr. Richardson was more than happy to oblige when informed how much he would earn for his cooperation.

"Of course, Mr. Saba. I understand," he replied. The doctor quickly assured Jamul all was under control. They would be in a wing that was totally apart from the general population.

Falk bent and twisted in his wheelchair, his hands and feet covered by the heavy rug. He wanted to yell at the doctor to call the cops, DHS, anyone.

Marco finished his breakfast, sat back and wiped his lips. "If Jamul is faking his abduction and hiding somewhere on the island, I'll bet it's first class."

"What do you mean?"

"That dude just does things like that—best of everything."

"And if he is a hostage where is he?"

"Don't know. No one does, right?"

"I think Joe tried to stop Jamul and something went wrong."

"You got pissed when I said that."

"Well, I've had time to think."

"Good. You want more coffee?"

The major came to their table. "What do either of you know about a guy called Grant, says he's DHS?"

Koski shook her head. "Oh, no. Why?"

"I got a call saying he's raising all kinds of hell at the airport. He says you're supposed to be working for him."

"Call Tom Stewart. He'll put you straight. Okay?"

"I don't have time for this, Agent Koski."

"Just one call. Trust me." The major blew out his cheeks and stormed across the room.

"C'mon, Marco. Time for us to move out." She pushed back her chair. Marco shrugged, gulped down his coffee and followed her.

Koski looked at the passing tourists enjoying their Easter holiday. "We passed an airport bus on the way down. Take it and find out where Grant and Nell are. Get her on her own." The sun was warming the air and moving the morning on. "You'll have to find where to catch the bus."

"No problem. What'll I do when I get Nell?"

"Both of you get back on a bus, go to our hotel and stay there. Grant will be on his own with the scooter. It'll at least slow him down. You do still have the cell phone Stewart gave you?" Marco tapped his shirt pocket. "Good. Give me a call when you get back to the hotel."

Marco mingled with the tourists and headed down the street toward the waterfront.

Marco was right, Koski thought. Jamul *would* seek a luxurious place to hole up in. Koski shivered slightly and fatigue swept over her. It was a little after ten. How long since she'd had a full night's sleep? At the Academy, they taught that sleep deprivation led to mistakes. She'd return to the hotel and instruct the desk to call her at four. Six hours sleep would make all the difference, bring her back up to speed. Besides, there were plenty of aggressive people out there searching.

Koski took a cab back to the hotel. Leaning back with her eyes half-closed, she was on the edge of sleep when the cab braked for a red light. Koski glanced over to a vehicle stopped beside them. The driver's face brought back a picture as sharp as if flashed onto a screen. It was the guy who was sitting in the Rav4 outside the hotel in West LA when she returned from her morning run.

"Driver, follow that Land Rover next to us. Let him get ahead then stay back. I don't want him to know he's being followed."

The cabby was startled and half-turned to look over his shoulder.

Koski held up her badge. "Do it now." Luckily there was little traffic and the driver quickly followed her orders.

"Driver, stay at least three cars back." They drove along a winding road leading into the hills. "Where does this road lead?" Koski asked.

"Heads out of town, past the Wrigley Mansion. You can see it up on the hill there."

She craned her neck and snatched a glimpse of the old house once owned by the chewing gum magnate. The traffic in front of them was thinning.

"What's up ahead?"

"Older houses, a couple of hotels then nothing until you get to the airport."

Koski leaned forward. "Deluxe hotels?"

"No. Mostly older houses that were converted into hotels over the years. Tourist hotels, you know."

Koski still saw the Land Rover about a quarter mile ahead.

"You part of the big search we're having?" the driver asked.

"I came over for some R&R. That guy ahead looks like my ex. He owes back pay on my alimony. I want to be sure."

The driver's eyes looked at her in the rearview. She knew he didn't believe a word.

"Could be your lucky day and here I was thinking the FBI could find anyone, anytime."

"Not true. We wouldn't need a most wanted list if it was."

The driver grunted and sped up as the Land Rover vanished around a bend ahead. Once through the curve, Koski saw the road ahead was empty.

Chapter 69

Falk sat on the bare wooden floor of a small stuffy attic. He was handcuffed to the foot of a metal-framed bed still shackled by leg irons. One hand was free from the manacles to allow him to eat and drink a meager lunch of bread and cheese. He'd taken stock of his surroundings and knew he was in a formidable prison with a thick oak door to the side, and a small skylight window above, the skylight ten feet overhead mounted flush in the ceiling.

The house was a stoutly constructed building from the days when stone and oak were the main materials and pride of workmanship mattered.

Falk had seen the luxury on the floors below in Jamul's quarters as he was hustled up to the attic. Now, as he chewed the remainder of his lunch, he knew he must escape. The longer he was a prisoner, the less chance he had of staying alive.

He sipped a mouthful of water from a tin mug. Falk removed the sliver of soap from his pocket, held it in the palm of his hand and spat a little of the water on it. Moving his free hand close to his cuffed one he tipped the water and soap into his upturned palm and rubbed both hands together, softening the soap. Then slowly massaging the slimy mixture onto his shackled wrist he started to manipulate it, pulling back slightly to free his hand. He repeated this several times, gritting his teeth against the pain.

There was only a little soap left but his hand was almost free. A few more tugs and he'd be out. The skin was raw and bleeding when he finally slipped loose. He washed the blood from his wrist with the last drop of water. Wasting no time, he tilted the bed nearly vertically against the wall beneath the skylight. Using the bed as a ladder, he inched upward, the leg irons slowing his movements.

The bed was shaky. Each movement made it shimmy. It could slide sideways at any moment and crash against the wooden floor, alerting those below. Inch by inch Falk eased upward, his eyes fastened on the glass skylight. Every fiber of his body was centered on getting to the window. He reached up, his fingers scant inches below the edge of the frame. The bed creaked and for a moment Falk thought it would go over. He reached out, touched the wall and waited. It held. He inched upward again. This time his fingertips touched the frame but he still needed at least another foot so he could work on the skylight and open it.

He saw the iron bar used to push open the window. Three holes were punched into it to enable someone to adjust the airflow into the attic. He needed to stand on the top of the bed. There was no room for error once he reached out and grabbed the iron device. He had to get the window open, pull himself up and through the opening.

He took a deep breath and steadied himself against the wall then reached up, grasped the iron lever and pushed. Nothing. It was jammed. Evidently the window hadn't been opened for years. Falk closed his eyes. His body ached with tension and fatigue. He had to open the son of a bitch—he had to.

He thought of smashing the glass with his shoe. No good. He could lose his balance and the sound of breaking glass was out. Holding the lever with one hand, he reached up and used the heel of his hand against the wooden framework. Flakes of dried paint dropped past his face. He hit against the frame three, four, five times and felt it move ever so slightly. Switching hands, he tackled the other side of the frame and felt it move a little more.

Encouraged, he thumped harder. The window opened half an inch then he felt a draft of air flow past his face. He pushed. Slowly the window yielded. With a final shove, it flung wide open, back against the roof. His fingers grasped the frame's edge as he sucked in cool air. He remained that way for a few seconds, gathering his energy for the arm-wrenching pull up and out of the window.

Focusing all his strength into his arms and shoulders, he took a firm grip and pulled himself up through the small opening until he had his head and shoulders outside. He slid onto the slate roof. He lay flat against the tiles a few feet from a brick chimney stack and sucked in lung-filling gasps. He crawled to the stack and sat with his back against the structure. He'd made it onto the roof but it was just the beginning of a dangerous journey to the ground and his escape.

Cursing the leg irons, he reached down and removed his leather-soled shoes. He tied the laces together and hung them around his neck. He needed secure traction. Confinement of the leg irons gave little room for error on a slate rooftop. In a crouched position, he moved to the ridge top and inched to the far end of the house, away from the rooms containing Jamul's entourage. He moved down the roof toward the edge at the back of the building that overlooked a large garden thirty feet below.

He quickly scanned the area. On the right was a kitchen garden with what looked like a tool or storage shed. Several rakes leaned against the wall. A wooden door was set into the brick wall. From his point of view he could see it led into a formal garden and beyond that a row of oak trees. He turned his attention to the immediate problem of getting off the roof in one piece.

Falk was relieved when he saw a sturdy iron gutter. He followed it along the eaves until he came to a drainpipe. Lying face down on the roof, he reached over, grasped the gutter and shook it. Solid as a rock. He gave silent thanks to the days when building materials were made to last.

Slowly he turned his body so he faced up toward the ridge, carefully lowered his legs over the edge, moving his feet as best he could in their restraints, trying to locate the drain. Inch by inch he lowered himself until he felt the drainpipe with the toes of his stocking feet, and edge of the iron gutter across his stomach. A few more inches and he'd be over the edge. Gripping the gutter, Falk lowered his body further until his feet were on either side of the drainpipe, the chain between the anklets conforming to the cylindrical pipe.

Grasping the gutter-to-drain connection with both hands, he started down. Suddenly he felt a tug and looked up to see one of his shoes jammed in the gutter. Quickly he reached up with one hand and tried to free it. There wasn't time, so he rotated his head and neck until the other shoe was swung free and dangled over the edge.

"Damn it." He started his descent hoping no one was in the garden to see him or hear the rasp of the chain as it slid down the pipe. When his feet touched the soil of a flowerbed, Falk shuffled toward a row of bushes and hunkered down.

Chapter 70

"We lost him!" Koski exclaimed, scanning the empty road ahead.

"I don't think so," the cabby replied. "See that row of trees ahead on the right? There's a driveway leading up to a private hospital. He must have turned in there. There's no other way he could have gone."

"Are you sure? I don't see any hospital."

"Yeah. I've been there a couple of times. Very secluded. The driveway is over a half mile long, big old house. Locals say it's a high-priced loony bin."

"Are there outside guards at the house?"

"Don't know. Never saw any when I was there. They do have closed-circuit television cameras at the gate. Do you still think that guy was your ex?"

She shook her head. "Guess not. I can't see him in a place like that."

"Like I said, it's high-priced."

"How high?"

"Folks say you could get a week at Betty Ford for what it costs for a day in that place."

"Then it wasn't my ex. He couldn't even get a job in a place like that. Let's get to my hotel."

Once in her room, Koski called Marco. "Where are you?"

"On the airport bus, almost back in town. We'll be at the hotel in five minutes."

"Fine. Come up when you arrive."

The excitement of what might turn out to be Jamul's possible hideout had removed all thoughts of sleep. She headed for the bathroom and a quick shower.

She was drying her hair when there was a knock at the door. "That you, Marco?"

"Me and Nell."

Koski opened the door and Marco and Nell entered. "You sounded excited," Marco said.

"I am. Sit down and listen up." She brought them up-to-date, including about the man in the Rav4.

"You think Jamul could be hiding out in that place?"

"I do. That guy in the Land Rover was my tip-off. He was outside our place in Hollywood then turns up here on Catalina and drives to a secluded place in the hills."

"You see him drive onto the grounds?"

"No." She twined the towel into a turban. "He was in front of us and when we went around a bend his car had vanished. The only place he could have gone was up to the house. Even the cabby thought so."

"And now you want to call in the troops and head out there?"

"Not exactly. If we go busting in with troops and police, and Joe is being held prisoner, his life wouldn't be worth a damn. They'd kill him."

"*You* want to go in and find out, right?"

"You're close. I need you and Nell as a diversion to allow me to get in and look around."

Falk glanced up at the roof and he saw his shoes hanging from the rain gutter. Crawling and keeping bushes between himself and the house, he wormed toward a wooden shed. A place to hide, take stock, and, if he was lucky, find something to cut the damn chain off the leg irons.

The door wasn't locked and several seconds later he was inside. It took a few moments for his eyes to adjust to the gloomy interior as he squinted around. He knew once they discovered he escaped, all hell would break loose.

There was the usual collection of garden tools and a small workbench. As he checked a dark corner, he noticed a set of bolt cutters half hidden behind a sack of mulch. He snatched them up and after three attempts with the cumbersome tool he was free.

On the back of the door was a set of raunchy-looking, mud-splattered Bib and Brace overalls. A straw gardening hat with a wide brim hung over them on the same nail. He decided he could make an escape disguised as a gardener. What better way than to wander through the grounds with a rake or hoe.

Falk unhooked the overalls, shrugged into them and pulled on the hat. Now he needed tools to look the part. He found a hoe and a rake then the best item of all, a pair of Wellington boots. He tipped them over to make sure there wasn't a spider's nest inside, shook them and noticed they were a size bigger than he usually wore. He pulled them on and stuffed the severed chains down among the old tools in the workbench drawer. At least now he could move in a more normal fashion.

Tugging the brim of the hat low across his forehead, he cracked the door open and looked outside—all clear. He shouldered his tools, stepped out into the garden and trudged around the side of the house toward the main entrance. Had no one noticed he'd gone?

Glancing up he saw his shoes still hanging in the gutter. Then he saw the man who'd driven them to the place. He was with another hulkish-looking character. They both looked agitated as they rounded the side of the building looking every way at once.

Falk stopped and began working on a flowerbed with the hoe, head down, paying close attention to his work.

The driver pointed toward Falk, said something and they parted. Hulky headed toward Falk, the driver going off in the opposite direction.

"Hey. You see a guy around here in leg irons?" the man yelled as he got closer to Falk, who didn't look up. He just kept on working, his heart beating faster than normal. Then Hulky was next to him. Falk glanced at him as if he'd just become aware someone was there.

"You deaf? Did you hear what I said?"

Falk shook his head and played dumb.

"Did a man go past here? Leg irons?" Hulky pointed to his own ankles thinking he was trying to communicate with some foreigner whose knowledge of the English language was somewhat lacking.

Falk grinned, nodded, looked at the man's ankles then back at the man and grinned inanely again.

"Dumb shit." Hulky shook his head and pushed past Falk who was once again busy hoeing.

Falk needed to get away from the private wing area. He waited a few minutes then slowly sidled his way toward the front of the building, raking and hoeing as he went. Keeping his eyes on his work, he finally arrived close to the front entrance.

Quickly scanning the car park, he noticed an old pickup truck parked alone, away from a group of up-to-date expensive automobiles. Shouldering his tools, he ambled to the lonely vehicle, threw the rake and hoe into the bed, opened the driver's door and got in. No yells or shouts. The owner of the truck was nowhere around and there wasn't a key.

Falk expertly hot-wired the engine to life, checked the gas gauge, released the hand brake and moved out. He was halfway down the long driveway to the main road when he saw a car approaching. Tugging the brim of his straw hat a little lower, he increased his speed. As the car passed, he took a glance at the occupants and almost swerved off the road. Koski was at the wheel. Both cars screeched to a halt. He saw her turn the car around and pull up beside him.

"Joe! I can't believe this. Get in. Quick."

Falk was in the car in seconds and she had the car in motion before he could close the door. Marco, in the back seat with Nell, leaned forward. "Hey, man. You look like a picture of my mother's brother when he was doing stoop labor in the San Joaquin Valley back in the fifties."

"Thanks."

Koski asked. "Where's Jamul?"

"Back there. Private wing of the hospital." Falk checked the rearview. "What were the odds of you finding me here?"

"A million to one. And if it hadn't been for a comment by a cab driver and a guy in a Land Rover, I'd still be looking."

"Stop the car," Falk ordered.

"What?"

"Stop the car. I don't want to leave the truck standing in the middle of the drive. Soon as they see it abandoned they'll know I was picked up. I'll follow you in the truck."

Imminent Danger

Chapter 71

The reports to Stewart's office on the mainland from around the island were dismal. DHS was still in a major search mode but with no results and no contact from Koski.

"Jack, every hour that passes diminishes our chances of finding them."

Wolf nodded and looked over at Pease, half-asleep on a sagging couch.

Pease opened one eye. "You said you were going to get me out of the country."

"Well, you'll have to wait a little longer, Mr. Pease. I have some pressing problems at the moment."

Pease sighed and closed his eye.

Marco made a suggestion. "It'd work out better if Nell and I drove the truck and followed you two back to the hotel. That way, if they show up, Nell and I can go off in a different direction while you and Agent Koski get the word to Stewart."

Falk agreed that what Marco said made sense. "Okay, Marco. Let's do it."

There still was no sight of any one heading down the long drive as Marco and Nell got into the truck. Marco was behind the wheel when Falk called out. "Hey, I forgot to mention there was no key. You'll have to..." Before he could finish Marco had the engine running.

"No problem." Marco waited until Koski turned left onto the road then started down the driveway. Glancing into the rearview, he saw a fast-moving Land Rover come suddenly into view. Marco stepped on the gas and turned right at the end of the drive.

The Land Rover was gaining on him and Marco knew he'd be overhauled in minutes.

"They're gaining on us," Nell murmured. Then the rear window shattered as a bullet went through the cab and out the windshield. Pulling to the right, Marco skidded to a halt on the dusty soft shoulder and a cloud of dust obliterated the truck.

"Get on the floor and stay there," Marco yelled. "Don't move."

A thin man and Hulky climbed from the Land Rover and walked toward the truck before the dust settled. That was when Marco backed up fast, hitting both men hard. They went down like chaff.

Marco leapt from the truck. Both men were groaning. Hulky groggily aimed an automatic at Marco who kicked it from his hand, scooped up the weapon and shot the man in the head. Thin man was face down, groaning. As Marco approached him he rolled over—an automatic in his right hand—and fired.

Marco stopped in mid-stride as the impact of the bullet into his right shoulder spun him to one side. Thin man took aim again but Marco, despite the agonizing pain in his shoulder, flung himself at the man on the ground as a second shot grazed his cheek. Marco's knee connected hard into the man's groin. He wrested the weapon from the man's grip with his left hand and shot him in the kneecap.

"Amigos, when the cops arrive tell them you were shot by an Islamic terrorist then show them your green card. Adios."

Nell was out of the truck at the sound of the second shot. She saw Marco getting to his feet and ran toward him.

"I said wait in the truck," Marco yelled.

"I know. Now it's time I got out of the truck. Look at you!"

Marco nodded toward the Land Rover. "Can you drive one of those?"

Nell held him around the waist and walked to the vehicle. "Sure, I can."

"Good. Let's get back into town and update Falk."

"You killed one and kneecapped the other!" Koski exclaimed as she examined Marco's flesh wound. "Another inch to the right and it would have shattered your collar bone."

"I know."

"It happened so fast, Koski. I've never seen anything like it," Nell said breathlessly.

Falk, cleaned up and wearing a change of clothes, came in from the bedroom. "Good job, Marco. I'm proud of you. There's a corpsman on his way over from the Coast Guard to patch you up."

"*I'll* feel proud when I have my money in a Swiss bank."

"I just got off the phone with Stewart. There'll be just a few details to clear up."

"Like what?"

"When Jamul is brought in and we find out who's behind all this."

"Man! Bringing him in won't do a thing except get a lot of big time lawyers into a pissing contest to see who can prove him innocent."

"He has to stand trial, Marco," Koski said.

"Do what you have to do, okay?"

Falk nodded. "You and Nell are going back to the mainland. Stewart's arranged protective custody for you both until we get Jamul. He also assured me he would see you get the original conditions you asked for. You've done a hell of a job, Marco."

The corpsman finished his work, and Marco was strapped into a sling and seated beside Nell.

"Koski and I are heading back to the Coast Guard station," Falk explained. "See you two on the mainland."

Once outside, Koski asked, "What's at the Coast Guard?"

"We're not really going there."

"Where are we going?"

"I know where Jamul is. If we get a task force charging into the hospital he'll simply say he'd been held captive by a terrorist who got away and the public will believe him. That's why I'm going to make Jamul a martyr."

Koski took a deep breath. "You mean…"

"Kill him. The report will read that his militant Islamic captor killed him. Think how the people will react. Their hero murdered."

Koski exclaimed, "You mean it, don't you?"

"Stewart has sanctioned the plan to be carried out by Cerberus, too much chance of a leak if done any other way."

"Where do I fit in, Joe?"

"Other than knowing the plan, you stay with DHS at the Coast Guard station. Stewart's orders."

"We're a team, Joe…"

"You'll have to sit this one out."

Koski's lips tightened. The idea of setting off to kill a man in cold blood worried her. Had Cerberus joined the rest of the world in casual "Wet Jobs"—removing people and manipulating the results to look like murder by someone else? Evidently, the answer was yes.

"When does it happen, Joe?"

"Tonight. I know the inside of the building." He tapped his cell phone. "I'll be notified if he tries to leave."

"I don't like it, Joe."

"I'll be fine." He put his arm around her waist and pulled her close. "I'll be okay." They embraced and kissed. She rested her head on his shoulder and wondered if he'd *asked* to go alone and not involve her in a premeditated murder.

Chapter 72

Officer Robert Gully went off duty while police, fire and emergency crews were placed on red alert until further notice. He returned to the Hollywood station, changed and headed up the San Diego Freeway to the San Fernando Valley. Local news constantly updated details of the attack.

As usual, experts said they had expected something like this. The government hadn't been vigilant and the DHS was unprepared. Gully snapped off the radio.

"Dammed media," Gully said aloud. "When will they learn they're preaching to the choir?"

As he topped the hill on the 405 and started down into the Valley, he checked the time. It was a little before five p.m. Harry Greenwood would still be at his place in Encino. Gully touched his jacket pocket, reassuring himself the bio weapon was safe. Harry would wet his pants when he saw what he had for sale.

The Rainbow Gold and Coin Exchange was on Ventura Boulevard in a two-story stucco office building. Greenwood told his clients he chose the location because it was safer than a storefront.

Customers knew it was for security reasons. Everybody had to buzz to get through the front door. The door opened into a steel cage with three security cameras. Someone on staff verified each client's name and checked it off in the appointment book. No one got past the cage without an appointment.

Gully parked on Havenhurst Avenue and walked down to Ventura. He thought it smarter to stay out of parking garages. They recorded in and out times, and license plate numbers were often captured on video, and he wanted neither.

He skipped the elevator and walked to the second floor. Greenwood's place was at the back of the building, last door on the right. He pushed the button and was buzzed into the cage.

"Hey, Bob. How you doing?" a tinny-shounding voice asked.

Another loud buzz and Gully walked into a thickly carpeted place of business.

Harry Greenwood was a heavyset man in his fifties. He stood at the glass counter next to a no smoking sign, a double-Corona cigar gripped between his large yellowed teeth. The cigar was unlit.

"Doing okay, Harry," Gully replied. "Like I said on the phone, I've got something to sell."

"You shoulda maybe told me what it was, like I asked you. You may have wasted a trip."

"Don't think so. We need to be in private."

Greenwood's thick eyebrows form a "V." "I can give ya five minutes."

"Fine."

"C'mon." Greenwood opened another electronically operated door and the two went into his office. The staff had already left for the day. Gully waited until Greenwood sat behind his gigantic oak desk. Reaching into his jacket pocket, Gully removed the bio weapon and laid it in the center of the desk.

Greenwood leaned forward in his chair. "What the hell's that? Ya playing games?"

"That, Harry, is worth millions."

"I don't have time for dumb jokes…"

"Wait. Let me demonstrate." Gully moved the weapon around on his forefinger until it was correctly positioned. "Now point at something in the room I can use as a target."

"Hold it. Whaddya mean, target?"

"Something you don't care about like that vase full of imitation flowers on the side table. They look like shit anyway."

Greenwood looked over at the vase and scowled. "Okay. Get to it. I ain't got all day."

Gully wasted no time. He simply pointed at the vase, touched his thumb on the recessed trigger and squeezed. The vase disintegrated.

Greenwood opened his mouth and the cigar fell in his lap. "What the fuck? Whaddya do?"

Gully shrugged. "I just gave you a demonstration of a weapon of mass destruction. It's yours for only $500,000—cash. With your connections you can triple that."

"I'll need details, Bob."

Gully told him all he knew about the weapon. Greenwood could sell it to the Russians or Chinese, who would take it apart and make their own.

Greenwood was impressed. He knew what Gully had would be easy to sell and offered the man $300,000, finally agreeing on $450,000. "Wait here. I'll have to go to the vault. I suppose ya want me to validate yer parking ticket, too," he rasped.

"No need, Harry. I didn't use the parking garage." Greenwood nodded and left the room.

Gully never heard the suppressed .45 Colt that sent a bullet through his head.

Harry Greenwood reholstered his weapon. He'd have one of his boys remove the body. It was good luck for him, and bad for Gully that no one saw Gully enter. He'd locate Gully's car and have it disposed of somewhere across town where it would look like some street punk had stolen and vandalized it. Greenwood picked up the bio weapon and slipped it into his pocket. He'd also make sure Gully's name was removed from the appointment book.

Imminent Danger

Chapter 73

As the nine millimeter slug went through Gully's head, Joe Falk walked through the main entrance of the private hospital he'd escaped from only hours before. This time he was dressed in suit and tie and carried a slim briefcase.

He crossed to the reception desk and introduced himself as Joseph Stewart, an attorney retained by a family in Pasadena. He was to personally check out the nursing home, meet with the director and confer in detail on all levels of the operation. The family sought assurance of complete secrecy in all matters. Falk handed his card to the receptionist. He had the card made less than an hour earlier at a local print shop.

"I'm sure dropping in unannounced is not the way you usually conduct business," Falk said with a smile. "May I speak with the head man?" He paused. "Or is it head lady?"

The receptionist smiled. "Head man is correct. Doctor Richardson. Doctor Victor Richardson. Please take a seat, Mr. Stewart. He's with someone. It shouldn't be too long."

Falk glanced in the direction the woman indicated before walking over to some couches and chairs arranged around a large fireplace. He noticed an old-fashioned elevator with an ornate iron pointer above the door. The pointer stopped on two.

Eventually the elevator door opened and Richardson stepped out. He paused a moment, saw Falk and headed toward him.

"Good evening. I'm Doctor Victor Richardson. How can I help you?"

Falk unfolded from the chair. "Joseph Stewart. I appreciate you seeing me without an appointment."

"Not at all, Mr. Stewart," he replied. "Let's go to my office."

Once seated, Falk began his speech. "I represent a family who needs to place their aging father into a private facility. The man is a well-known figure in the business world. His family doesn't want anyone to know he's here. The multinational corporation he heads would lose millions if the stockholders even thought their investment was in a company with a sick man at the helm."

Falk continued. "The story being released is that he's going to be fishing in the far west and will be unreachable."

The doctor had heard many reasons over the years and this was as good as any.

"So we're looking at least a month. Correct?"

"Possibly six weeks. It all depends on how much security and secrecy you can provide."

"Of course." Richardson looked as if he was mentally toting up the cost.

Falk took out a small pad and pen. "I jotted down a few questions. I'll ask the questions and make margin notes. It'll be easier for both of us." Falk didn't want him to see the questions were nothing but scrawl he'd jotted before leaving the hotel.

"Fine. I'll walk you through the facilities and you can ask questions as we go."

"Good idea, doctor."

The receptionist glanced up as they walked past, quickly picked up her phone and then tapped a few digits. "We have someone taking a tour with Doctor Richardson. The visitor's business card says he's a lawyer. Do you want me to check out the number?"

Jamul's face darkened. "No. Whoever answers will know we have doubts about him. I'll take care of it." Jamul put down the phone. "He's back," he said softly.

Less than an hour after moving into the private quarters at the hospital, Jamul's men had visited the receptionist and other key personnel. He made them an offer they couldn't resist. They were to report any unusual visitor activity and would be well paid.

Now the call from the front desk was paying off.

"I can get backup," Brasinov said.

Jamul shook his head. He needed to keep a low profile. As long as he had someone with him whom he could kill and say he was the terrorist that had abducted him, he felt secure in fooling the authorities.

"What do I do if it's the agent?"

"Kill him. Find Falk's partner and bring her to me," Jamul said calmly. He went into the bedroom, took a bio weapon from his bedside table and adjusted it beneath the forefinger of his right hand. He removed his old man wig and beard and again was his imposing self.

"As you can see," Richardson suggested, "in no way do we resemble an ordinary nursing home. We think of our patients as guests." He was right. The interior had little resemblance to an institution. It looked more like what it once was—a gracious home.

"Our security is non-intrusive. We have a silent alarm system that is directly connected to police headquarters in Avalon."

They approached a graceful wooden staircase curving to the upper floors. There were oil paintings of stern-faced men gracing the wall and staring with disdain at anyone using the staircase. Richardson noticed Falk eyeing the portraits as they ascended.

"Past owners. They came with the place."

"Interesting." Falk's mind tried to figure the location of Jamul's quarters from where he was standing. They'd walked down long corridors with many twists and turns and he was no longer sure of his bearings.

"My client instructed me to inquire about private quarters away from the general populace."

Richardson stopped on the stairs and looked over his shoulder. "All of our guests have total privacy. They can remain in their quarters as long as they wish. We have all the amenities possible to take excellent care of them."

They continued and Falk knew as soon as he got the opportunity to look out of one of the upstairs windows he'd be able to orient himself as to

269

where he'd been when he made his escape.

"I was asked to look at rooms with a view, preferably facing south."

The doctor smiled. "Ah, a view of the ocean. Good choice. This floor is perfect." He nodded toward one of the windows. "Allow me to show you." Standing side by side Richardson pointed out details like a tour guide.

"We're located on a high point on the island that's surrounded by over three hundred acres of native land, wild and unspoiled. Buffalo herds, bison to be exact, roam freely. They've been breeding since their transfer from Wyoming in the 1920s to make a western movie. The magnificent beasts remained after the film was completed and over the years became native to the area. We're very proud of them."

In the distance, the Pacific twinkled in the evening sun. Falk recalled catching a glimpse of the sea as he worked his way along the roof ridge before descending the drainpipe. He knew immediately where Jamul's quarters were.

"Another important factor is the lack of traffic or noise. We are five miles from Avalon via the canyon road. Guests can walk or be wheeled about without breathing tainted air. " The doctor's mobile chirped. "Excuse me." Richardson moved away, leaving Falk time to solidify his plan. Jamul was on the third floor of the maximum privacy wing. Evidently Jamul had not attempted to leave after Falk escaped. He must have been secure that he arranged everything so he could remain in seclusion despite any search of the house. If they did close in on him, he could always say he was being held hostage.

"Sorry about that, Mr. Stewart."

Falk waved his hand. "I understand. You're a very busy man." He glanced at his watch. "I wonder if I'd be allowed to wander around on my own to get the feeling of the place. I have hard taskmasters to report to."

"I can have one of my security people accompany you. I'll instruct them to stay back, not bother you but still have you in sight. You do understand?"

"Of course, Doctor. I'd be concerned if you hadn't suggested it. In fact, I'll be sure to mention your concern for your guest's safety and security when I complete my report."

"Very well. I'll see to everything at once." The doctor opened his phone and spoke rapidly. He looked up with a smile. "All taken care of. He's on his way."

Imminent Danger

Chapter 74

Falk and Richardson gazed out across the hills. They heard footsteps. Turning, Falk saw a pleasant looking young man approaching, late twenties, medium build.

"Here's Keith now," Doctor Richardson said. "He'll answer any questions you have. I'll be in my office if you need me."

"Thanks, Doctor. I won't take long."

"No problem. Regulations you know." Richardson headed to the elevator.

"Are all the rooms on this floor occupied?" Falk asked.

"Most of them," the young man replied. "Let me check. I have a list." He removed a sheet of paper from his pocket. "There are two vacancies on this floor."

"I'd like to see inside to get an idea of the size. The people I work for will have a lot of questions."

"Sure. Which one would you like?"

"Sea view, definitely."

"Okay." He indicated a door down the hall on the right. Removing a bunch of keys, the man opened the door and stood back. "Go ahead. Take your time. Look around."

Falk went straight to the back of the apartment and checked the rear windows that looked out on to well-kept gardens and wild countryside. Moving slightly to his left, Falk could see the edge of the wing he had escaped from. It was one floor higher and much further back from where he stood.

Now he had a better understanding of the layout. He'd have to get rid of the security guard and find a way to get into Jamul's quarters. The heavy drapes still in place gave him an idea. Pulling them aside, he checked the stout cords that opened and closed them. He took a penknife from his pocket, reached up as high as he could and cut the cords down. He wrapped them around his waist and buttoned his jacket. Falk waited so it looked like he was checking all the rooms before he rejoined the guard.

"Nice apartment," Falk said, "but not private enough. Is there anything more remote from the rest of the house?"

"All the apartments are safe and secure, Mr. Stewart."

"I have no doubt. My people want *absolute* privacy. Let's keep looking. Perhaps the top floor will have something to offer."

"Full, sir, I'm afraid. It's always full. They have the best views."

"I noticed there's a wing attached. I saw it from the back windows of the apartment I was just in. Is that part of the hospital?"

"Old and drafty staff quarters. No guest would want to stay there."

Falk shook his head. "Seems like a waste. I'm sure it has a great view and is very private. I think Doctor Richardson is missing a bet not using it for his patients."

"You'd have to talk to him about that, sir."

"I will. I'll walk through the third floor and that'll be all, I think." Falk pointed to the elevator. "Let's ride up."

The man pulled open the elevator door and stood aside. Falk stepped back in the car and unbuttoned his jacket. He removed the cord from around his waist as the man busied himself closing the door and attending to the old manual controls. It happened fast. The cord looped up and over the young man's head and tightened around his throat. "Relax. I'm not going to kill you but you will be out of sight for awhile."

Falk applied just the right amount of tension to the cord until the man passed out and slumped to the floor. He wound the cord under the man's arms and around his chest. The elevator was at the third floor.

Looking up, he saw the escape hatch on top of the car. He took one end of the cord between his teeth. He jumped up and grasped the ledge of the

274

opening. Falk placed the soles of his shoes against the wall and stretched until the top of his head was touching the grillwork of the hatch cover, then pushed. The grill moved and Falk continued pressing through until he was on top of the elevator looking down at the guard. Using all his strength, he grasped the guard's collar, dragged him through the hatch, and laid him on the car roof.

Gasping from the exertion, he removed the cord, cut it into lengths and bound his victim's hands and feet. The man groaned and Falk knew he was going to be okay. Nonetheless, Falk removed a handkerchief from his pocket and stuffed it into his mouth. The light from the elevator illuminated a ledge set into the elevator shaft. It looked like a work area for the repair technicians. He pulled the guard onto the ledge and pushed him as far back as was possible.

"If you can hear me, remain still. Don't try and move or you could fall three floors. I'll tell the authorities where you are. When the time is right, you'll be rescued."

Falk then dropped a length of the cord through one of the holes in the escape grill, let it fall into the car and then lowered himself down. He eased the grill cover back into place by jerking on the cord then pulled the cord free and stuffed it into his pocket. Glancing up he made sure everything looked normal before pressing the button for the ground floor.

Leaving the elevator and glancing toward the reception area, he saw a man seated at the desk. His head was down and he appeared to be engrossed in paperwork. Evidently the shifts changed while he was on the upper floors. Falk walked across the foyer and down a long corridor toward the wing containing Jamul's apartments.

Two nurses approached, laughing and talking to each other. They didn't seem to notice someone wandering the corridors. Perhaps the suit and briefcase made him appear legitimate. He nodded as they passed. So much for Dr. Richardson's so-called super security.

The polished tiles beneath his feet suddenly ended. It was replaced by wall-to-wall carpeting that was thick, soft and expensive. He recognized the place where Jamul and his party had stood when Dr. Richardson and the nurses greeted him as he sat twisted in the wheelchair. Now the place had an unearthly quiet like a church at twilight.

Jamul turned the bio weapon on and off with his thumb as he slowly calmed down and glanced up at a flat plasma screen television hanging on the wall. The picture was in sharp, crisp color and showed the corridor leading to the door of his suite. One of his men covered Jamul from the bedroom. Anyone entering the suite put themselves in a deadly crossfire zone.

On the second floor of the wing Falk suddenly felt a shiver run through his body. It was his personal built-in alarm, an endowment that had saved his life several times. He was being watched. He glanced back then retraced his steps to a door marked Dispensary. In seconds, he picked the lock, entered and switched on the light then locked the door behind him.

It was a small, windowless room. Falk ran his eyes over the shelves of chemicals and bottles. Six oxygen tanks stood in a row against one wall. He examined their gauges—full. Then he checked a natural gas outlet attached to a Bunsen burner. A telephone stood on a desk. Falk quickly memorized the number. He turned on the gas, opened the valves on all the canisters and once he heard the steady hiss exited the dispensary.

Falk backtracked to the ground floor and left by a side door. Dusk had turned into night and he silently moved around the side of the house and stood in the deepest of shadows.

The guests were at dinner and the security guard was safe on his ledge. Falk took out his cell and called the number of the phone in the dispensary. He kept the cell at his side and concentrated his gaze on the second floor wall near the dispensary.

Suddenly a dull thump came from the building, followed immediately by a blinding flash as the wall split apart into a gaping hole. A gush of yellow orange flame leapt into the darkness. The fire alarms clamored throughout the building. Lights came on, shining from every window. Falk knew Jamul had to come out and was ready for him.

The floor heaved beneath Jamul's feet when the huge explosion blew the dispensary wall across the gardens below. A second later, his bedroom door flew open and one of Jamul's men staggered into the living room and leaned against the wall. Jamul pointed and thumbed the recessed trigger on the bio weapon. The man's eyes widened for a second before crumpling to the carpet.

Jamul walked into the bedroom and retrieved his white wig from the dressing table. He put it on and checked in the mirror. It was time for Jamul to leave—alone.

Moving quickly, Jamul went into the corridor and ran in the opposite direction from the cloud of billowing smoke. Ahead he saw a lighted sign above an emergency exit. He pushed the bar, thrust through and started down a set of stone stairs.

At the second floor he was suddenly among other guests trying to make it down the last flight and to the safety of the outdoors. He immediately transformed into the bent-shouldered old man. No one could recognize him as the famous Jamul. He would be even less noticeable once outside.

Falk watched the guests stream from various exits and stand in huddled groups as the nurses and orderlies checked on those in need. He had picked the right fire exit, knowing Jamul would head away from the original source of the disaster. He saw him, head and shoulders taller than the rest.

Staying in the shadows, he moved closer. In the distance, he already heard the sound of fire and emergency vehicles. Jamul had edged his way toward the far side of the building. He was going to run for it. Why? Falk wondered. Now was the perfect time for him to come forward and claim he escaped his captors.

Falk saw Jamul look over his shoulder as if undecided whether to return, then he started to move in the opposite direction. Perhaps he sensed Falk was nearby and decided to postpone his grand entrance for a later, safer time. It was at that moment their eyes met over the crowd. Falk saw a quick flash of a smile as Jamul turned and vanished into the darkness.

Police and ambulance personnel wheeled their vehicles around the building, screeching to a stop in an untidy group in front of the hotel. Red and swirling blue lights added to the confusion as two TV trucks rolled into the scene.

Imminent Danger

Pushing his way through the crowd, Falk followed. Jamul was already out of sight, somewhere in the blackness of the wild open land surrounding the hospital.

Falk took out his nine millimeter, clicked the safety off and moved forward into the blackness.

Brasinov, standing apart from the crowd, watched Jamul and Falk vanish into the night.

His orders had been to bring the agent's partner to Jamul. He always obeyed orders.

Chapter 75

Stewart wasn't able to contact Koski. Calls to Coast Guard, Avalon over the last two hours reported the same. Stewart wondered if he'd made a mistake in separating his two best agents. It was possible that Falk had disobeyed orders and taken Koski with him to kill Jamul. They had both bent a few rules in the past.

Stewart tapped a rapid tattoo with his fingertips on the desktop, wondering if the serenity of his own retirement would even match a small part of what Pease could look forward to. Pease had agreed to give full details of his bio weapons to the U.S. government in exchange for protection by the Federal Witness Protection Program and a home in Switzerland.

A saying from Stewart's schooldays ran through his mind. "*The extremity of justice is extreme injustice.*" As he tried to recall who had written the quotation, his phone rang.

"Stewart." He tilted back his chair and closed his eyes as he listened to the voice. Then he let the chair return to all four legs. "Goddamn it, Grant. I've had it with you. No. I don't know where Falk is and if I did I'd warn him to get as far away from you as possible.

"You and that damn scooter are being recalled to Washington, under close arrest if need be." He listened to the splutter and blather from the other end. "Grant. Take my advice and go home. Take workers' comp for a few weeks."

Slamming the phone down, he muttered, "Take a prick out of the news media and put him in the DHS and you have a prick in the DHS."

Coast Guard Catalina phoned Stewart and informed him of the

explosion and fire at the convalescent home. Stewart immediately arranged for his party, including Pease, to get over to the island at once. Stewart felt hampered by having Pease with his group but knew safety called for him to be under Cerberus protection at all times.

They crossed by high speed Hovercraft from Marina Del Rey. Due to FAA rules, The Airport in the Sky on Catalina closed at sundown.

The radio crackled and the voice of the major in charge of the search reported that a security guard was rescued from inside an elevator shaft at the hospital after an anonymous phone call had given his exact location. The man suffered ligature marks on his neck and a major sore throat but otherwise was in good health. He said he'd be able to identify his attacker.

Standing beside the radio operator, Stewart made a mental note to be sure the man and Falk never meet face-to-face. He reached for a microphone and toggled the switch.

"Are all the residents accounted for, major?"

"I was informed there are two dead, sir. One by a gunshot wound and the other was an apparent heart attack. An African diplomat also is missing."

Stewart pinched the bridge of his nose. "Diplomat? What do we know about him?"

"Very little at the moment," the operator replied. "The doctor who runs the place is hesitant to say too much. Says his guests, as he calls them, demand privacy at all times."

"Did he now. Well, he's going to find out that during a nationwide red security alert, he'll be fully debriefed and *will* answer *all* questions. Get right on it. Let me know the outcome." Stewart went on deck and squinted through the darkness and flying spume as the boat raced toward Avalon's glowing lights.

Falk trailed through the darkness after Jamul. He was able to catch an occasional glimpse of his quarry but never close enough to be sure he didn't miss when he fired.

Suddenly the smell of ozone filled his nostrils and a branch above his head snapped and fell to the ground. For a moment Falk thought the tree had been struck by lightning. There was no rain or sign of a thunderstorm. Then it came to him. Jamul had a bio weapon! The ozone smell was the particle beams from the high frequency laser blasting through the damp night air. There wasn't any sound but the dampness could have caused the odor when the weapon fired.

Falk squinted trying to see any movement ahead. Nothing but blackness. A wisp of fog swirled in from the Pacific to add to the problem. He sank into a crouch and waited. Jamul had the advantage. He was a black man on a black night with a weapon that made no sound to give away his position. Falk realized he'd been suckered into the chase—a chase that wouldn't end until one of them was dead.

When Jamul faded away from the crowd at the hotel, he moved toward town. Falk could see the soft glow of Avalon in the distance. Jamul had to move. As long as Falk remained hunkered down Jamul could make his escape.

Falk laid flat on the earth and belly crawled to an oak tree on his right and again peered into the darkness. At least he had something between him and the bio gun. How far did it shoot? Could its particle beams penetrate a tree?

Then he heard a sound. A snuffling and crunching that was slow and deliberate. The sound got closer, moving in on either side of him. The darkness was suffocating. He couldn't see anything. The sound was nearer now and an even darker mass loomed beside him. He felt the sudden warmth of hot breath and animalistic snorts. He remained rigid as four huge bison, their humped shapes looming, slowly grazed their way through the grass. Falk felt his blood run cold. If provoked, one of those brutes could stomp him to death in seconds.

Now the smell of ozone mixed with the pungent odor of the beasts. One of the bison stopped in mid movement, buckled at the knees and heeled over, crashing to the ground a few feet from Falk. The others made a deep rumbling sound, pawed the ground and charged forward at an amazing speed for such ungainly-looking brutes.

Staring ahead, Falk saw a figure, backlit by the distant glow of light from the town. It rose from the ground and ran crashing through the brush and thick grass. Falk noted Jamul had gotten rid of his wig to guarantee complete camouflage in the darkness. The ground around them shook and vibrated with the thud of charging bison as others in the herd came bursting through.

Quickly Falk went around the oak and stayed on the lee side as the rest of the herd streamed by. As the last animal passed, Falk ran across the side of the hill toward town. In the distance, he saw car headlights as they drove up the canyon. Falk scrambled down the steep slope toward the road, grasping tufts of thick grass to stop himself from sliding headlong into the canyon. The bison were nowhere in sight. He wondered how such large beasts could vanish so quickly.

Falk grunted as his ankle connected with a thick clump of gorse and a sharp pain ripped up his leg almost toppling him. He regained his balance and made it to the roadside.

What was Jamul's plan? Announce he'd escaped his captor during the evacuation at the hospital? Falk watched for any sign of movement alongside the canyon. Cars passed, their headlights momentarily lighting the sides of the highway. Keeping in the shadows, he edged his way down the narrow canyon road toward Avalon.

The road was about five miles from town. Both men were in good shape. They could be in the heart of Avalon in less than an hour. Falk lengthened his stride, gritting his teeth, and trying to ignore the growing pain in his ankle.

Chapter 76

Stewart stepped ashore dockside in Avalon and headed straight for the Coast Guard station. Crescent Street was awash in tourists enjoying the evening. He noticed the famous Casino Ballroom ablaze with lights. The building had once been the mecca of the big bands since the 1930s and 1940s and continued entertaining young people and their choices of music to the present day.

A large poster in a store window announced the music of the 1940s would be playing that very evening at the Casino.

Stewart pushed through the doors of the Coast Guard station and found people moving in all directions. He saw the major in conversation with Falk and immediately joined them.

"Tom, we've got zilch," the major growled.

Stewart secretly wondered if perhaps he'd made a mistake in concentrating on Catalina. Jamul could've gone almost anywhere. "What did you hear about the African diplomat?"

"All we know is he was listed as 'Mr. Saba and party'."

"And party?"

"Yes. The doctor finally came clean. He said there were five in the party, all men, one of them in a wheelchair."

Falk grimaced. "That was me. Now all we have is two dead men; one supposedly dead of a heart attack."

"Damn it, Major," Stewart said. "Jamul escaped from under our noses. Hundreds are combing the island and he still escapes!"

"There was a new report of two men, one shot dead and the other kneecapped. The police are questioning the wounded man as we speak. Jamul can't get off the island without us knowing," the major said defensively.

"Right. There are several thousand people out there, major." Stewart jabbed his thumb over his shoulder in the direction of Crescent Street. "They'll all be going home after an Easter weekend by ferry, private boat, airplane, you name it. You think we can check all of them?"

"We can try, sir."

"Trying isn't good enough. We have to nail his ass before the tourist exodus starts tomorrow morning. You've had all boats checked, shops, private homes, anyplace anyone can hide out, right?"

"Including some places that we might hear from later who want to sue us for invasion of privacy."

"Let them. Okay, Falk. Bring me up-to-date."

Chapter 77

Stewart boiled after Falk finished his story. "You let him get away!"

"I didn't *let* him, Tom. A bison stampede and utter darkness can throw one's aim off."

"Well, you'd better get that ankle taped up. We still have a chance of finding him. Then you can finish what I sent you to do."

A Coast Guardsman came by with two cups of coffee and handed one to each of them.

"Thanks," Falk muttered and grimaced as the tape grew tighter around his ankle. He placed his weight on it. The corpsman had done a good job. The pain had lessened.

"He can't be too far away. I wasn't far behind him when I lost him." He checked his watch. "Now he's about twenty-five minutes ahead of me."

The crowds were still heading toward the Casino Ballroom. Stewart nodded out the window. "Big night tonight at the Ballroom. That place will be full. They can handle over three thousand five hundred on the dance floor."

Falk glanced toward the famous landmark. It was lit up with hundreds of bright twinkling lights, a beacon attraction for music and lovers. He turned to Stewart.

"What's going on there tonight?"

"Big Band music," Stewart answered. "A salute to the music of the 1930s through the 1950s and a pain in the ass for security. We're checking everyone who enters. Why?"

"A hunch," exclaimed Falk. "Jamul made his debut as a singer in New

York City years ago in an amateur contest at Radio City Music Hall. It was his first step into big time. He sang a Frank Sinatra classic, won first place and never looked back."

"You think he's hiding in the crowds at the Ballroom? He'd never make it through security."

"No. I think he'd purposely go there to make a statement. He wants to show everyone he's escaped from his Islamic captors, strut in the limelight and be adored by his fans."

Koski had returned to her hotel after Falk left on his assignment. She was flipping through old magazines in the foyer. Killing time wasn't one of her usual pastimes. Finally she went up to her room and watched late breaking news on TV until she tired of the sameness of all the talking heads.

She tried reading a paperback but tossed it aside after a few chapters. Instead she decided to freshen up, change and go down for an early dinner. She was almost through with her dessert when a man pulled a chair away from her table and sat down.

Koski froze and her heart beat faster. Brasinov sat opposite her, his black eyes glinting and a thin smile on his thin cruel lips.

"Good evening, Ms. Koski. Where is Agent Falk?"

"He wasn't hungry. What do you want?"

"Please, don't let me interrupt. Finish your dessert then we can talk about our days in Vienna."

Koski didn't want to talk about the time she and Falk had been involved with Brasinov on one of their assignments in Austria.

"Actually, I'm here to take you to someone who will make you a household name."

"I don't want to go anywhere with you." Koski set down her fork and spoon.

"As you would guess, I have a gun aimed at you. Please, no heroics. We'll leave together like a civilized couple."

Koski knew she had no choice. When they sauntered from the dining room, she felt the hard metal snout of an automatic touching her ribs.

The melodious beat of the band already oozed throughout the ballroom by the time Falk arrived at the stage door. Stewart called ahead and advised DHS security that Falk was to liaise with them backstage.

Once inside, a surly stage manager met Falk. "I hope you're the last one. I have a show to tend to." Falk assured him he was. "Good. I'll give you a quick tour then you're on your own. C'mon."

Together they walked through what seemed organized chaos to Falk. Cables snaked across the floor, ropes and scenery. Everything had an odd, temporary look about it—a circus waiting for the last act so they could pack up and move out.

"Up there are what are known as the flies." The stage manager pointed upward and Falk gazed at a maze of wires, ropes with sandbags attached, motorized rigging equipment and a rack of spotlights attached to a catwalk fifty feet above their heads.

"No one's working up there tonight. Having just the bands we've no need for backdrops or scenery. C'mon, you can see the band on stage now." Falk heard the brass blaring as they neared the wings. The stage manager tugged Falk's sleeve. "Wait here." The stage was brightly lit and members of the orchestra were hard at work. Falk tried to squint out across the footlights but the glare made it impossible.

"Where are the others from DHS?" Falk asked.

"Dunno. I told them to do whatever they had to do. Just stay out of my way." He looked over his shoulder toward the ropes and scenery then checked his watch. "I gotta go. You look around. Be careful. It's easy to get hurt if you don't keep a sharp eye open."

"Thanks." Falk again looked out into the darkness beyond the footlights then into them. Was Jamul out there? Where was Koski? Was it possible Jamul had her? The singer's plan began to take shape in Falk's mind.

The band started up with a new number. At the first few notes the audience clapped and whooped then settled down to enjoy the thumping rhythm. "Chattanooga Choo-Choo" was leaving track twenty-nine as Falk eased back into the shadows. He quickly called Stewart's cell phone to tell him it was possible Koski had been abducted by one of Jamul's men.

Fifty feet above, he reviewed the catwalk with its sandbagged weighted ropes and pulleys. He knew that was the place to be; a bird's eye view. He moved deeper into backstage. *"Nothin' could be finer than dinner in the diner,"* the vocalist crooned, as Falk found the permanent ladder attached to the wall that enabled him to ascend to the catwalk. Rung by rung, he made his way upward, his eyes fixed on his destination fifty feet above.

Pulling himself onto the narrow walkway, he heard the singer belt out the last few lines...*"until I tell her I'll never roam— Oh, Chattanooga Choo-Choo carry me home."*

The audience cheered and whistled. They enjoyed the trip back through the Golden Age of Big Band music. Falk edged to the center of the catwalk and looked down. He had the best view in the house amid a faint smell of grease, paint and dust. Five minutes to intermission.

Shortly before intermission, a four-seater electric golf car whined along Crescent Street to the Casino Ballroom. Jamul was seated next to the driver, a wide brimmed straw hat pulled down low across his forehead. In the rear, Brasinov sat next to Koski, a gun pressed into her ribs.

The driver pulled the golf cart into a parking lot and Jamul handed him a wad of cash. "Find someone backstage who'll open the stage door for five hundred dollars or whatever it takes. We'll wait there."

Jamul held Koski's arm in a steely grip outside the stage door and inhaled deep breaths of cool sea air. "This place holds thousands of people. We'll go on stage during the intermission, announce I've made an escape and introduce you as my savior. They'll go crazy. Enjoy the adoration when it sweeps across the footlights, Agent Koski."

Koski remained silent, her hair ruffled as wind from the Pacific swept around the building. She shivered and pulled her jacket tightly around her.

Five minutes later they were inside looking up at the huge art deco ceiling. Recorded music played and the crowds milled around waiting for the second half of the show. The next of the Big Bands readied themselves behind the stage curtain. Three minutes to show time.

Chapter 78

Jamul was excited. The tiredness and stress that had plagued him since leaving the convalescent hospital was gone. Now, amid the magic of the music and the electrical vibes from the huge assembly, he came alive, anticipating when he would move forward, mount the stage and announce his escape.

Nodding to his driver, Jamul pushed forward. Koski was still held in his grasp beside him. Inch by inch they moved closer to the stage.

"Now," Jamul said calmly and without hesitation walked up a short flight of steps at the side of the stage. It happened so quickly and smoothly no one seemed to notice until Jamul was center stage with Koski. Jamul's driver had also gone on stage behind the curtain. Seconds later he appeared with a floor mike and set it in front of Koski and Jamul. Jamul removed his hat. With a flourish he skimmed it out into the audience and tipped the mike closer.

"Good evening, ladies and gentlemen. This is Jamul speaking. I am back."

For a few seconds the audience was stunned. Some who had been heading for the bar stopped and turned at the sound of his voice. Those still in the ballroom recognized the tall powerful figure at once. It *was* Jamul!

"I am no longer a hostage of the militant Islamic Jihad. I am free thanks to this tiny person beside me. Agent Susan Koski, FBI." Koski stared at the floor. "I came here at once to announce my escape."

He paused with the skill of a smooth politician. He saw the audience was over the shock of his sudden appearance. They leaned forward, hanging on his every word.

"How'd you get away, Jamul?" a voice from the audience called.

"Let me just say that Agent Koski was my savior. You can read the details later."

"Sing for us, Jamul. *Sing*," a voice called. Within seconds it became a chant. "Sing for us, sing for us…"

Jamul wore a smile of joy on his face. He shook his head and waved his arms. It was no use. They wouldn't take no for an answer. Jamul leaned into the mike.

"Okay. Just one song." The chant had shortened to "sing, sing, sing." The curtain slowly opened as the musicians scrambled to their seats, eager to play for Jamul. The audience stomped and cheered when they saw the band on stage.

Jamul waited as the audience settled down. "Thank you. Thank you. It was a night such as this many years ago when I stood for the first time in front of a large audience in an amateur talent show backed by a Big Band." He turned and indicated the orchestra, at the same time giving them a deep bow. Then facing the audience, Koski still at his side, he continued.

"I sang a Sinatra ballad that night, 'Luck Be a Lady Tonight.' It turned out to be lucky for me back then. Later, it became my signature tune. I'd like to sing it for you tonight."

Thunderous applause, cheers and whistles slowly quieted as the orchestra started the introduction. Jamul looked down at Koski and began singing. Falk had witnessed the unbelievable scene below as if it were a dream. Jamul was on stage with Koski at his side! He was only fifty feet away, yet so far. He couldn't just shoot the man in front of thousands. There also was Koski to think about. Jamul had her in close beside him. He would have to wait.

Jamul finished to a wild applause. He held his arms out wide as if embracing the audience. At the same time he threw his head back and looked up to see Falk staring down from the catwalk. Jamul's mind, the satanic side, immediately went into action. With automatic reaction he thumbed the trigger on the bio weapon as he held his arms wide. The first shot went wild, missing Falk by several inches. As the laser zapped into the wall he scrambled for cover, causing the catwalk to swing wildly.

The smile was gone from Jamul's face now. He signaled for the curtain to close as shouts from the crowded ballroom called for more. Koski twisted free from Jamul, jumped from the stage into the crowd and vanished. She had seen him fire upward and for a moment had even caught a glimpse of Falk as he threw himself down on the catwalk. She had to get backstage.

Imminent Danger

Chapter 79

Jamul had to kill them both. He didn't want anyone to dispute his story of getting free from the fake hostage situation. He hurried into the wings to the sound of wild applause, followed by Brasinov and the driver.

"Falk's up there." Jamul pointed and ordered Brasinov, "Kill him." He turned to the driver. "Find the woman. She mustn't get away."

DHS agents came swarming toward Jamul as the two men vanished to carry out his orders. Jamul immediately went into his hero role.

Koski jostled and pushed her way through the crowds, working her way back toward the wings. When she finally squeezed backstage, she saw Jamul surrounded by well-wishers from the DHS. She knew at once she'd be wasting her time if she tried to communicate with them. They were as charged up as the damn audience.

Slipping unnoticed past the admiring crowd, she moved along the wall looking up at the catwalk to see if Falk was still there. That's when she saw Brasinov halfway up the ladder. She started up after him.

Brasinov was concentrating on the long climb and never knew Koski was behind him until he felt a grip on his ankle. He jerked around, looked down and tried to kick her free. Taking a chance, Koski reached with her other hand and grabbed his waistband. She was now thirty feet up holding on to nothing but the man. If he fell, they'd both go crashing to the floor.

Brasinov held the ladder with one hand and reached for his gun with the other. Koski saw the muzzle aim toward her as he tried to steady himself for a shot. Releasing her grip on his ankle, she grasped tight to the ladder and removed her hand from his waistband. She reached between his legs, grabbed his balls and pulled down with all her strength. Brasinov growled like a wounded animal and dropped the gun as Koski held on like a vise.

The man was in agony and tried to reach back and grab Koski. When he did, she snatched his arm and pulled him off the ladder, leaning inward, head tucked in tight as Brasinov plummeted over her, landing with a sickening crunch on his head.

Trembling, Koski continued her climb, pulled up onto the catwalk and lay gasping for breath.

Falk was at the far end of the long catwalk and turned quickly when he felt the movement. Then he saw it was someone laying flat. Koski.

She clung to him as he spoke softly. "I have to finish my assignment, Koski." She nodded.

"If Jamul leaves here he'll still be useful to the cell, no matter what we try and prove. His fans will believe him. You heard them just now. They idolize that swine. Think of all the other millions around the world."

She nodded. "I know. It has to be now."

"Go down the ladder at the far end of the catwalk." Falk pointed. "It's close to an exit. Wait there and stay out of sight. We're going to have to move fast when I join you. Okay?"

"Be careful, Joe. Jamul's driver's down there and he has a gun."

"Okay. Now hurry. Call Stewart and tell him to have a car at the back of the ballroom when we come out." He handed her a phone. "Call just before you go down the ladder. Now move out."

She took the phone, kissed him and made her way along the slightly swaying catwalk.

Falk watched until she reached the end, made the call and vanished down the ladder.

The driver stood on the outer edge of the DHS men as they milled around Brasinov's crumpled body. He'd seen Koski on the catwalk then lost sight of her but knew he had to obey orders and stay with Jamul. He caught Jamul's eye for a split second but it was enough for him to catch the almost imperceptible shake of Jamul's head that indicated he abort the order to hunt down Koski. The driver turned and left the building as Koski crouched, hidden behind a piece of scenery.

Falk removed two items from his pockets that Stewart had supplied him with prior to leaving the Coast Guard station: a smoke grenade and a long barreled .44 Magnum fitted with a sound suppressor. He checked the smoke grenade and replaced it in a side pocket. The time had come. Moving to the middle of the catwalk, he steadied himself against the railing and stared down. Jamul was in the center of a crowd. Not an easy shot.

Removing the grenade from his pocket, Falk hooked it onto his waistband, took a couple of deep breaths then riveted his eyes on his target. Curling his finger around the trigger, he took careful aim and squeezed. A muffled "spit" and Falk saw Jamul's head snap back in a spray of blood. He scooped the grenade from his waistband, pulled the pin and tossed it into the center of the group.

Falk scurried along the catwalk and down the ladder to the exit. Thick smoke from the grenade filled the backstage area as Koski pushed the door open. Together they burst into the cold night air as Stewart pulled up in a car. In seconds they were both aboard the vehicle and Stewart drove out of the lot and headed into a maze of small back streets.

Stewart glanced in the rearview. "There's a helicopter on the way. We'll rendezvous at a prearranged spot near the center of the island."

Koski moved closer to Falk as the car roared through the darkness. Falk had carried out his orders; assignment complete.

Worldwide Media had covered Jamul's shooting. Talking heads discussed the event non-stop. Messages poured in from around the world praising God for sparing Jamul's life. Medical reports went into detail on how close he came to death. A half-inch closer and Jamul's carotid artery would have been severed and he would have died instantly.

There was no mention in the first medical bulletin that the bullet had severed his larynx and he would never be able to speak again. Jamul was destined to live out the rest of his life as a mute and his fans would forget him. The Islamic cell had no further use for his fame as cover. Now he'd live forever taunted by the memory of the opening verse of the last song he sang to his adoring fans.

They call you lady luck
But there is room for doubt.
At times you have a very
Un-lady-like way—of running out.

A military helicopter lowered to its pad at the Van Nuys Airport in the San Fernando Valley. Koski and Falk were heading back to the FBI office in Reno.

"The story that Jamul had escaped, been hunted down and shot by the terrorists held together well," Stewart said. "I suppose shooting from a shaky catwalk fifty feet above the target was the reason you weren't able to get a perfect head shot. Right, Joe?"

The helicopter touched down amid a cloud of dust. They bent their heads against the backdraft as Falk and Koski prepared to dash for the aircraft.

Falk yelled to Stewart, "Absolutely, Tom." He gave a quick wave and grabbed Koski's elbow. They dashed across the apron, heads low, and climbed aboard. They both had their headsets on by the time the copter swooped across the San Fernando Valley, gained altitude and headed toward Reno.

Koski glanced back toward Los Angeles. "Glad we were able to give Nell her interview. She earned it."

"Yeah and Marco got his Swiss bank account and into the witness protection program."

"Nell told me she was going to get the Toyota Rav4 she always wanted as soon as she sold her article."

Falk grunted. "Marco said he and Nell were going to get married. Maybe he'll want a Ferrari. He can afford it."

The helicopter leveled off and the landscape below changed to rugged hills. The snow-capped Sierras glinted in the distance.

Koski snuggled close to Falk and rested her head on his shoulder.

"Do you think Stewart believed you, Joe?"

"About what?"

"Missing a head shot at fifty feet?"

"A very difficult shot from a shaky unstable platform, my dear."

"Yeah, right," she said softly.

Stewart watched the helicopter dwindle into the distance then snapped his fingers. "Grafton."

"Who's that?" his driver asked.

"I've been trying to recall who wrote a certain quotation and it just came to me. Her name was Grafton. Sue Grafton. It was in a detective novel. Her protagonist paraphrased the famous Roman orator Cicero, who said, '*Summum jus, summa injuria*'. 'Extreme justice is extreme injustice'."

Imminent Danger

If you enjoyed *Imminent Danger* consider the first book in the Falk and Koski adventure series, the Kindle genre bestseller, *Who's Killing All the Lawyers?* by A. G. Hayes...

Lawyers are being murdered by laser-driven arrows. The FBI believes that someone is training a Native American militia to take over the economic system in the U.S. Joe Falk and Susan Koski are assigned to find the hired killer and The Fox, the real force behind the killings.

...and also the second book in the Falk and Koski adventure series, *The Judas List* by A. G. Hayes.

Between the end of World War II and the winter of 1975, a 700-year-old prayer book, a key and a faded blueprint came to light in Vienna, and began a 25-year search for Nazi Herman Goering's treasure. In modern day Vienna, American agents Koski and Falk must go undercover to locate the treasure and the Judas List—a compendium of individuals and organizations that financed WWII, and, in it's aftermath, now intended to manipulate world finances to bring about the Fourth Reich. But the Americans aren't the only ones looking for the list and the treasure. So are ex-Nazi, the Bosnians, Russians and, most recently, Muslim militants.

Imminent Danger

About the Author

A. G. Hayes studied television writing at UCLA. He has published short fiction, including *Cover Up*, *Not a Penny Pincher*, *Home*, *Payment in Full*, *Small Wonder* and *Guided through a Mine Field*, and written scripts for CBS TV and other television production companies. He lives in the Sierra Nevada Foothills and spends his time writing and traveling to nearly every part of the world. He has used personal experiences gained during service with the British intelligence in Eastern Europe and the Middle East to enrich the characters of his protagonist teams. He is the author of the Kindle genre bestseller, *Who's Killing All the Lawyers* (Savant 2011) and *The Judas List* (Savant 2012).

Imminent Danger

If you enjoyed *Imminent Danger,* consider these other fine books from Savant Books and Publications:

Essay, Essay, Essay by Yasuo Kobachi
Aloha from Coffee Island by Walter Miyanari
Footprints, Smiles and Little White Lies by Daniel S. Janik
The Illustrated Middle Earth by Daniel S. Janik
Last and Final Harvest by Daniel S. Janik
A Whale's Tale by Daniel S. Janik
Tropic of California by R. Page Kaufman
Tropic of California (the companion music CD) by R. Page Kaufman
The Village Curtain by Tony Tame
Dare to Love in Oz by William Maltese
The Interzone by Tatsuyuki Kobayashi
Today I Am a Man by Larry Rodness
The Bahrain Conspiracy by Bentley Gates
Called Home by Gloria Schumann
Kanaka Blues by Mike Farris
First Breath edited by Zachary M. Oliver
Poor Rich by Jean Blasiar
The Jumper Chronicles by W. C. Peever
William Maltese's Flicker by William Maltese
My Unborn Child by Orest Stocco
Last Song of the Whales by Four Arrows
Perilous Panacea by Ronald Klueh
Falling but Fulfilled by Zachary M. Oliver
Mythical Voyage by Robin Ymer
Hello, Norma Jean by Sue Dolleris
Richer by Jean Blasiar
Manifest Intent by Mike Farris
Charlie No Face by David B. Seaburn
Number One Bestseller by Brian Morley
My Two Wives and Three Husbands by S. Stanley Gordon
In Dire Straits by Jim Currie
Wretched Land by Mila Komarnisky
Chan Kim by Ilan Herman

Who's Killing All the Lawyers? by A. G. Hayes
Ammon's Horn by G. Amati
Wavelengths edited by Zachary M. Oliver
Almost Paradise by Laurie Hanan
Communion by Jean Blasiar and Jonathan Marcantoni
The Oil Man by Leon Puissegur
Random Views of Asia from the Mid-Pacific by William E. Sharp
The Isla Vista Crucible by Reilly Ridgell
Blood Money by Scott Mastro
In the Himalayan Nights by Anoop Chandola
On My Behalf by Helen Doan
Traveler's Rest by Jonathan Marcantoni
Keys in the River by Tendai Mwanaka
Chimney Bluffs by David B. Seaburn
The Loons by Sue Dolleris
Light Surfer by David Allan Williams
The Judas List by A. G. Hayes
Path of the Templar - Book 2 of The Jumper Chronicles by W. C. Peever
The Desperate Cycle by Tony Tame
Shutterbug by Buz Sawyers
Blessed are the Peacekeepers by Tom Donnelly and Mike Munger
The Bellwether Messages edited by Daniel S. Janik
Purple Haze by George B. Hudson
The Turtle Dances by Daniel S. Janik
The Lazarus Conspiracies by Richard Rose

Soon To Be Released

The Hanging of Dr. Hanson by Bentley Gates

http://www.savantbooksandpublications.com

www.ingramcontent.com/pod-product-compliance
Lightning Source LLC
Chambersburg PA
CBHW051242260626
47162CB00002B/562